Kevin –

Just Reme[illegible]

You knew [illegible]

Keep Hope Alive!

Tom Terbush

12.19.12

MW01707088

MissingLid
BOOKHOUSE

The Following: Beneath the surface of Beniwan

Published by Missing Lid Bookhouse
www.missinglid.com

ISBN: 978-0-9838068-0-6 (paperback)
ISBN: 978-0-9838068-1-3 (e-book)
ISBN: 978-0-9838068-2-0 (hardback)

Library of Congress Control Number: 2012918707

Copyright © 2012 by Tom Terbush

Book cover art and design, illustrations, and inside page design by Nathan D. Fisher
& Sci-Fi Book Cover Designer
www.scifibookdesigner.com

Additional support provided by JPED Publishing Group, Colorado Springs, CO.

All rights reserved. No part of this book may be reproduced or transmitted in any form or by any means, electronic or mechanical, including photocopying and recording, or by any information storage and retrieval system, without permission in writing from the publisher.

Printed in the United States of America
2012 – First Edition

The Following

Beneath the Surface of Beniwan

By Tom Terbush

For Judah, Ora, Ariah, Ezekiel,
Joseph, Aiden, Avarie, and Aubryn

May your lives be filled with love,
best friends and heaps of adventure.

Table of Contents

WYND

A few years ago, I met a young man while trekking through the mountains of Colorado. It was one of those gorgeous autumn mornings when the yellow aspen leaves barely twitch in the breeze and the smell of fresh mountain air penetrates the soul. As far as I knew, I was the only person on the trail that day. There were no other cars in sight when I pulled into the parking lot about an hour before. I hadn't seen or heard much of anything, or anyone. Then, out of nowhere, I heard footsteps behind me. I had just climbed a series of switchbacks and there hadn't been anyone on the trail below me. Perplexed, I turned around. To my surprise, a young man in his early twenties was jogging up the path.

I kept moving forward at my slow-but-steady pace, and pretty soon, the guy caught up with me. I politely stepped to the side to let him by, but instead of passing me, he slowed down and began walking with me.

"Good morning," I said, through my heavy breathing.

"Ho there!" was his energetic reply.

His complexion was unusually pale, except his cheeks, which were flushed from the crisp morning air. He had a pleasant smile and his penetrating eyes seemed to look deep inside me. I had a strange feeling he knew what I was thinking, but that was impossible. I pushed the thought aside.

We struck up a conversation while I took a much-needed break at the next switchback. I sat down on a log to dig for my water bottle, and was able to get a good look at him for the first time. He was grubby, wearing one of those South American poncho-things with a hood. The more we talked, the more I wanted to know. Who was he and where did he come from? His accent was like nothing I'd ever heard. It definitely wasn't Spanish or Portuguese.

We started up the trail again and came to a fork in the path. I anticipated an exchange of farewells and this would be the last I ever saw of him. Instead, he continued behind me – step-for-step. As we walked, we talked about all sorts of things, like the mountains we had climbed and the countries we had visited. But soon we ran out of small talk.

Finally, I asked his name.

"Wynd," he said.

"Wind?"

"Wynd with a 'y'," he replied.

"Are you from around here?"

"No, I'm a traveler. I don't have a real home. My home is wherever I am – and today I suppose it's . . . Colorado!"

OK, that was a little weird. Maybe he was the product of some '60s couple who spent a little too much time at Woodstock. *Who names their kid Wind?* All that aside, I had to admit I was beginning to like him. He had an engaging personality and I couldn't shake the feeling that I knew him from somewhere.

The day flew by and we had a great time on the trail. We summited our mountain, a 14,000-foot peak, and arrived at the parking lot before sunset. I had accomplished my goal without being deterred. In fact, with Wynd along, I made it down even earlier than expected.

We said our 'farewells' as I fumbled through my day pack for my car keys. I was exhausted, starving, and needed something cold to drink. And, there was the long-anticipated reward of famously-bad Mexican food just a few miles down the road. I accidently dropped my keys and stooped to pick them up. When

I looked up, Wynd was walking down the dirt road toward the highway.

"Do you need a lift?" I asked.

"That's all right, I can get where I'm going."

"Really, it's no problem. I can drop you in town. I'm headed to Miguel's for a coke and burrito."

He nodded and smiled.

Thirty minutes later, we were sitting at a sticky yellow table in a dark Mexican restaurant, exchanging more stories.

Somewhere between the outrageously good guacamole and my second taco, the conversation turned a little . . . funky. I was telling him one of my few genuinely 'funny' stories about being stranded in Nepal when he interrupted me.

"You should have transported out of there," he chuckled.

Maybe I didn't hear him right. What did he say?

"Did you say 'transport'?"

"You know . . . you should have sent yourself somewhere else."

This was too bizarre. I couldn't just leave it there; so I pressed him for more, expecting a rational explanation – or at least some kind of clarification. But the conversation just kept getting weirder.

He began to tell me stories about these kids with extraordinary powers – how they could see in the dark and transport to other places. Maybe the exertions of the day or the altitude were affecting my brain, but his stories were too fantastic to be real. Every now and then, I would burst out laughing. But his expression never changed. He appeared to be serious.

The hours flew by and the busboy was forced to ask us to leave. It must have been after 2:00 in the morning. My mind was on overload. The last time I had felt like this was after watching *Star Wars* for the first time. I was intrigued by the world of possibilities Wynd described. They were all fantasies, but the thought of altering my current reality was compelling.

We shuffled out the front door to the parking lot. I headed to my car and Wynd walked along the front of the building.

"Keep hope alive!" he yelled as he waved goodbye. Then he stepped around the side of the building.

"Wait!" I yelled, "Let's get together tomorrow."

I ran to where he had been standing and looked around the corner. There was nothing but an open field for hundreds of feet. He was nowhere to be seen. *That's odd.* I looked for him behind the restaurant but he wasn't there. I circled the restaurant a few times just to make sure I wasn't going crazy. I even went back inside and asked the server if she had seen him. Nothing.

Now, I consider myself a fairly levelheaded person. I love a good sci-fi flick, but this shook me up. I drove to my hotel and lay awake most of the night trying to figure out what had happened. The more I thought about it, the more impossible it seemed. In the morning, I returned to the restaurant and walked around it in full daylight. There was no place he could have been hiding. He had simply disappeared.

I went inside to order a cup of coffee. As I sat at the counter, the waiter from the night before handed me a poncho.

"Your friend left this here last night," he said.

Well, at least I knew I wasn't dreaming.

I never saw Wynd again, but nothing has ever affected me so much as the day I spent with him. His stories were so compelling that I began to believe they might actually be true. You just can't make up stuff like that.

So, I wrote this book. It's my attempt to capture what I can remember of the stories he told me that night.

Beniwan

The sun darkens to a dirty orange and wearily lowers itself onto the horizon, melting into the landscape. It is nightfall in Beniwan. As this tired world nears the end of its life, the once-vivid colors of creation have faded to dull, dirty versions of their former selves. The sepia skies, muddy green plants and faded flowers slip into the shadows as the two moons of Beniwan begin their descent. They make their final bow and a dense blanket of clouds stretches across the sky, blocking any remaining light. A gentle mist begins to fall, saturating everything.

Then comes total black. All of life slows to a halt, waiting for the clouds to lift and the light of the stars to return.

Two tribes inhabit Beniwan, the Keeon and the Kinsmen. Their origins are the same but when they parted ways generations earlier, the Keeon became the overlords of their meek and gentle cousins.

Over time, the Keeon rule has developed into a system marked by aggression, arrogance and domination of their subjects. Obtaining position and power is so highly valued that cruel and ruthless acts against their own people are commonly practiced.

The Keeon live separate from the Kinsmen in the large walled cities south of The Sands – a vast desert covering hundreds of miles. Their architecture is massive and imposing. It is believed to be impenetrable. The government also assigns small peacekeeping troops to police the Kinsmen in the villages north of the great dunes. They exact a heavy tax of grain and textiles from the inhabitants. This helps provide for their extravagant taste in housing, clothing and food.

It is rumored that there are 'free' Kinsmen tribes living in the steep northern mountains. It is not known if the stories are true but the Keeon's fear of high places make the reports plausible.

The Kinsmen are simple folk who dwell in the fertile plains beneath the Avion mountains. They are humble and hard working, content to spend their days growing crops and creating beautiful fabrics. The men are skilled and intelligent artisans, capable of constructing anything – except for weapons.

All Kinsmen despise the thought of violence. This mindset opened a way for Keeon domination and it has kept them enslaved for generations. To ensure the upper hand, Keeon law forbids the possession of all weaponry by the Kinsmen.

Over time, the Kinsmen have become a fearful and superstitious people. The origin of these fears in unclear, but they have permeated the culture. Stacking rocks, killing birds or going inside of holes is forbidden. They never cross a river alone, and always wear bright colors to ward off evil spirits. The Keeon have fed and exploited this weakness, making their control of the people almost effortless.

In spite of all this, the Kinsmen put their hope in something they call 'The Legends.' These fantastic and exciting stories have been passed down from generation to generation. Most Kinsmen don't believe the stories are historic, but they follow the life-principles illustrated in them.

The Legends tell of an ancient race of people who inhabited Beniwan, long before Keeon rule. The Paddor, or 'Ancients' as the Kinsmen call them, possessed extraordinary powers and governed the world in wisdom, peace and justice.

They were friends and protectors of the Kinsmen for many centuries. Then, for no apparent reason, they left Beniwan and moved their entire race to a new world. The Legends don't explain what prompted their mass exodus, but every version tells of the 'Great Departure' – when the Paddor disappeared in a single day.

Every so often, a fieldworker will unearth a mysterious object while plowing. This starts people wondering if The Legends might be true. Whenever this happens, the Keeon waste no time in declaring the object evil and destroying it.

There are small pockets of Kinsmen who gather in secret to recount The Legends. They speak in hushed tones of a profound hope – the hope that one day The Ancients will return to Beniwan and deliver them from their oppressors.

In the humble village of Maidenton live seven children who are the best of friends.

Lucas Beeman, or Beem as his friends call him, is fourteen. He is the oldest of the seven. Kinsmen tradition requires that he take responsibility to protect the younger children whenever they leave the village. Although this adds some pressure to Beem's life, he doesn't mind. He always manages to get everyone home safely by the end of the day.

Beem is a good-looking boy with kind brown eyes

and an innocent face. He is the tallest of the children but only tops Pria by a bit. She insists his unruly mop of auburn hair gives him an unfair advantage.

Beem has developed quickly in the last year. His once-spindly arms have become muscular from working alongside his father. Everyone knows he will one day make an excellent harvester like his dad. He is smart, capable and good with people – making him an excellent choice for a supervisor position when he gets older.

Beem's best and worst trait is his vivid imagination. He has a unique ability to invent the craziest stories. His friends love going on the fantastic adventures he dreams up whenever they are together. His parents find this gift annoying because they never know which world he's living in – real or imagined.

Pria Limm is thirteen. She is tall and thin with long golden hair. She ties it back with a bright red ribbon, which is her favorite color. Her eyes are deep green and her skin is so fair it is almost translucent. She catches the attention of the village boys, but is unimpressed by their admiration. Her friends just see her as Pria – nothing more or less.

Her greatest desire in life is to one day be a mother. She loves young children, especially babies. In all of Beem's adventures, she takes the role of 'mom.' Her knack of giving good advice, or a timely word of caution, consistently keeps them out of trouble. Beem appreciates this because he would be the one to receive punishment if anything were to go seriously wrong.

Pria is a brilliant cook. Her love and knowledge of herbs and spices turns even the simplest of foods into a feast, but her gifts aren't limited to the kitchen. She is also a skilled artisan, able to weave the most intricate patterns on her family's loom. She was recently invited by the weaver's guild to teach them her new 'double twill' technique.

Pria is confident for her age, doesn't mind taking responsibility for the younger children if the need arises, and she likes being in charge.

Jinkmin and Mylan Spin are eleven-year-old twins. This is something of a rarity in their society because Kinsmen families are only allowed one pregnancy. The brothers are almost identical in stature and even in their facial features, but if you look closely, Jinkmin's dark eyebrows are thicker and his chin isn't as defined as Mylan's. Their appearance is where all similarity ends.

It has been a long time since the children have called them by their given names. Among their friends, they are known simply as Jinx and Spinny.

Jinx is the picture of average. Skinny and gangly, it's as if he hasn't grown into his skin yet. He has straight black hair and freckles. Nothing about him makes him unique or memorable to the outside observer – his brother makes sure to remind him of this. Consequently, he is often overlooked when something is being planned. He's not sure if this happens by accident or if Spinny intentionally leaves him out.

Jinx seeks after the attention and respect of the others, but his attempts usually backfire. He is accident-prone, so they started calling him Jinx and the nickname stuck.

Beem looks out for Jinx. Even though he's clumsy, he picks himself up without complaining and takes the teasing in stride. Beem respects him for it, and does everything he can to make sure he is included in their adventures. When they are out playing, he is often distracted by new discoveries and plods along at a slower pace than the rest of the children.

Spinny, on the other hand, is a fireball. He is lean, muscular and can't stop moving. His eyes are wild and blue with a sparkle of mischief behind them. He has the same black hair as his brother with a few less freckles.

He is usually the cause of the latest catastrophe, but Beem takes it all in stride. They first met when Spinny was three and have been best friends ever since.

Jinx is the firstborn of the twins, making him the favored child, and the one their parents put in charge. This infuriates Spinny. He is constantly driven to prove himself. Everything is a competition to him so he outruns, out-throws, and out-yells the other children – except for his nemesis, Trince.

Trince Tummins is *almost* twelve, so she says. She is strong, athletic, and can hold her own with any boy. Her pretty face is framed by long black curls that bounce as she walks. Her eyes are deep brown and flash with passion, especially when she is challenging Spinny in his endless competitions. She always manages to put him in his place, which results in frequent bickering between them.

Trince has a zeal for living and loves a good adventure. She has just come into the time of life when girls start having feelings for boys. When these emotions confront her, she pushes them away or ignores them altogether.

Stalwart 'Wort' Cromwell is eight. He is short and round-faced with a pasty complexion and small grey eyes. His coarse brown hair is cut short and combed flat. The other children often poke fun at him because he is a bit of a stick-in-the-mud. He prefers playing at home with his building blocks to a good tromp through the woods or a climb up Broadside Hill. The love of his mother's rich, baked desserts, combined with his aversion to all physical activity, has left him flabby and out of shape. He tires easily and gets grumpy when their hikes get too steep. But he hates being alone, so he usually ends up going along on his friends' expeditions. The Cromwell's have made good money through their farm mercantile, which has made Wort's life better than most Kinsmen. His parents have spoiled him; so his attitude can be demanding at times. He has learned to get his way by whining. While this has worked to manipulate adults, his friends are wise to his tactics. They refuse to let him get away with anything when they play together.

Wort's one consolation is being able to boss around Meekus, the youngest of the seven.

Meekus Tivley is only six. He is small but unusually strong for a boy his age. He has chubby cheeks, straw-colored curls and large blue eyes. He can find the good in any situation and often acts more mature than Wort. He takes Wort's bossing with good humor. Besides, Beem or Pria always come to his defense if Wort gets too nasty.

Meekus loves playing with the older kids. His favorite thing in the world is going along on Beem's make-believe adventures. He hates for them to end and always begs to play a little longer whenever it's time to go home.

Meekus is brave for his age and tries hard not to cry, even if he's bleeding from a scraped elbow or chin. Everyone likes him so much that he has become like a little brother to them. They fight to have him on their team whenever they play Throw-Stick or Charge the Wall.

Today the children decide against playing in the woods outside Maidenton. Instead, they head for the summit of the flat-topped hill between the village and the mountains. This mesa is farther away than the woods, and takes longer to get to, but once you're on top, it's paradise.

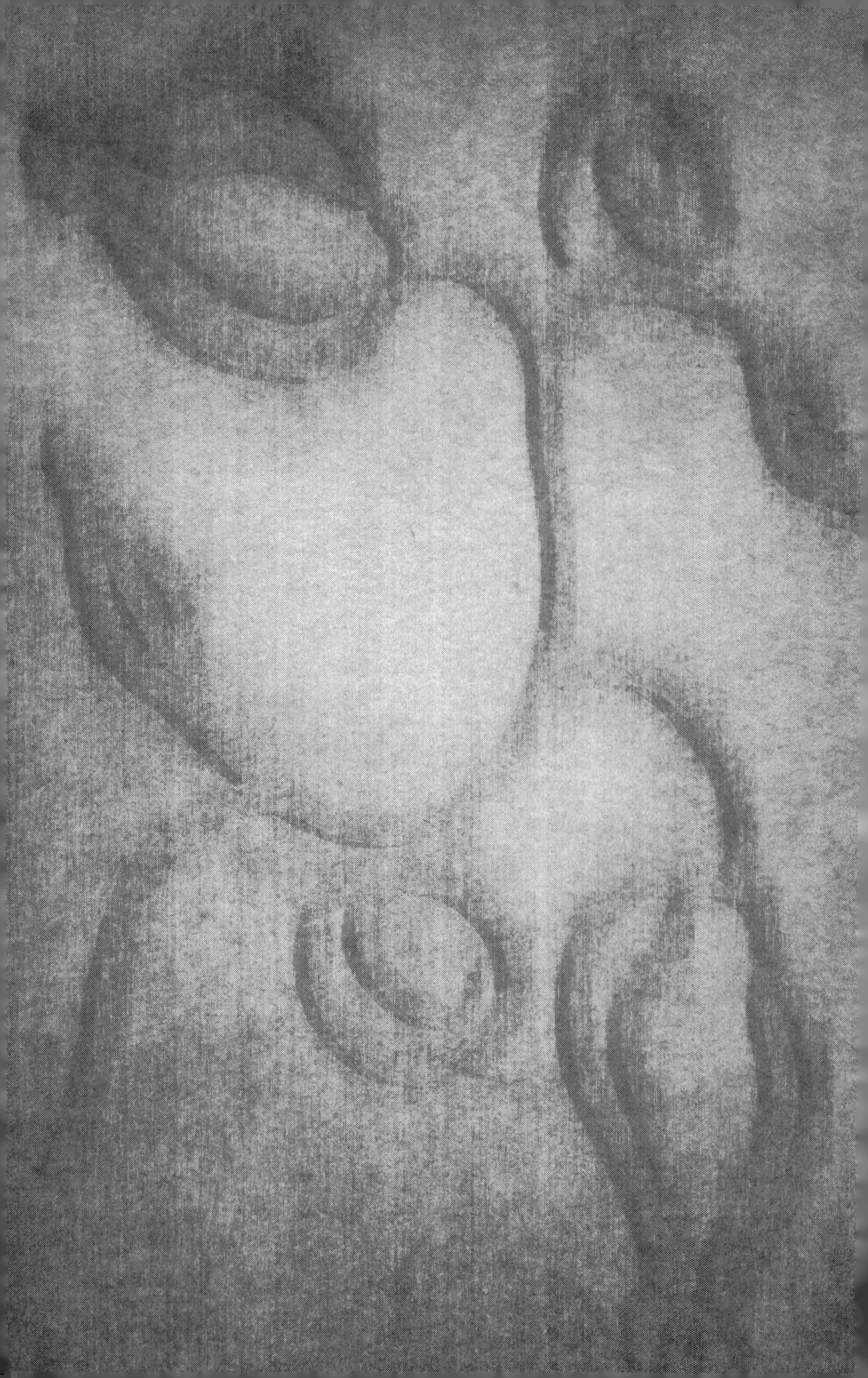

1

The Hole

Should they go in or not? It was driving them crazy. Wort didn't hesitate.

"We can't go in! Holes are evil. We have to stay away from holes!"

"You're only saying that because that's what you've been told," argued Pria, "You're such a momma's boy."

"I think he's scared," taunted Trince as she poked his arm.

Wort slapped her hand away.

"I am not!"

Within seconds, arguments were flying. Some of them wanted to go in the hole, some wanted to report it and others just wanted to pretend they had never seen anything at all.

The children had been taught from an early age that holes were evil. They didn't exactly know why, but Kinsmen had always been superstitious about such things. Regardless of their beliefs, the children had discovered a hole. If they didn't report it immediately, they would be breaking the law.

Spinny was excited about the prospect of adventure – a *real* one this time. He picked up some rocks and threw them into the opening to see how deep it was.

"Come on, let's go in!" he urged, "I doubt if it's very deep."

Each time Spinny tossed a rock inside, they could hear it ricochet off the wall of the cavern and then again farther down.

The dark fissure that lay at their feet was two feet across and six feet long. It was nestled between a dead tree and a large boulder. It didn't look intimidating, and beside the fact they couldn't see the bottom, everything was familiar – just rocks and dirt.

"I'm scared, Beem. What should we do?" squeaked Meekus.

"Yeah Beem, what are we going to do?" echoed the others.

Beem hesitated. He knew the grown-up thing to do would be to march straight in to the village and report the hole to the committee. But something tugged at him to take a peek inside.

"It's just a stupid throw-stick," announced

Jinx. "I've got another one back at my house we can play with."

"It's *my* stick!" Meekus retorted, "And it's not stupid! If you hadn't thrown it so hard we wouldn't even be here."

"Hey!" interjected Spinny who was still trying to get their attention, "Think about it. There could be all kinds of great stuff down there. The throw-stick could be sitting right next to a hidden treasure – maybe around that big boulder."

He threw in another rock.

Beem stared down the valley at the thatched rooftops of Maidenton, lost in thought. The noise of the arguing children faded into the background. He imagined his father lecturing him to tell the committee everything. But he couldn't shake what Pria had just said to Wort, 'Holes are evil because that's what we've been told.' What is it that makes something evil? He looked back at the crack in the ground, then up to the grassy summit where they had been playing. No one from the village ever ventured this far. Chances were their discovery would remain hidden forever. He stomped his foot to get everyone's attention. He had made up his mind. They would forget the whole thing and go play a new game somewhere else.

Before Beem could announce his decision, a peculiar sound came from the hole. Spinny's latest toss produced a shattering crash that echoed from below. Apparently, the rock had broken something to pieces in the darkness. The children stared wide-eyed at each other.

After a short pause, Trince yelled, “That’s it! I can’t take this anymore. I’m going in.”

She grabbed a branch covered with dried leaves and told Spinny to light them.

“I’m going in too,” he announced.

A mischievous smile crossed his face as he sparked his flint to the wad of wooly grass he had collected.

“I’m not sure that’s a good idea,” cautioned Beem, “What if . . .”

“Oh, come on Beem!” argued Trince.

She stood, hands on hips, glaring at him.

“You know you want to go in there.”

A spark leapt from the flint and ignited the wooly-grass, transforming it into a glowing blue flame. Trince held the branch to the little fire until the leaves began to crackle and burn. She glanced up at Beem, and threw the whole thing into the void.

“Now come on!” she demanded.

Meekus and Wort yanked on Beem’s cloak.

“What are we going to do?”

“Everybody quiet down for a second,” Beem yelled, “I’ve made a decision.”

The clamor subsided and the children turned their attention to Beem. Even though they were of differing opinions, they all trusted his advice. Not just because he was the oldest, but because he had earned their respect. They would go along with whatever he decided.

Beem looked back toward his home and then again at his friends.

He cleared his throat and with the hint of a smile announced, “Let’s be about it!”

The children knew exactly what this familiar statement meant. A buzz of excitement broke out. They were about to embark on another great adventure!

They loved the fantastic quests Beem dreamed up whenever they were together. Just a week before, they had rescued a princess from the dreaded Keeon prisons on the far side of The Sands. Once they fought twenty battalions of enemy forces to return the mythical treasure of the domes to the Kinsmen. Every mission ended victoriously – even against incredible odds. The adventures were make-believe of course, but to their active imaginations, it was hard to tell the difference.

This time would be completely different. The hole they were about to enter wasn’t imaginary. It was real. And there were real laws they were going to break if they didn’t report it. Ignoring the hole was one thing, but to actually climb inside was taking the children to an entirely new level of risk – especially for Beem.

Beem took Meekus and Wort by the hand. He knew they would be scared. His firm grasp gave them courage as they approached the opening. Trince and

Spinny were already inside, climbing over the first large boulder. Pria and Jinx would bring up the rear.

Spinny made himself a torch by scrunching handfuls of wooly-grass between three small tree limbs. He bound it together with some twine. The natural oils in the wooly-grass would burn for hours, allowing them to see in the dark. Jinx made a similar torch to light the rear of the expedition. Pria, who was always thinking ahead, shoved some extra wooly-grass in her cloak just in case one of the torches burned out. Even though their previous adventures had been pretend, they were able to use the skills they had developed and practiced over the years.

The path they were on, if you could call it that, was a jumble of large rocks, dirt, and the occasional dead tree limb. It was a steep decline, right into the belly of Broadside Hill. Fortunately for the children, the chasm wasn't very large. They discovered they could easily descend by pushing against the tunnel walls as they lowered themselves off the boulders. Every time they would bump their head or shoulder against the side, a small avalanche of dirt would tumble down the shaft in front of them. They didn't pay much attention to the instability of their surroundings because none of them knew anything about holes.

They advanced through the murky torchlight as Trince continued to toss the burning branch down the shaft. It did a good job illuminating their surroundings, but Beem was anxious someone from the village might see the smoke.

Broadside Hill was about a mile and a half to the north of Maidenton, on the far side of a large grassy field. Nobody from the village ever climbed up there, which made it the ideal environment for adventures. The children loved playing on the top of the large hill. More often than not, they ended up there whenever they were together. There weren't many trees on it, so you could see everything from its long, flat summit. It was also the ideal place for playing games like throw-stick. The children considered Broadside their own private wonderland. Discovering the hole that day was just one more surprise that fed their hunger for adventure.

Above them, the cave entrance framed a narrow patch of murky sky. The deeper they descended, the more obscured the sky became, until they could no longer see any signs of the outside world.

Spinny was in rare form. He chattered on and on, describing everything he was seeing as he led the team forward. He pointed out roots growing from the dirt and unusual bugs none of them had seen before. They decided to avoid the bugs thinking they might be poisonous – maybe that's why holes were evil. In the end, they saw nothing that would explain why they shouldn't be allowed in holes.

As they continued forward, their excitement began

to fade until Spinny cried out, “There it is! I found the little culprit!”

He had spotted the throw-stick. It was lying right next to where Trince had just dropped the burning branch. Its brightly painted stripes stood out against the drab surroundings of the tunnel. He jumped from the rock he was on, landing next to it.

“WHUAAAHH!” he cried, almost backing into the fire.

Something near the bottom of the rock had startled him, but the rest of the children couldn’t see what it was.

“Wow, did that give me a scare!” he yelled.

“What is it?” screamed Meekus.

“It’s an old animal skeleton.”

In an instant, the mood of the children changed from curious to uneasy. Wort and Meekus decided it was time to go home. They clung even tighter to Beem. Pria didn’t like the idea of dead things either and asked if they might turn around. Beem shouted to Spinny to toss up Meekus’ throw-stick so they could be on their way.

“Here you go, Cry Baby.”

Meekus reached out to grab it but noticed something was wrong. He moved out of the way just before it hit him.

“That’s not funny, Spinny!”

“What is it?” asked Pria.

“A stinky old bone!”

Spinny was already laughing.

"Come on, Spinny," scolded Beem, "Let's get going."

"I don't think so. We didn't come this far to turn around now."

"That's right Beem," added Trince, "We're on an adventure. Remember?"

"It's not that simple," retorted Beem, "You aren't looking at a year in Punishment House if you're caught."

"At least let us look around a bit first," pleaded Trince as she jumped off the rock.

"Eeww!" she yelled when she spotted the skeleton.

The bones weren't white and clean like the ones you find in the woods. They were a dull brown with bits of skin and fur still clinging to the skull.

"That isn't a very nice greeting," she grimaced.

"What does it look like?" Meekus asked nervously.

"It's the skeleton of some sort of animal," she replied, "Maybe a grommel or something. It probably fell in here and couldn't get out."

The younger ones let out a sigh of relief.

"All right you two, take a quick look around and let's get out of here," ordered Beem.

Before he could give his next directive, he was jostled by someone trying to get by.

"What's going on?"

"I can't let those guys have all the fun," said Jinx as he squeezed past Beem.

He climbed down to the last boulder and positioned himself to join the others.

"Make room," he yelled, motioning for them to stand aside.

"Don't bother," said Spinny.

He had just kicked the burning branch to the edge of the cave, illuminating the bottom.

"There's nowhere to go but back up," he said.

"The one chance for a real adventure and all we end up with is a stupid pile of bones," whined Trince.

"Well at least let me see the bones," said Jinx, refusing to be left out of the discovery.

Trince and Spinny moved to the side, making enough room for Jinx to land. He inched to the edge of the boulder and hopped off. In that moment, time seemed to slow down.

Jinx's feet hit the cave floor and kept going. The surface gave way beneath him, filling the tunnel with the deafening roar of rocks and dirt crashing into an unknown chasm below. Everyone was screaming as a choking cloud of dust filled the air. The blast extinguished the torch and the branch. Then there was silence.

After what seemed like an eternity, Beem called out anxiously, "Is everybody all right?"

The sound of coughing and a few moans echoed from the darkness.

"Trincy!" screamed Pria.

There was no response.

"Hand me the other torch," Beem shouted.

Pria struggled to navigate through the aftermath but was able to deliver it to him safely.

"Stay here with the boys until I figure out what to do."

The younger ones were trying to be brave, but nothing could stop their sniffling as they fought back tears.

Beem slid down as far as he could to assess the damage. As the dust settled, he could see a layer of old wooden poles sticking out from the sides of the tunnel. They appeared to be part of a structure but were now splintered and broken away, leaving only a few protruding stubs. Below that was complete blackness. The most shocking discovery, however, was Trince. She was still clinging to the cave wall on the far side of the gaping void. Her feet were barely perched on two snapped poles. She was paralyzed with fear, unable to speak.

"Trince," Beem said, with as much assurance as he could muster, "Hold tight 'til I can get to you. Are you all right?"

She turned her head enough to make eye contact with him.

"I – I think so," she managed to whimper, "But I feel like I'm going to fall."

Beem scanned the cave for anything that might

help – nothing. He took off his belt. He and his friends had often used them as ropes to climb trees or descend embankments.

"Toss me your belts," Beem instructed Meekus and Wort.

They quickly tossed them to Beem who tied them together, creating a lifeline just long enough to reach Trince.

"What happened?" groaned Spinny from somewhere below them.

His words echoed through the enormous cavern.

"Careful!" yelled Beem, "Any sudden movement you make could cause another collapse. We can't risk burying Jinx."

Beem worked his way down the tunnel to rescue Trince. He wedged his feet and fists into the crack formed between the cave wall and the large boulder. He held one end of the rope in his mouth until he got as low as he could.

"Lishen Trinsh," he said through clenched teeth, "I doan shink I can get owr to you, but I shink I cn lowr you down to Shpinny."

He shoved his left foot as far into the crack as it would go. With his left hand, he grabbed on to a lip of rock inside the opening, allowing him to hold the rope with his free hand.

"Spinny, can you catch Trince?"

"Not yet. I need to climb to the top of this pile first.

It's kind of hard to see down here."

Beem's voice softened.

"Are you ready, Trince?"

"I think so."

"Try to sit on those poles."

Trince turned around so her back and the palms of her hands were against the side of the cave. Her trembling legs threatened to buckle beneath her. Slowly, she slid down the wall. When she was as low as she could go, she looked over at Beem with tears streaming down her cheeks.

Beem swung the rope across the opening. After a couple of failed attempts, she was able to grab the end.

"Great!" gasped Beem.

Trince endeavored to sit on the broken poles. But, as she made her final adjustment, her foot slipped. She landed on the ledge with a thud.

"Ahhh!" she cried, trying to steady herself.

Then came the sickening sound of cracking wood. All at once, Trince was swinging over the darkness of the cavern. Beem yelled in pain as the sudden weight threatened to pull his arm out of joint. Trince tightened her grip on the belt as she swung back and forth through the blackness.

"There's nothing below me! My feet aren't touching."

She fought the panic but waves of trembling weakened her desperate hold on the rope.

"I'm trying to get to you," shouted Spinny, "But my foot is stuck. Keep holding on 'til I can get there!"

Beem gasped as Trince's weight gradually pulled his hand from its hold.

"Beem!" cried Trince, "I can't hold on. I'm slipping!"

Terror gripped her. All she could see was the looming darkness below.

"Hold on!" yelled Spinny.

The rope crept slowly through her hands. She tried to tighten her grip but within seconds she could feel the end of Beem's belt sliding through one hand and then the other. She screamed in horror as she fell into the blackness.

"Noooooooo!" yelled Beem, feeling the abrupt release.

In a split second, she landed on the pile of debris. It had only been inches from her feet. She sat down and began to laugh and cry at the same time. Beem let out a groan, pulled himself back on to the boulder and sat down. There was a sharp throbbing in his left hand. He touched it and realized it was bleeding. In spite of the pain, he felt a rush of relief knowing Trince was unharmed.

Everyone's attention now turned to Jinx. Where was he? Was he hurt – or worse? How would they ever explain this to their parents? The seriousness of their situation began to sink in as they realized this *real* adventure might not end like their make-believe ones.

Pria, Wort and Meekus worked their way down to where Beem was sitting. He was trying to gather his thoughts.

"We need to find Jinx. I will never forgive myself if he's hurt."

"He's got to be okay." assured Pria.

She tried to push back the fear.

The children were startled by a brilliant flash of light coming out of the blackness below.

"What was that?" shouted Beem.

"I need to get my foot loose," groaned Spinny, "I'm starting a fire so I can see what I'm doing."

Spinny scraped his flint again and another flash lit up the cavern. Soon a small flame emerged from the pile of sticks and leaves he had gathered, emitting a soft glow. The fire provided warmth and a sense of comfort for their frayed emotions.

"Trince," yelled Beem, "Throw me Spinny's belt. I'll see if I can make a rope long enough to get down."

"Don't you mean get *up*?"

"Both," he said, "Hey, Spinny! Can you see Jinx?"

"I thought I saw him a minute ago. Hold on."

Spinny looked down at the bottom of the pile where he thought he had seen his brother – but the firelight revealed he wasn't there.

"It's not him!" Spinny exclaimed. "But, I could have sworn I saw him."

Beem felt a cold chill come over him.

"Oh, please don't let Jinx be buried under all this stuff," he whispered.

Both Spinny and Trince began calling Jinx's name. It was strange to hear the echo of their voices bouncing around the cavernous space. It had to be enormous. Their eyes strained to see where they were but everything was totally black beyond the flickering light of Spinny's dwindling fire. They felt small and vulnerable. No matter how loud they cried, there was no response from Jinx.

Trince picked her way through the jumble of boulders and wooden poles, trying not to fall or loosen any of the debris. She crouched next to Spinny and together they worked out a plan to free his ankle. He remembered from other adventures he could lift very heavy objects by using a lever. It didn't take Trince long to find a tree limb suitable for the job. She shoved the branch into the gap where Spinny's leg was wedged, and pulled down on the free end. The branch let out a loud creak as the mound slowly opened its jaws. He jerked his leg free.

"Ahhh!" he gasped, rubbing the compressed skin around his ankle.

Trince scrambled to the top of the pile with Spinny's belt and tossed it to Beem who was watching from above. Soon the six of them were standing at the bottom of the cave staring at Jinx's bloodstained cloak lying in the rubble.

"Something's not right about this," stated Pria, "Jinx was wearing this when he jumped off that rock. How could it just come off?"

"I know he was lying there earlier," said Spinny, "I'm sure I saw the outline of his face and hands."

"Jinx!" yelled Beem into the darkness, "This is no time to be playing a joke. We need to get out of here. The adventure is over!"

No response.

Wort whispered to Pria, "I told you holes are evil. We shouldn't have come down here!"

"Holes aren't evil," countered Beem. "That's only what the committee wants you to think. They just don't want us to fall into one and get hurt – like we just did. I think we proved their point today. The best thing for us to do is find Jinx and get home. Agreed?"

"Agreed," echoed the children.

Pria held the torch close to the ground where they noticed two things. First, they found a small puddle of blood confirming Jinx's location. They also noticed the floor under their feet was perfectly flat and smooth. Meekus bent down and wiped his hand across its dusty surface. It glowed with the reflection of the torchlight. None of the children had ever seen anything like it. They bent down and touched the cool, smooth surface, fascinated by the discovery.

"What is this place?" asked Trince.

"It's some sort of room or building," said Pria.

Meekus couldn't stop rubbing the floor.

"What's this made of?" he asked, "It's so smooth and shiny and cold and hard – and swirly."

"It's like the river rocks down by the mill," Spinny deduced, "It must be stone . . . a stone floor?"

"A stone room." said Pria, pointing to a nearby wall.

The light of the torch danced off its polished surface.

"Enough about that! We must remain focused," interrupted Beem, "The task at hand is to figure out what happened to Jinx. He's hurt and we need to find him as soon as we can. This is not good."

"Hey, if he's bleeding," responded Spinny, "We should be able to track him."

"Look over here," said Trince.

She pointed to some footprints tracked across the dirty floor. Every few feet there were small drops of blood.

"There's our first clue!" said Beem mustering his confidence, "Now we're getting somewhere."

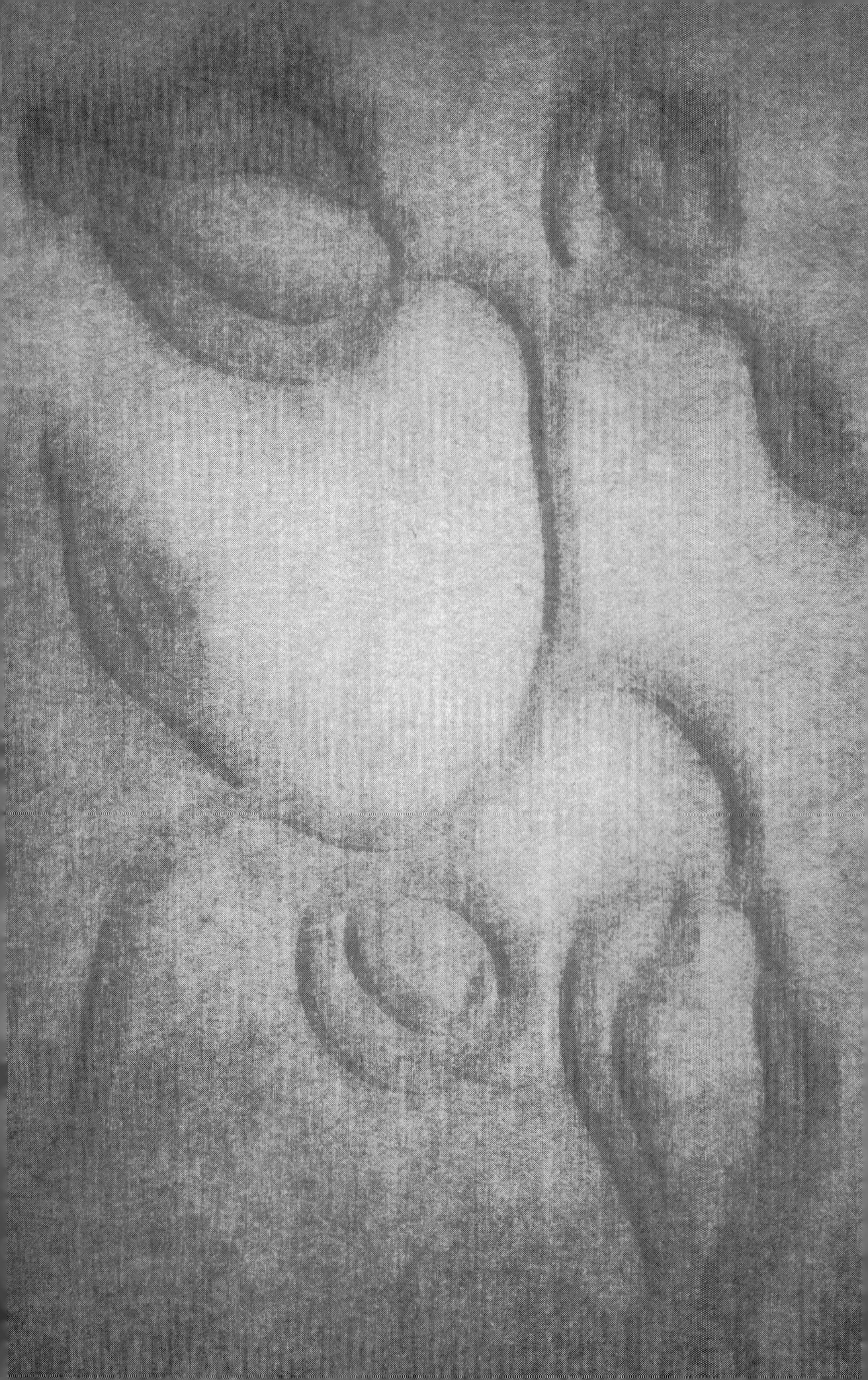

2

Where's Jinx?

The fog in Jinx's mind slowly lifted. He began to hear unfamiliar sounds – distorted and distant, as if his head were under water. He thought he recognized Beem's voice, but the muffled words didn't make any sense. He didn't know what had happened to him, and he had no idea where he was.

All at once, he felt the pain. It coursed through his body like lightning, causing his teeth to clench and every muscle to tense. He attempted to roll on his side, but the agony intensified. His only option was to lie motionless.

He strained to open his eyes, but discovered they were crusted shut. His left eye eventually opened wide enough to see a blurry, flickering light.

Everything was wrong. He knew he was in trouble.

Fear flooded Jinx's thoughts. Realizing his condition, he took a deep breath, pushed back the pain and forced himself to remember what happened.

We were all playing on Broadside Hill . . . and then we lost the throw-stick . . . and then . . . ohhh.

The images of the morning came rushing back.

We fell through the floor of the hole. I must be at the bottom – all broken in pieces.

"Mmmmph!" he moaned, but no one could hear his weak cry.

He tried again, but the effort to call out was too exhausting. He decided it would be best to lie still. The others would find him eventually.

To his surprise, it wasn't long before someone discovered where he was. The person knelt down next to him and began tending to his wounds. The dust was wiped from his face and his cloak was carefully removed. Slowly, a pair of hands patted down the length of his arms and legs. He thought this was strange until he realized they were checking for broken bones. Jinx struggled once more to speak, but the best he could eke out was a whimper.

The stranger never said a word. He went about his business as if he had done this sort of thing before. Jinx didn't pay much attention. He was just happy to be found.

The next thing he knew, his arms were gently folded

over his belly. In one smooth movement, he was lifted and cradled in the arms of his caretaker. The rescuer then began the delicate task of maneuvering through the chaos of logs and boulders. As he moved down the rubble, it became obvious to Jinx the arms carrying him didn't belong to Beem or the others. They felt more like the strong arms of his father. He wondered if Beem had gone to the village and found someone to help.

As soon as the two of them were on solid ground, Jinx was whisked away. He could feel the cool air moving across his face. The voices of his friends faded, disappearing behind them. The only sound remaining was the plodding of the man's feet across the ground. He tried to open his eyes again but everything was pitch black. He figured they must have swollen shut.

Fear seized Jinx again. Why wasn't this person talking? Why didn't the others follow? Where was he being taken? Fear turned to panic, but there was nothing he could do to escape the clutches of the stranger. All he really wanted was to be home playing with his dog. Tears began to flow.

After what seemed like a long time, he was carried down a flight of stairs, but it made no sense. Wasn't he at the bottom of a hole? Finally the stranger stopped, placing him gently on a cold hard surface. Jinx didn't like how it felt and struggled to get up but the pain was too much.

He could hear objects clinking together and the

quiet shuffling of items being moved about. Then, as quickly as they started, the noises stopped. The stranger whispered something he didn't understand and slipped away. Jinx was all alone.

His mind began to taunt him.

"You're dead," it whispered.

Jinx strained to hear something . . . anything.

I wonder if I've been carried off by a spirit.

He hated the idea of being left in a state of nothingness, but strangely, the cold surface beneath his back brought him comfort.

I can't be dead; I can feel this.

The silence was suddenly broken by a buzzing noise, followed by a loud crack that echoed around him. It startled him at first but eased his thoughts about being dead. A faint light appeared, revealing the walls of a room. He realized his good eye had been open the entire time.

The room he was lying in began to get brighter. The walls themselves were emitting the light. Cobwebs hung from peculiar objects, and dust covered everything. As he was taking in his surroundings, the stranger walked past. Without a word the man began a flurry of activity as he set about tending to Jinx's wounds. He moved quickly, taking different ointments and applying them to Jinx's injured body. Jinx tried hard to stay engaged, but in the end, the pain took over. He slipped into unconsciousness.

Spinny figured out the footprints were heading in two directions, and they were much too large to be Jinx's. Whoever had made them had entered the room, picked up Jinx, and left the same way.

"Who would take Jinx?" Pria cried, "That's crazy!"

"Holes ARE evil!" yelled Wort, turning to Meekus in terror, "I bet Jinx was taken away by a sorcerer who is going to eat him. He's probably roasting him right now."

"Stop it!" screamed Meekus.

"Quiet, Wort," scolded Beem, "You don't know what you're talking about. I'm sure Jinx is being helped by a friendly person."

Beem desperately hoped his words were true.

"Explain how this person could carry Jinx in the dark," asked Trince.

"That's right," agreed Spinny, "I never saw a torch. Maybe these footprints aren't a clue at all."

Pria bent down and touched one of the drops of blood. It felt sticky as she smeared it across the floor leaving a long red streak.

"This is still fresh," her voice trembled, "This has to be the right way."

There was so much blood on the floor they could only imagine the worst.

Jinx's rescuer became concerned that the boy's injuries were too extensive to be mended. The treatments weren't enough to stop the bleeding or repair the broken bones. The man stared at the boy's limp body. A string of saliva dangled from the corner of his open mouth. He feared the child would soon be dead.

Going back to Maidenton would only result in more problems for the children. They had to find Jinx. They were afraid his life depended on it. They would have to follow the mysterious set of footprints disappearing into the black.

They banded together and set off across the giant room. The vast space made them feel exposed and vulnerable. Staying close gave them a much-needed sense of security.

At the far end of the room, they discovered a huge archway carved into one of the massive walls. Beneath the ornate stonework was a large passageway leading them deeper into the mountain. The footprints continued forward.

The expansive hallway was lined with piles of unusual objects and furniture. Everything was coated in a thick layer of dust. The eerie scene was nothing like the adventure they had imagined when they set out that morning.

Spinny and Trince were out in front as usual, exploring some of the dark abandoned spaces. Everyone was worried about Jinx, but at the same time, fascinated with their surroundings. Trince picked up a bowl shaped like a flower. It reflected a bright red glow from the torch as the others approached. When she held it to the light, it became transparent. She carefully wiped the dust from it with her skirt.

"This is beautiful!"

Her heart leapt with joy at the discovery.

"Put it down, Trince," ordered Beem, "We don't have time for that."

She reluctantly set the bowl back, hoping she might find it again on their way out.

They continued to call Jinx's name, but heard nothing but the echo of their own frightened voices. To his amazement, Spinny noticed a dim light just beyond them.

"Come on!" he yelled, "There must be a way out of here."

"Wait!" snapped Beem, "Do not get separated from the group!"

Trince and Spinny ran down the hall anyway, making sure Beem could still see them. They found themselves looking down a twisty stairwell with light coming from below.

"Jiiiiiiiinxx!" shouted Trince.

. . . still no answer.

The man heard Trince's voice and realized time was running out. He went to the door and closed it tightly. The thought of the boy's friends finding him dead was unacceptable. And if he were to be discovered, it could be disastrous for them all. There was only one thing left to do.

The man was unsure if this was the right time, or even the right person, but he would need Jinx to be awake in order for everything to work properly. He gently slapped Jinx's cheek causing his head to roll limply to the side.

He leaned over to his ear and whispered loudly, "Son, I need you to wake up."

There was no response.

His last resort was to use the smoke. He had never

heard of anyone doing this with an unconscious person before. He wasn't even sure if it was possible, but it was his only hope. The man reached into his cloak and pulled out a cloth bundle. He unfolded the frayed fabric revealing several small wooden sticks. He pulled one out and carefully returned the others to his cloak. He lit the end of the stick and blew out the flame. A small plume of smoke arose from its glowing tip. He rolled Jinx on his side and held the burning ember before his face.

"If you can hear me . . . breathe it in."

After a few minutes, the man lifted Jinx's eyelid with his thumb and looked intently into his eye.

"Come on, son," he whispered.

Moments later, Jinx's eye began to sparkle and glow. Delighted with the result, he dropped the stick, rolled Jinx on his back and placed his hands on the boy's temples. The man's head tilted slightly backward. He stood motionless, eyes rolled back, as if in a trance.

The trauma of their quest was taking its toll on Meekus. A normal day for the six-year-old was playing with his friends and trying his best not to cry from a scraped knee. Following a trail of blood through a dark cavern was beyond anything he could have imagined. He wanted to go home.

"Jinx, come on – answer us!" he yelled, "Where do you think he is?"

He gazed up at Beem, with complete trust, believing he would figure out what was going on.

"I don't know," Beem responded.

He tried to remain strong for his friends but struggled to restrain his own frustration.

The children hurried down the hall and completely missed the room with the closed door.

The man's eyes returned to normal and he scanned the room to make sure they were still alone. He leaned over the table and took Jinx's hand in his own.

The man:	*Can you hear me?*
Jinx:	*Yes I can hear you. Is this a dream?*
The man:	*No, this is real. Listen carefully. You're unconscious and your body is about to die. You need to transport. Do you understand what I mean?*
Jinx:	*Yes. I know what transporting is . . . and I know how to do it. This is very*

	strange. How do I know these things? What is happening to me, and who are you?

Jinx began to get frightened. Part of him was curious about this influx of strange information, but at the same time, he questioned if this voice could be trusted.

The man:	*I am an Ancient.*
Jinx:	*An Ancient? That's impossible. Wake me up. I want to go home.*
The Ancient:	*There is no time! Now listen to me. You were in a bad accident, and you need to transport. Think, son, think.*
Jinx:	*Alright . . . I understand. Transporting will heal my body.*
The Ancient:	*Right. Now, think of a place close by where nobody will see you reappear.*
Jinx:	*The top of Broadside Hill.*
The Ancient:	*Good – picture that in your mind and don't let go of my hand.*

"Everybody stop!" yelled Spinny.

The group came to a halt, wondering what the problem was.

"Something's wrong," he continued, "There are plenty of footprints in the dust but I don't see any more blood."

Trince poked her head in a doorway a few feet in front of them.

"Hey! The footprints end in this room and turn around."

Beem fought his rising frustration and fear. He couldn't get the terrible scenarios out of his mind.

How could I have missed that? I'm supposed to be a leader.

"Good catch, Spinny," said Beem, "We'll need to retrace our steps – and pay better attention this time. Look for anything unusual. There are too many footprints now."

The children headed back in the direction from which they had come. Trince and Spinny pushed their way to the front again.

"Stop it, you two!" Beem yelled, "This is not a game."

They ran ahead anyway. This time, Spinny noticed the closed door and grabbed the handle to take a look inside.

"What's in here?"

The Ancient could hear the children rattling the door.

The Ancient: *Are you ready, son?*

The door flew open with a bang. The man looked up to see two shocked children standing before him.

"Aaaaaaah!" screamed Trince as she beheld the strange man with fire in his eyes.

The Ancient: *Now!*

Jinx and the man vanished from the room.

"WHAT?!" yelled Spinny as he witnessed the impossible.

He attempted to back out of the room, but tripped and fell to the ground. In complete panic, he began kicking and clawing his way into the hall.

"No way – there is no way!" he yelled.

The others ran to the door to see what was going on. In the center of the room was a metal bench smeared with blood. Along the walls were counters covered with strange-looking bottles. One of them had tipped over, leaving a stream of yellow liquid dripping to the floor. Spinny sat dumbfounded with Trince clinging tightly to his arm.

"What is it?" asked Beem as he touched Trince's shoulder.

They both jumped in surprise, glaring at Beem and utterly speechless.

"What happened?" he asked again.

All at once, a flood of words and wild gestures bombarded him. It was impossible to understand.

"We were just – and the door – when he saw us – there was blood – then his eyes were – when Jinx looked – they were on fire and disappeared – gone – just like that," and Spinny snapped his fingers.

"What happened?" asked Meekus as he tried to sort out the jumble of nonsense.

"I don't know," said a bewildered Pria, "Something about Jinx and another man and now they're gone."

"Trince," Beem said calmly, "Only you talk this time. Tell us what you saw . . . slowly."

"All right," gasped Trince, "So – Spinny opened the door and there was this man looking at Jinx who was lying on that bench over there. And, then he looked at us."

"And his eyes had fire coming out of them!" added Spinny.

"Just Trince!" Beem yelled as he held his hand over Spinny's mouth, "Now, go on."

"So," she continued, "The man's eyes were on fire or something. They were glowing and had sparks moving around in them. I don't know. Anyway, as soon as he saw us they both vanished."

The other children didn't know what to think of such an outlandish story.

"So where did they go?" asked Wort in disbelief.

"No!" stressed Spinny, "They disappeared.

One second they were right there and the next – they were gone."

"This is too much!" declared Beem, "I don't think you saw what you think you saw. There must be a hidden passageway. Everyone look around. See if you can find an exit. This place is starting to play tricks on our minds."

The children began to explore the room, banging on walls, opening cupboard doors, trying to move the bench, jumping up and down on the floor – but there was no way out except through the door they had just entered.

"What's this?" exclaimed Meekus picking up something from the floor.

"It's a twig," replied Wort.

"I know it's a twig, but look – its smoking."

Meekus began to blow on the tip, watching it glow red.

"Let me see that," said Beem.

The others continued looking for clues while he examined the stick. He inhaled some of the smoke. At first, the pungent smell took him by surprise. But as the fragrance lingered, it became sweet and intoxicating.

"This smells really good," he thought.

Beem liked the smell so much he took several whiffs before setting it on the metal bench.

"So now what?" asked Pria.

Beem turned to Trince, "Are you sure you saw Jinx?"

"I know what I saw, Beem," she said adamantly, "Besides, Spinny was right beside me. He saw the same thing."

"Everything she told you is true," he concurred, "The man with the eyes, Jinx on this bench, and they both disappeared. It sounds impossible, but that's what happened. I swear it."

"This is not good."

Beem felt himself growing more and more impatient. If he didn't bring Jinx home, alive or dead, the whole village would soon be asking questions.

I am headed for Punishment House for sure.

"No, it's going to turn out just fine," said a voice in his mind.

For a brief moment, a blanket of peace surrounded him. He didn't know why, but he felt like everything *would* be just fine. His thoughts were interrupted by Pria shaking him.

"I said . . . we can't stay in here forever, and you looked straight through me. Are you all right?"

Beem gathered his thoughts.

"Y-you're right," he agreed, "We need to find our way out of here."

"But what about Jinx?" asked Meekus, "Are we going to give up looking for him?"

"No, of course not. I know we can find him. On our

way out, keep looking for clues . . . like this stick."

Beem picked it up and turned to Trince.

"This has to mean something."

As he lifted it to his face, Trince screamed in horror. She struck his chest with her fists, shoving him away.

"What's wrong with you?" asked Beem.

All she could do was stare at him in shock. Pria ran to her side.

"What is it, Trincy?"

She pointed at Beem's face.

"His eyes . . . his eyes were just like that man's eyes."

"What are you talking about?" argued Spinny, "His eyes don't look anything like that man. They look just fine."

"No!" retorted Trince, "When he was looking at the stick, Beem's eye's changed."

Spinny took the twig from Beem's hand and held it in front of his face. To everyone's amazement, his eyes began to glow.

"Impossible!" Spinny yelled as he stepped back.

"What's happening?" asked Beem.

"It's true. Trince was right. Your eyes are just like that mans."

"I saw it too," said Pria, "Something happened to you!"

Meekus ran to Pria and held tight.

"Give me that thing!" Beem demanded, snatching the twig from Spinny.

He walked to a nearby mirror, cleaned its dusty surface and slowly lifted the stick to his eyes. As he did, they began to emit a dazzling light.

"What is going on?" he whispered in disbelief.

He reached up with his other hand, trying to touch the sparks coming from his eyes.

"Ahh!"

"What happened?" cried Meekus.

"I poked myself in the eye."

"I'm scared," he whimpered.

"Don't be afraid," Pria reassured, "Things will work out – real soon. Right, Beem?"

"Yes . . . absolutely!" he said as he stepped away from the mirror, "Everything is going to be just fine."

A realization came over Beem. He actually *believed* what had just come out of his mouth. He didn't know why he thought that, considering their circumstances, but he somehow knew Jinx was safe. They simply needed to get out of the hole. Beem extinguished the burning stick and tucked what was left into his pocket.

"It's time we get going," he said to Meekus with an affirming smile.

The children were encouraged by Beem's words. He led them forward with a newfound confidence. They made their way back down the hall, and up the stairs toward the large room where their adventure had started.

"Hey Beem!" yelled Pria, "Wait a second. We can't see."

"Yeah," added Spinny. "Let me light the torches."

Beem stopped and looked back at the others fiddling with their flints.

"Trince, come over here."

Beem watched as she felt her way along the walls, trying not to trip.

"How dark is it in here?" he asked her as she approached.

"What are you talking about?" she replied.

"How far can you see right now?"

"I can see the boys lighting the torches back there."

"What about in the other direction?"

"I guess I can make out a few dark shapes. But everything else is just black – like 'total black'."

Beem looked in the same direction and could see everything, just as if the hallway were fully lit.

"So you can't see that chair?"

"What chair?"

"The clunky one next to the tapestry."

"Wow! You can see that? You have good vision. All I can make out is a big blob."

She pointed to a large chest only a few feet in front of them. The chair and tapestry he was pointing to were at the far end of the corridor, thirty feet away. A sense of wonder overtook him as he realized what he could do.

"Trince," Beem whispered, "I can see in the dark."

"What do you mean?"

"I mean I can see all the way down this hall as if it were day."

"You're starting to scare me, Beem!"

"Hold on," he said.

He began to blink and cover his eyes.

"That's strange," he exclaimed.

"What?"

"It only works with one eye."

"Which one?"

"The one still hurting from me poking it."

"Well, maybe you should poke out your other eye," Trince joked.

Beem reached up to touch his other eye.

"Ouch!"

He paused and focused.

"Hey, you're right! That worked!"

Beem began to play around with his eyes. Every time he touched them, they would turn on or off the ability to see in the dark.

"Come on, Beem, I was just kidding."

"Joke all you want, I can see all the way down this hall," he said, "I'll prove it to you. Wait here and I'll come right back."

Trince heard his footsteps fade into the distance.

"Hey, Trincy," called Pria, "What are the two of you doing up there in the dark?"

"Nothing," she replied with a note of uneasiness, "Beem says he can see in the dark. That's all . . ."

Beem raced down the corridor. He could see everything – details and colors. It was amazing! He felt a flood of excitement as the cool air exhilarated him. For a moment, he forgot all about his problems.

Suddenly his foot caught something, launching him into the air. He tried to recover, but he hit the floor hard and slid across its smooth surface. He stood up, rubbing his bruised elbows. Beside him was a small chair tipped on its side. He glanced at it a second time and realized it didn't have a shadow.

That's odd.

Then a flash of understanding came to him. Without a source of light, there was nothing to create shadows. He decided it would be best to move slower until he learned how to determine distances and depth. His new gift had not come with instructions.

He passed under the ornate archway and entered the great hall where they had first fallen in. He advanced in awe, taking in the immensity of the room for the first time.

Along each of the walls were tall, intricately carved columns. Where the pillars met the ceiling, the design split into three narrow arms that spread out across the ceiling in a web-like pattern. In between the crisscrossed tapestry was the same polished stone that seemed to be everywhere.

At the opposite end of the room was the mountain of debris where the massive ceiling had caved in. He spotted Jinx's cloak. His plan was to bring it to Trince to prove he could see in the dark.

Before he did anything else, he decided to make sure he wasn't imagining the whole thing. He stopped in the center of the room and touched his eyes again. Instantly, all was completely black. He waved his hands in front of his face but couldn't see a thing. He turned the other direction wondering if he might make out the torchlight from the others, but there was nothing.

He touched his eyes a second time . . .

"Whuuuh!" he screamed.

Walking toward him was Jinx. His clothing was torn and bloody, but he appeared to be unharmed. Next to him was a man – whose eyes seemed to be on fire.

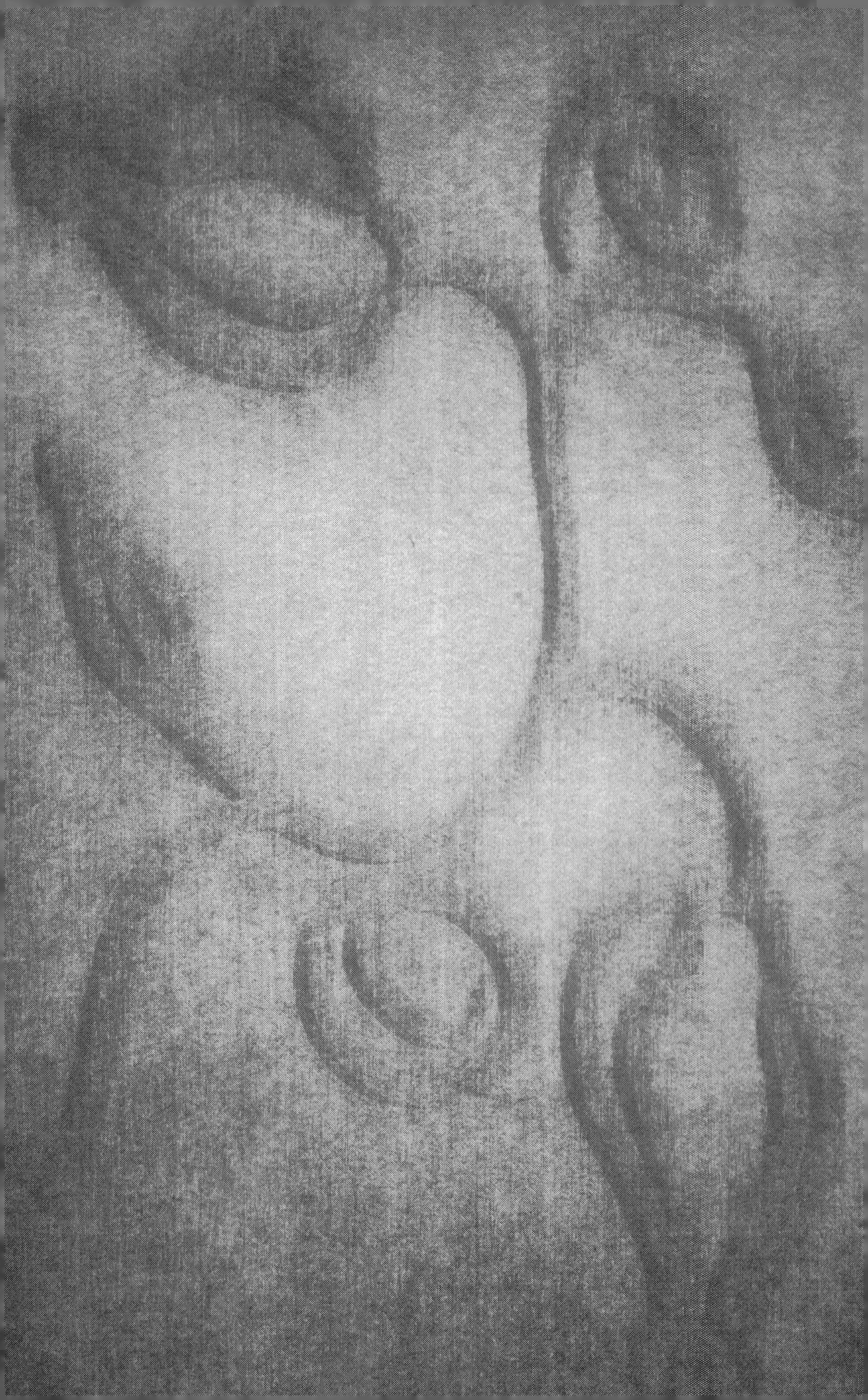

3

The Legends Are True

Pria made an effort to establish a sense of order without letting her fears become obvious. It had been far too long since Beem ran off alone. Now that he was missing, it was her responsibility to get everyone home safely.

The children continued to call Beem's name, but were answered by an eerie silence. It felt as though the darkness was creeping in from all sides.

"Something must have happened to him," admitted Trince.

"Either Beem is lost or he's had an accident," announced Pria, "In either case, we're not going to stay here and do nothing. I think it's time to get help."

They all agreed.

Meekus and Wort held tightly to Pria's hands as they made their way forward. The flickering torchlight created distorted shadows as they passed through the hallway. Their fascination with this place was now gone. It had been displaced with fear, bordering on panic. Without Beem's calming presence, the slightest noise sent them reeling. Meekus began to cry, and he kept wiping his nose on Pria's sleeve as they walked along.

Because Beem was the oldest of the seven, it would have been his responsibility to explain about Jinx. If anyone were to get into real trouble, it would have fallen on him. But now that he was missing, everyone knew they would share in the consequences. Even worse, one by one, they were beginning to disappear. Wort's comments about 'holes being evil' now held a note of truth.

"Can you see us, young man?" asked the stranger.

Beem backed away from the man with glowing eyes.

"Who are you and what do you want?"

"Calm down, Beem," reassured Jinx, "Hey, can you touch-talk too?"

"What are you talking about?"

Beem's heart was beating so fast he thought it would explode.

"And . . . and how did you get better? Am I hallucinating?"

Jinx ran to Beem and looked intently into his eyes.

"You can see me can't you?"

"Of course I can see you. You're standing right in front of me. But who is that guy?"

Jinx smiled.

"That . . . is Mr. Lyndal Froam. He is the man who saved my life."

"Pleased to meet you, Beem," he said.

Lyndal smiled warmly and offered Beem his hand in greeting. Beem was confused. He was overjoyed to see Jinx again – even more relieved that he was alive, but he didn't know what to make of this mysterious man. His reasoning told him to be cautious but another voice inside him told him to trust.

"Well?" asked Jinx, "Are you going to take his hand or not?"

Beem hesitated for a moment, then reluctantly held out his hand. The man took it with a firm grip that startled Beem. He pulled back in fear but the man held tightly.

Lyndal: *How is it you can see in the dark?*

Beem shook his hand free as if it were on fire and backed up again.

"How did you do that?" he demanded, "Are you

some kind of witch or something?"

"Did he touch-talk you?" asked Jinx, "I can do that too! Watch this."

Jinx grabbed Beem's hand.

Jinx:	*I can talk to you by touching your hand*

Beem gawked at his friend in astonishment. How could these things be happening? The reality he knew so well was being shaken apart by new possibilities. He couldn't decide if he should panic or get really excited. His curiosity got the best of him and he decided to give it a try.

Beem:	*Can you hear me?*
Jinx:	*Yes – isn't this great!*
Beem:	*I'm not sure. Can he hear what we're saying?*
Jinx:	*I don't think so*
Beem:	*Who is he? What does he want?*

"He's an Ancient!" Jinx said aloud as he released Beem's hand.

"You mean from The Legends?" sputtered Beem.

He remembered some of the crazy folklore his mother had told him growing up.

"It's true!" Jinx replied, "He's like a billion years old. He gave me the powers."

"But the real question is . . ." interrupted Lyndal, "How did *you* get the powers?"

Beem whispered to Jinx.

"How do you know if we can trust this guy?"

"C'mon Beem, he saved my life! What else could you ask for?"

"I don't know," Beem sighed in frustration, "This is all too confusing. I mean, look at him, he's not normal."

"Tell me young man . . . what does normal look like?" asked Lyndal, "Would it be easier for you if my eyes were like yours?"

Lyndal closed his eyes tightly and opened them again. They no longer emitted the sparkling light.

Beem was hit with the realization that his eyes looked just like Lyndal's when he saw them in the mirror. 'Normal' was taking on a new definition.

"I'm sorry sir," he apologized, "I didn't mean to insult you, I'm just a bit overwhelmed right now . . . *and* a little scared."

As soon as he said those words, Beem began to relax.

"It's all right," Lyndal reassured him, "I understand. But, I would still like to know how you received the powers."

"To tell you the truth, I don't know how I can do these things. I didn't even know I could talkytouch until just now."

"But you did figure out you could see in the dark."

"Yes, but that just happened a few minutes ago. I

came running in here to prove it to Trince. Oh no! I need to get back to the others right away. They must be wondering where I am."

"They'll be fine," said Lyndal, "I can feel it."

"That's strange; I feel the same way too, but it doesn't make any sense. I've been gone far too long. They must be worried."

"You have the powers all right, but you don't even know what you have . . . or how to use them. Would you like me to give you some understanding about your new abilities?"

Beem knew he should return to the others, but was fascinated with what was happening.

"I – I guess so," he replied, "But I really need to get going. I'm responsible for them."

"This will only take a few minutes," Lyndal explained, "I think it would be best."

Lyndal didn't hesitate. He went straight to Beem and placed his hands on his temples. Before Beem could question what was happening, his eyes rolled back as volumes of information, knowledge, history, and understanding were transferred to his mind. After a few minutes, they were both back to normal. Beem was now fully aware of what was happening.

"I smelled the smoke from the stick!" he blurted out in amazement.

He dug through his cloak for the little stub of wood.

"It was still smoldering when we found it. That's

how I received the powers."

Beem was thrilled by this sudden revelation.

"I must have dropped it in the chaos of taking care of Jinx," Lyndal explained, "May I please have it back?"

"Of course."

Beem handed it to Lyndal.

"I don't think it would be wise for me to be here when the others arrive. We've all had enough excitement for one day."

As soon as Lyndal finished his sentence, Beem heard his name being called in the distance. The boys turned around to see the approaching torchlight illuminating the corridor.

"Do you have to go?" asked Beem, turning back to Lyndal.

He was no longer there.

"Just remember, Beem," warned Jinx, "you and I aren't like Lyndal. He can transport as often as he wants, but we have limits. Lyndal told me over and over – 'Don't waste a transport. Only do it when you're desperate – life and death.' Understand?"

"Yes – I think so," answered Beem.

They could hear the sound of running feet and soon Spinny and Trince were standing at the entrance to the large room looking around. Beem cupped his hands around his mouth and yelled as loud as he could.

"We're over here!"

The two of them ran toward Beem's voice until they could see him and Jinx running to meet them.

"Jinx! You're alive!" yelled Spinny.

He noticed the bloodstains on his ripped clothing.

"So, what happened to you? Is this some sort of joke?"

"No joke. I was dead, but now I'm alive again. Look at me," he said laughing, "I'm brand new!"

Years of bickering and competition instantly dissolved as Jinx hugged his brother for the first time. Trince was caught up in the moment and joined the two boys in a group embrace.

"Oh, Beem!" she cried.

With tears of joy, she ran to him, threw her arms around his neck and hugged him fiercely.

"Everything you told me about Jinx was right. I'm so sorry I didn't believe you," said Beem.

"I knew I wasn't crazy. But what happened – how did you get here?"

"It was incredible," Jinx replied, "I have so much to . . ."

"Beem!" yelled Pria as she and the two boys entered the room.

"It's Jinx!" screamed Meekus.

The three of them dashed across the room to their friends and embraced. Meekus ran circles around them yelling, "It's Jinx, it's Jinx – he's alive!"

Wort shook his hand.

"Well at least you're not dead. Now, shouldn't we be going?"

"You're right!" Beem said, "We need to get everyone home right now! I don't have enough time to tell you all that happened today. But you must know the man with the fiery eyes is no ordinary man . . . he's an Ancient."

The sun was setting as they emerged from the fissure in Broadside Hill. They were tired, hungry and disheveled. The sky was already a burnt orange color, signaling the final hour of the day. As quickly as they could, they scrambled down the hill, said hasty good-byes, and ran to their homes. If they were lucky, there was a slight chance they could see each other the following day.

Beem had to take Meekus and Wort home first, so he would arrive at his house even later than the others would. Along the way, he instructed Wort that if he told his parents about going in the hole, he would never be allowed to play with them again. Wort agreed and promised to keep quiet.

By the time Beem got home, his father was already seated at the kitchen table. Dinner had been served. According to Kinsmen tradition, the father was always the last to be seated for the evening meal. Anyone late to the table would be sent to their room without food. Beem looked at his father's stern expression, hung his head and headed to his room. In addition to experiencing the greatest adventure of his life, Beem had gone all day without eating. He was ravenous. The aroma was almost too much to bear as he walked past the kitchen. He longed for a taste of the red sausages steaming on the serving platter.

He washed up, put on his nightclothes and climbed into the hammock that hung in the corner of his room. He gathered his pillows around him as he did every night, nestling in for a well-deserved sleep. As his bed gently swung back and forth, he began to smile. He could hardly believe the events of the day. The more he thought about it, the more incredible it seemed. Then, out of nowhere, a thought crossed his mind.

I can record the events of the day in my memory.

Beem sat up in surprise. He knew he possessed another new power.

This must be part of the information Lyndal imparted to me.

Exhaustion immediately gave way to excitement and he decided to give it a try. He touched his fingers to his temples and began to record the events of the day, just by thinking them:

> *This is my first attempt at logging something into my memory.*

> *Today I met Lyndal Froam. He's an Ancient . . . like the ones in The Legends. He says he was born 163 years before the mass departure. That would make him more than 2000 years old. It seems impossible, but I believe him.*

> *Most people think The Legends are nothing but folk tales. I used to think they were just bedtime stories. I had no idea they might be true. All of that changed today.*

> *Lyndal gave Jinx and me special powers and the ability to know how to use them. It's strange but I like it. Now that I know The Ancients are real, I will learn everything there is about being one.*

> *That's all.*

Beem opened his eyes, wondering if anything had happened. He touched his temples a second time and repeated the process. After a few seconds, they popped open.

"That's great!" he said aloud.

Every thought he had stored was there, word for word, exactly as he had logged them.

Tomorrow I'll try to transfer this to Jinx.

Tap, tap, tap. Beem's bedroom door swung open and his parents stepped inside.

"Lucas," scolded his father, "What was so important that kept you out so late? You know you are supposed to be home *before* dinner."

"Yes, sir," Beem replied sheepishly, "I know I should be home on time. I'm sorry I was so late. It was such a great adventure, I lost track of the time."

"What was it this time?" his mother asked, "Rescuing the princess again?"

"No," said Beem, "We found our way inside an underground building where we met an Ancient, and he showed us how to see in the dark and how to talk without speaking."

Beem held his breath awaiting their response to the truth he had just confessed.

"I'm glad you're having fun with your friends," she continued, "but you can't keep coming home late. I'm afraid you're going to have to do some extra chores tomorrow. Maybe that will help you remember to keep track of the time. Your imagination is no excuse for breaking the house rules."

"And you're the oldest," reminded his father, "You are to set an example for the other children. So, when you're finished with your chores I want you to apologize to all the parents. Understood?"

"Yes, I understand."

His parents left the room, chuckling about the fantastic story Beem had just told them. He nestled back into his pillows and smiled as he stared at the rough wooden beams above him. He felt such joy and hope, two unfamiliar emotions among his people.

A few minutes passed and his door opened again. His mother set a small plate of food on his desk.

"You can clean the dish in the morning," she said softly, "Just be sure to get plenty of sleep tonight, you'll have a lot to do tomorrow."

He climbed out of bed, ran to his mother and gave her a big hug. She kissed him on the forehead.

"Good night, Lucas."

"Good night."

Beem wasted no time devouring the pile of cold sausages. It tasted marvelous. He could never understand why food, even cold food, tasted so much better after a full day of adventures. He popped the last bite of meat in to his mouth, sucked the sweet and tangy chutney from each finger and licked his plate clean. He could have eaten two more platefuls, but he was content for now.

The next morning, Beem's father burst into his room.

"Wake up young man! You have a lot to get done today. You might as well get an early start."

Beem peered out through his sleepy eyes. It was still dark. He could make out the blurry outline of his father standing in the doorway, already dressed in his work clothes.

"What's this?" his father asked as he noticed the empty plate sitting on the desk.

"Mom brought it to me last night," Beem mumbled.

His father walked out of the room muttering, "That woman spoils the boy."

Beem rubbed his eyes, stretched, and began to dress. He was a little groggy from experimenting with his new abilities all night. Even with the lack of sleep, and chores looming ahead of him, he felt energetic. He had found a new sense of purpose.

His goal was to get everything done as quickly as possible. He cleaned the dishes, put them in the cupboard, swept the lower level of the house, tidied his room so you could actually see the floor and scrubbed both washbasins. His mother was impressed with Beem's willingness to work and even more so that he did it without complaining.

When the sun reached midday, she decided to give him a break. She gave him a handful of coins and a shopping list.

"I need you to run to the square for me. There's more than enough to buy everything on the list," she instructed, "and a little extra so you can get yourself some lunch."

Beem kissed her on the cheek and headed for the door.

"Don't forget to come back before dinner!"

"I won't!"

Beem set off for the square. Instead of staying on the path in front of the homes, he ran through each front yard, leaping over the hedges defining their borders. He cleared the last bush and turned onto the main path leading to the shops.

Spinny was playing in front of his house when he saw Beem run by.

"Ho there!" he shouted and jogged over to meet him, "So did you get into trouble?"

"Yup, I have to do chores all day and then apologize to everybody's parents. Did you and Jinx get in trouble?"

"I didn't, but Mom keeps interrogating Jinx. We were pretty lucky our Dad wasn't home. Anyway, how come you're allowed out so soon?"

"I'm running errands for my mom and getting something to eat. Want to join me?"

"Sure, as long as I get a taste of whatever you get."

The boys walked into Maidenton's busy center square. It was filled with noisy shop owners and women buying supplies for the day. The square was an open-air bazaar located across the main bridge to the village. Along one side were two-story buildings hosting a variety of shops along their ground floors with residences above where the merchants lived. In front was a large public area where pushcarts were wheeled in every morning by local vendors. For as long as Beem could remember, they were always the same carts, owned by the same people, and parked in the same spots. Brightly decorated awnings and vibrant canopies above the pushcarts made the square a wonderful bouquet of colors. It was a festival of sights, smells and sounds.

On the opposite side of the square was Punishment House. The ominous structure stood out as a constant reminder of the ever-present Keeon rule. Its stark façade was positioned to be seen from all of the public areas around the square. Its presence was resented by the entire community.

Beem decided it was best to eat first and then shop. On the way to their favorite food stall, he noticed Trince with her mother.

"Mrs. Tummins!"

"Well if it isn't Mr. Beeman. I see you are out and about today."

"Not really. I have to do chores all day. I'm just down here picking up some things for my mother. But, I wanted to apologize for yesterday."

Mrs. Tummins stopped and looked him in the eye.

"Well?" she stated, "Go on."

"I'm very sorry for keeping Trince out so late yesterday, Mrs. Tummins. It was completely my fault. I'm the oldest. I should have known better. It won't happen again."

"Well I have to tell you," she scolded, "Trince's father is not happy with you. It may be a couple of days before you two can play together again."

"I understand. If I were in his shoes I would be . . ."

"All right, fine," she interrupted, "Don't get carried away. Apology accepted. Now what are you supposed to be doing?"

"I have some things I need to buy," he said, pulling the wadded up list from his pocket, "but I was going to eat first."

Trince pulled on her mother's arm and with her most forlorn expression begged, "Please?"

"Oh, all right, but only because Beem apologized, and don't go running off. I want to see you both sitting at that table right over there."

"Thank you, Mrs. Tummins," exclaimed Beem.

"Yeah, thanks, Mom!"

She took Beem's arm and the two of them ran toward Spinny who was waiting near the vendors.

"Wait!" Mrs. Tummins yelled.

She pulled out some coins and handed them to Trince.

"Don't buy cakes with this. You need a proper meal."

"Yes Mom."

The three children headed to their favorite food stalls, bought what they liked, and returned to the table. Trince had an enormous appetite since she had missed dinner the night before. She consumed her food with enthusiasm and then helped herself to Beem's.

"I love food," she said as she stuffed a wad of grilled bread in her mouth, "I almosht fainted lasht night when I wazj shent to my room."

"Did you get in much trouble?" asked Beem.

"Of course," she said, "I'm not allowed to leave the house by myself for three days."

"Ohhhhhhhh – that's horrible," teased Spinny.

"I suppose you didn't get in trouble at all," she asked.

"You're very smart . . . for a girl," he retorted.

Trince leaned over the bench to punch him.

"Stop it you two," cried Beem intercepting her arm, "What we need to do is figure out how to find The Ancient again."

"You mean that creepy guy from the hole?" asked Trince, "I thought I was seeing things when he and Jinx disappeared."

"Yeah," added Spinny, "I don't ever want to see that guy again."

"I felt the same way when I met him," said Beem, "I thought he was a witch. But, when I got to know him, he turned out to be amazing. He knows things – important things, and I think he wants to help us. Besides, he saved Jinx's life! All I know is, I have a bunch of questions I want to ask him."

The three of them began strategizing about how to get back inside Broadside. Spinny thought they should sneak off while nobody was watching, but under the circumstances that would be impossible. Beem concluded it was best to wait until their parents had calmed down. But he was anxious to talk to Lyndal again.

It wasn't long before Mrs. Tummins had finished her shopping.

"You boys should start thinking about getting home," she reminded them, "You've been here quite a while."

"You're right!" answered Beem, "I don't want to be late today!"

He stood up and gathered his things.

"See you later, Trince."

"Bye."

Beem told Spinny goodbye and headed into the produce area. This was one of Beem's favorite places in the village. The brightly colored awnings made kaleidoscope patterns on his arms as he walked underneath them. It was magical. Each cart had its own unique personality. Some were jammed with trinkets while others were lined with the most sumptuous food. The wonderful smells of rich spices and baked breads were mouthwatering.

He also enjoyed negotiating a good price with the vendors. He considered it a personal challenge to barter a price even lower than his mother could. As he stopped to admire a mound of freshly baked bread, he heard an unfamiliar voice from the other side of the cart.

"We need to talk."

Beem couldn't see beyond the pile of bread, so he maneuvered around the display for a better look. Standing opposite him was a tall thin man. Beem tried to see his face, but the hood of his cloak was pulled up, making it impossible.

That's odd. Why would someone have their hood up in the middle of the day?

Beem knew better than to talk to strangers so he turned to walk away. But something inside him said to wait. It was the same voice he had heard several times since the previous day's adventure. He made sure the bread vendor was close by in case something went wrong.

The man approached and extended a shaky wrinkled hand in greeting. Strands of long grey hair hung from under his hood.

"Hello, young man."

Beem refused the man's hand.

"Do I know you?"

"Sure you do. We met yesterday."

He was lying. The only person he had met on the previous day was The Ancient, who was a much younger man.

"That's impossible," said Beem, "I've never seen you before."

He turned to leave but the man reached out and seized his hand. Beem looked up in astonishment. The man positioned himself so he could see inside the hood.

Lyndal: *It's me, Lyndal*

His eyes were glowing under the shadow of his cloak.

Beem: *How can that be? You look so old.*
Lyndal: *We need to talk, but not here. Meet me on the bridge during total black . . . tonight.*

Lyndal released his hand and disappeared into the crowd.

"Well are you going to buy something or not?" asked the bread vendor.

Beem, still shocked, turned and smiled at the baker.

"Oh . . . uh yes," he stuttered, "I'm sorry; I didn't get much sleep last night. I'll take this one."

Beem shoved the bread into his shoulder bag and gave the man the full price without even haggling. On his way to the next vendor, he tripped over a basket of vegetables spilling its contents everywhere.

"I'm never going to get a good night's sleep again," he moaned as he chased after a renegade melon.

Thoughts of shopping, completing his chores, apologizing to the parents and then sneaking out that night were overwhelming. But there was so much he wanted to know he was willing to make the sacrifice.

As soon as Beem's chores were completed, his mother escorted him from house-to-house as he made his apologies. Every mom was understanding and accepted Beem's repentance with a firm, 'That's all right, but don't let it happen again.'

When they arrived at Spinny and Jinx's home however, things didn't go so smoothly. The two boys stood silently next to their mother as Beem recited his speech. Marlyne Spin glared at him, unmoved by his words and turned her attention to Illie Beeman.

"That's all fine for him I suppose, but I want to know exactly what happened yesterday," she snapped, "Jinkmin's clothes were torn to bits and there was blood all over everything. You can imagine how horrified I was when he came through the door. Something strange is going on and I intend to get to the bottom of it."

Beem's mother looked at him with great concern.

"Is this true?"

Beem tried to think up a reasonable story they might believe, but the voice – The Wisdom inside him – instructed him to tell the truth.

"I don't think you'll believe me if I tell you, Mrs. Spin."

"Try me, and let's see what I believe or not. Jinkmin, you and your brother go inside."

Jinx shot Beem a knowing glance. Without a word, the brothers turned and went in the house.

"Go on then!" Marlyne ordered.

"Well," he began, "We were all playing high-stick up on Broadside Hill when Jinx threw it over Meekus' head. It flew over the side of the hill and landed . . . inside a hole."

"Why didn't you tell me this last night?" demanded Mrs. Beeman, "You know we could *all* get in trouble if you don't report a hole, especially if it's on Broadside Hill."

"Yes, I know," he continued, "but it was a great adventure to see if we could find the stick, and there was something down there. When we went in, it all came crashing down. That's how Jinx's clothes were ripped up. I'm sorry Mrs. Spin. I'll pay for the ruined clothes."

"I can't believe you would allow my son to go into a hole like that," Marlyne argued, "You're the oldest,

Lucas. You know the laws. You're old enough now to pay the penalty for breaking the law."

"Yes, Mrs. Spin. I understand and I promise it will never happen again. I am truly sorry."

"All right, then. Now go stand over by the hedge, I want to talk to your mother alone."

Beem quickly obeyed. He watched his mother and Mrs. Spin converse in tense, hushed tones. Finally, the women clasped hands in agreement and Marlyne Spin went inside. On their way home Beem's mother explained the situation.

"Lucas, I want you to stay away from Broadside Hill from now on. There are plenty of other places to play with your friends without having to go up there again, understand?"

"Yes ma'am."

"Now listen to me," she continued, "Nobody else needs to know about the hole you found – not even your father. I want you to forget you ever saw it."

"But what about the other kids? They might say something."

"You are the oldest," she replied, "They will go along with whatever you tell them. I'll explain things to the mothers. It will be all right – you'll see. By the way, Lucas, thank you for telling the truth to Mrs. Spin. Apparently Jinkmin told her the same story last night."

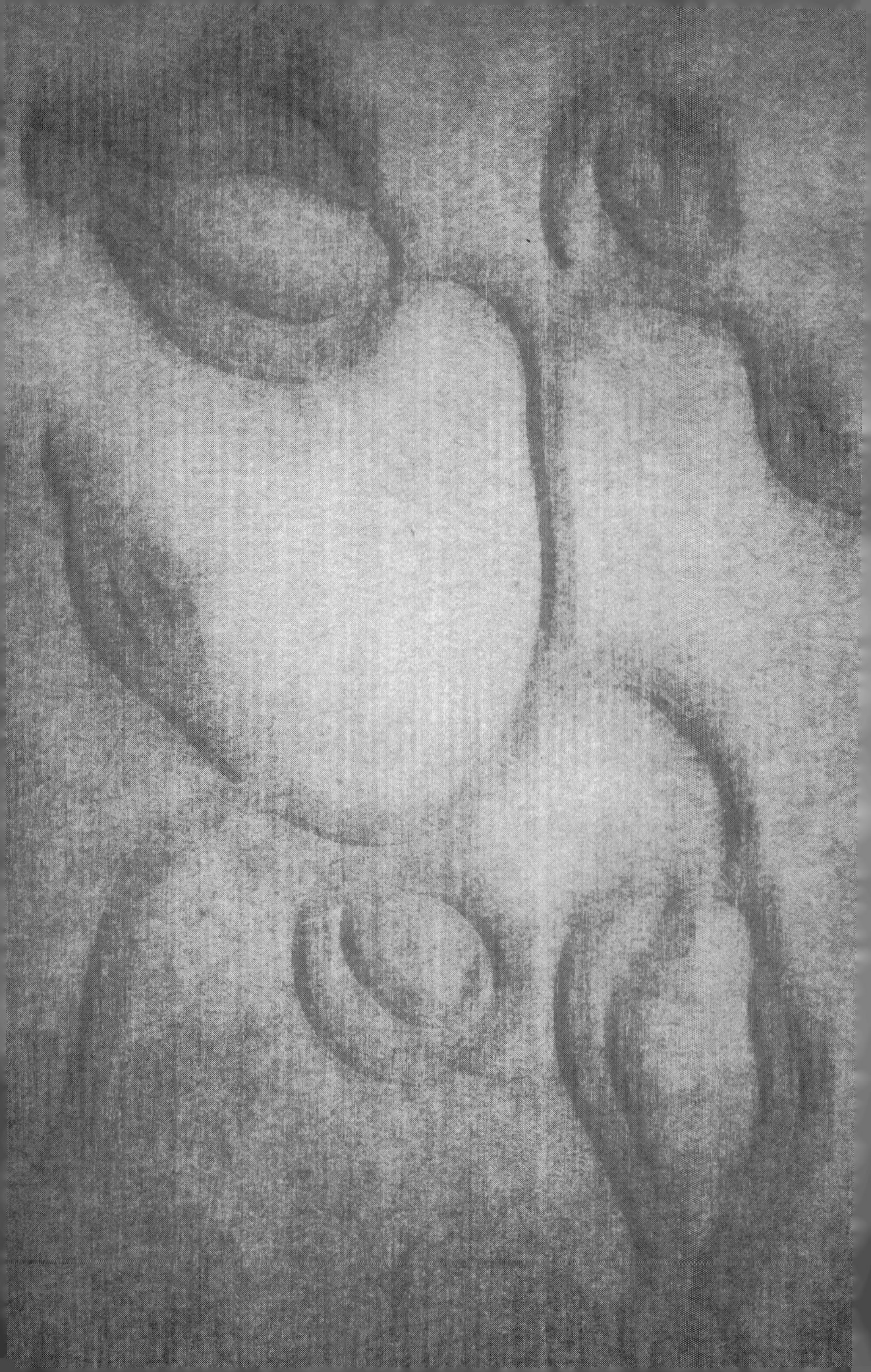

4

TWO PRIVATE MEETINGS

Beem tossed in his bed while he waited to sneak out of the house. He strained to look out the window, but couldn't determine if both moons had set. It was already dark, so he knew it would be soon. He lowered himself from his hammock and tiptoed across the room for a better look.

The rooftops of Maidenton were barely a shadow against the blackening landscape. The only light left in the sky was a dim glow filtering through the clouds near the horizon. He could barely hear the drizzle from the night mist as it lighted on the roof, collected into little drips and fell from the cornice. He knew within a few minutes everything would disappear in the black. At last, it was time for him to go meet with The Ancient.

He activated his night-vision, changed into his clothes and slowly opened the door.

From down the hall came the muffled vibrations of his father's snoring.

This is perfect. The noise will hide any sound I make walking through the house.

With every snore, Beem made a quick dash and then stopped, waiting for the sound to start again. After what seemed like an eternity, he made it to the front porch and closed the door silently behind him.

Without his new ability to see in the dark, it would have been impossible for Beem to move another inch. Every night, at the same time, a dense blanket of clouds filled the sky as Beniwan's two moons dipped below the horizon. The cloud cover blocked any remaining moonlight as the mist in the air saturated everything for the next few hours. It was now utterly black and very damp. Beem pulled the hood of his cloak over his head and set off to meet Lyndal.

It was strange to walk around in the black without a torch. Beem wondered if he might be the first person to have ever done it, but then remembered that Lyndal had been doing it for centuries. Nevertheless, he imagined he was a great explorer trying out a new navigation tool for the first time.

During the black, nothing dared move around for fear of injury. Every so often Beem would discover a small animal sitting in the middle of the path. It was fascinating to walk right next to one without it scurrying away.

It was also amazing the way his night-vision made the mist appear. The whole atmosphere shimmered with tiny flecks of light. The ground glistened with moisture as well. It was like walking on a carpet of diamonds.

Beem was careful not to make any noise as he walked along. The slightest sound would trigger the village dogs barking. That, in turn, would cause the residents to light torches to investigate. He decided to stay in the middle of the path where the ground was hard and free of twigs.

Within a few minutes, Beem was walking across the square. He had never imagined the market area void of its hustle-bustle of activity, noises and smells. When he reached the center, he climbed on top of one of the eating tables to take it all in. The realization hit him that nobody would ever know he was there. For some reason, this made him feel powerful.

At the far side of the square, he could see the bridge. Standing in the middle was a man leaning against the rail. It had to be Lyndal. As Beem approached, the man lifted his head revealing his glowing eyes.

“Beem,” he whispered, “I’m so glad you came.”

The sound of the running water was enough to mask their whispers. They would be able to converse without having to touch-talk.

Beem looked down at the river and was mesmerized. The water had been transformed into blobs of dim light slipping through the rocks and gliding over precipices, merging and breaking apart as they slid down the channel. It was like nothing he could have imagined.

"This is one of my favorite spots in Maidenton," said Lyndal, "I love to come here and stare at the water."

"I see what you mean," exclaimed Beem, "Everything is so different. It's better somehow."

"I suppose so, in some ways. The problem is there's no one to share it with."

Lyndal paused for a moment.

". . . until now."

"So, what did you want to talk to me about?" asked Beem, "'Cause I have some questions for you."

"How about if we find a dry place to talk?" suggested Lyndal.

"Okay, but I can't be gone for very long. My parents will kill me if they find out."

"I understand. I promise you'll be home before the clouds break up."

They made their way across the square and into the residences. Beem thought they might be going to a house in the village. Instead, they followed a path out of town into the Western Woods. Within minutes, they were among the huge trees at the bottom of the valley.

Lyndal pointed out sticks and other objects to avoid. Beem decided it was easiest to place his feet exactly where Lyndal had just walked, playing a very practical game of follow-the-leader. Eventually they came to a clearing where the ground was covered with mounds.

Lyndal abruptly left the path and jumped on top of a large rock peeking through the ground – then on to a second rock. He motioned for Beem to follow. Lyndal had devised a way to cross the clearing without leaving any signs of his presence.

Midway across the uneven landscape, Beem could see a small plume of smoke bubbling out of the ground. It crawled along the surface, dissipating into the air. He followed Lyndal until they arrived in the middle of the clearing, near the source of the smoke. Lyndal pointed to a place where two large rocks rested against each other leaving a small gap. He sat down, lowered his legs into the opening and slid inside the hole.

"Come on," he whispered.

Beem nervously followed suit and soon his toes found solid ground inside. He looked back through the opening and surveyed the surrounding field, marveling at how amazing the last two days had been. It seemed more like a dream than reality, but somehow Beem knew *this* was what he was made for.

"This way," instructed Lyndal.

He maneuvered through the small passageway.

"We can speak freely now," he said, "We can't be heard down here."

"Where are we?"

"This is my home when I'm in Maidenton. I have places like this near other villages too."

They shimmied around a boulder and Beem could see part of a smooth rock wall similar to the ones he had seen earlier. A portion of it had collapsed, leaving an opening large enough to pass through. A warm glow was coming from the other side. He stepped in and was filled with awe as he took in the marvelous shapes and colors surrounding him. It was like the rooms he had seen in the underground complex, but without dust or cobwebs.

"Take off your shoes and I'll stoke the fire," said Lyndal.

The floor of the room was completely covered with animal skins, rugs and pillows. Beem buried his toes in the soft, thick fur as he studied a series of pictures hanging on the wall. At the far end of the room, the remnants of a fire smoldered in the hearth. Its glowing coals reflected off the polished walls. Lyndal placed a fresh log into the embers and stirred them with the poker. The wood quickly ignited and the whole room came to life.

"Make yourself comfortable and I'll fix us something to drink."

Lyndal pulled out the large kettle that was hanging over the fire. He poured in some white liquid from a small barrel sitting on the hearth. It sizzled, sending a plume of steam into the air. Beem inhaled the sweet aroma and smiled with delight. He watched Lyndal add spices and richly colored liquids to the brew. Soon the pot was simmering over the fire. The two of them reclined on large, embroidered pillows next to the crackling flames.

"What do you think about your new powers?" asked Lyndal.

"I think they're fascinating. I've been experimenting with them – except for the transporting thing. I've been wondering though, what are they for? It's exciting to see in the dark, but in the end, what's the point? The only thing I've accomplished is missing out on a good night's sleep."

"Yes, that's true," laughed Lyndal, "but what if I told you these powers could save you, your family and your friends."

"Save us from what?"

Beem's curiosity was sparked.

"From the Keeon," he continued in earnest, "Wouldn't you like to live your lives free from their control?"

"I don't know. I didn't think that was possible."

Lyndal pulled the pot from the fire and poured its creamy contents into two mugs. He stirred the mixture vigorously until a foamy head formed on each drink and handed one to Beem.

"Ahhh," Beem sighed as the warm liquid filled his mouth.

His first sip left him with a large foam mustache.

"Wow! This is fantastic," he said, taking another swig. "What is it anyway?"

"It's a recipe handed down by The Ancients. You are the first Kinsman to drink this for many centuries."

"I wish I could have this every day," said Beem, licking his lips.

Lyndal smiled and refilled Beem's empty mug.

"What if I were to tell you that living free of Keeon rule is possible? Wouldn't you want that for yourself and the people you love?"

"I guess so, but it seems pretty far-fetched. I mean, how can a couple of kids and one Ancient take on an entire empire of trained soldiers? Besides, the Kinsmen have always sought peace. War only means death and destruction. That's what our tradition tells us."

"True enough," Lyndal agreed, "But peace without freedom is still slavery. You've never tasted freedom. You think that keeping the Keeon law is your only option. But those laws are there to cover up the truth and keep you under their control. Two days ago, you thought The Legends were make-believe. Now you're living them. That's the freedom the Keeon don't want you to have. Freedom always comes with a price and sometimes that price is the lives of those fighting for it. But it's a precious gift worth the sacrifice.

Think about the advantages you now possess. You can maneuver in the dark, and communicate without making a sound. You can even transport and no one can do a thing to stop you. Don't you think these skills can help free you from your captors?"

"I don't know. I've never considered it – until now."

Beem's head was spinning with new ideas and possibilities.

"I lived during the time of the Paddor rule, before the great departure. We numbered in the millions. All the tribes lived together in peace – Paddor, Kinsmen, and Keeon. We used our powers for the benefit of all, which was enough to ensure freedom and equality for everyone. It was only when the Paddor left this world that the Keeon became aggressive and began to subjugate the Kinsmen. They only succeeded because there was no one here to stop them. As you said, the Kinsmen have always been peaceful – but they have not always been slaves."

Lyndal took a long drink from his mug and continued.

"Imagine if the Kinsmen were to become like the Paddor. Life could return to the way it was before the departure."

"I don't know. You're talking about things I never thought possible."

"Well, think about it, Beem. You and your friends could usher in a new way of life, a new race of people, a new time of peace and prosperity."

Beem sat silent, lost in thought.

"If you and your friends accept, I will prepare you for what's ahead. I will give all of you the powers and teach you how to use them. But if you don't want to do this, I will simply move on to another village. Everything will go back to the way it was – except you and Jinx will possess the powers."

Lyndal walked to the entrance and gathered their cloaks. They retraced their steps through the woods and down the path until they could see the houses on the outskirts of the village. Lyndal stopped and clasped Beem's hand.

Lyndal:	*This is a far as I go tonight.*
Beem:	*When do you need an answer?*
Lyndal:	*Meet me in the square at lunchtime, in two days. If you're there, I'll find you. If not, I'll consider your answer to be no. One more thing . . . this is more than an opportunity for freedom. I'm offering you life, real life, as you've never imagined it before.*

Lyndal's eyes sparkled with intensity. Beem nodded, and released his hand. As he walked back to the village, his mind exploded with more questions. Lyndal's invitation was too fantastic to be true, but the powers Beem now possessed opened a world of possibilities.

We could do anything . . . anything!

Beem made his way through the village without a sound. He loved how easy it was to get around in the dark. As he turned onto the path where he lived, he stopped in his tracks. His stomach turned in horror. A dim flickering light was coming from his bedroom window. Oh no! Someone was awake and had discovered he was gone. He imagined his father waiting angrily for him in his room.

I'll be sent to the fields for sure. Everything Lyndal just offered me is now impossible.

To his surprise, he heard the voice of The Wisdom. It told him to go home and be truthful.

That's crazy!

He heard the voice again and this time it came with a sense of peace. His fears subsided. He decided to go home and face the consequences. He ran down the path, hopped over the hedge, and landed squarely on a stick. SNAP! The sound seemed deafening as it broke the silence of the night. Immediately a dog began barking, creating a chain reaction of noises throughout the village. Beem hurried to the front door and slipped inside.

"Illie?" called his father, "What's going on out there? What are you doing up at this hour?"

"Don't worry," responded his mother, "I'm talking to Lucas. The dogs must have awakened you."

"Come back to bed," he ordered, "It's too late to be talking to the boy."

Beem cautiously approached his room. Peeking in, he saw his mother sitting at his desk.

"I'll be right there," she replied, looking straight at Beem.

Beem tiptoed into his room, placed his shoes on the floor and removed his cloak. He turned to his mother, nervously awaiting her response.

"I need to know what's going on, Lucas. What could you possibly be doing out there – in the middle of the black!"

"Am I in trouble?" he pleaded, "Are you going to tell Dad?"

"That depends on what you tell me. But what concerns me the most is you haven't shared any of this with me."

He stood silent, struggling with what to say.

"Don't you trust me?" she asked.

"Yes, of course I do. It's just that I don't think you'll believe me if I tell you the truth."

"Lucas," she sighed, "We have always shared everything with each other. What would be so strange I wouldn't believe you? Are you seeing a girl?"

"A girl? Of course not – the only girls I know are Trince and Pria."

"If it's not a girl, then what is it? I need to know."

Beem hesitated and fiddled with some dirt under his thumbnail. All at once, he felt The Wisdom again, urging him to tell the truth.

"Do you believe The Legends?" he blurted out, "I mean, do you think they're true . . . not just stories?"

His mother's eyes widened with curiosity.

"I guess so," she said thoughtfully, "Yes, I do believe they're true. But what does this have to do with you being outside just now?"

Beem swallowed hard and mustered his courage.

"I need to show you something. Don't move."

Beem picked up his mother's lamp, placed it in the hallway and closed the door. The room was completely dark.

"OK, mom," he continued, "how many fingers am I holding up?"

"Lucas, what's this all about?"

"No. Come on; tell me how many fingers I'm holding up."

"I don't know," she said in frustration, "I can't see a thing in here without the lamp"

"Take a guess!"

"All right . . . I'll say three."

"Wrong. Try again."

"This is silly, Lucas, you know I can't see your hands."

"All right then," Beem said, "You hold up your fingers and I'll guess."

She held up two fingers.

"I really don't see what this is . . ."

"Two," Beem announced.

She paused.

"That's right – That was a lucky guess."

"Try it again," he said.

She held up her other hand adding two fingers.

"Four."

She changed the number.

"Eight . . . One . . . Six."

"How are you doing that? Is this some sort of trick?"

She held both hands behind her back.

"Now how many?"

"I can't tell," Beem said, "I can't see behind your back."

"Lucas! You're beginning to frighten me."

"One more thing," he continued, "Pick up the book that's on my desk and open it."

She groped around until she found the book.

"Now, point to somewhere on the page."

Beem began to read.

". . . in the mountains. The first thing, however, is to keep sight of your partner . . ."

"Good," he said, "Now, don't move your finger."

Beem brought the lamp back in the room and set it next to her. His mother looked down. Her finger was on the text he had just read.

"I don't understand. Are you telling me you can see in the dark?"

"Yes, and a whole lot more! The Legends are true, mother – all of them. I met one of The Ancients."

Illie Beeman sat dumbfounded by what she had just witnessed. Could The Legends she secretly cherished really be true? She began to get excited.

"What do you know about The Ancients?"

"More than I could tell you in one night. The history of the island cities alone would take me a couple of hours. Is there something specific you want to know?"

"Let me see . . . There's so much . . . Oh, I know. What is . . . ' The Wisdom'?"

"How do you know about that?"

"Just tell me what it is," she insisted.

"Well . . . I guess the best way to describe it is like a voice . . . only it's in your head, or maybe in your heart. It tells you important things, especially when you're not sure what to do."

Illie's thoughts were flooded with what she had learned about The Legends over the years. She struggled to connect what she had heard with what Beem was telling her.

"Are you all right?" Beem asked.

"Yes. I'm fine."

She sat quietly for a minute, trying to take it all in.

"Lucas," she said, "I want you to get something for me."

"All right."

"Take care not to wake your father. He doesn't

need to know about this. In the kitchen, to the right of the tall cupboard where the floor meets the wall, is a hidden compartment. Lift up the floorboard and bring me the little box."

She passed the lamp to Beem.

"I don't need it. Remember?" he said with a smile.

Beem tiptoed through the hallway, down the stairs, and into the kitchen.

What could she be hiding? And why doesn't she want Dad to know?"

He crouched next to the cupboard and ran his hand across the floorboards. They were so close together there was no way to lift them. As he shifted his weight, he pressed down on the end of one board and the other end popped up. Success! He slid it to the side and reached in. Tucked underneath was an old cloth bag wrapped tightly around a box.

He quickly returned to his room and handed the mysterious container to his mother.

"Close the door." she instructed, "This is only for your eyes."

They sat in the middle of the floor with the lamp between them. His mother untied the strap and opened the bag. Inside was a small blue metal box with peculiar symbols pressed into its surface.

"That's funny," Beem said.

"What?"

"I think I understand this writing."

"Really?"

She handed it to him for a better look.

"To my beloved," he read, "How I wish you would come away with me."

"Oh, that is amazing . . . truly amazing," she gushed. "Where did you get this?"

"It's a secret heirloom."

Illie took it and with great reverence held it next to her heart.

"At one time this belonged to one of your relatives."

"Really? Who would that be?"

"I'll show you."

She opened the lid. The interior of the box was lined with red velvet, embroidered with tiny vine-like patterns. There was a man's ring, a sash, some maps, a thin book and a picture frame. His mother picked up the picture and cleaned its surface with her nightclothes. She gazed in wonder at the image.

"I'm always amazed when I look at him. This is no ordinary drawing. It's as if he were standing there, right behind the glass."

"Do you know the person?"

"I've never met him. That would be impossible. But I know who he is."

She passed the picture to Beem.

"This is a picture of my great, great, great, great, grandfather."

"Wha . . . ?" Beem gasped.

The image was remarkably life-like, unlike anything he'd ever seen. Stranger still, the man in the picture was his new friend . . . Lyndal Froam.

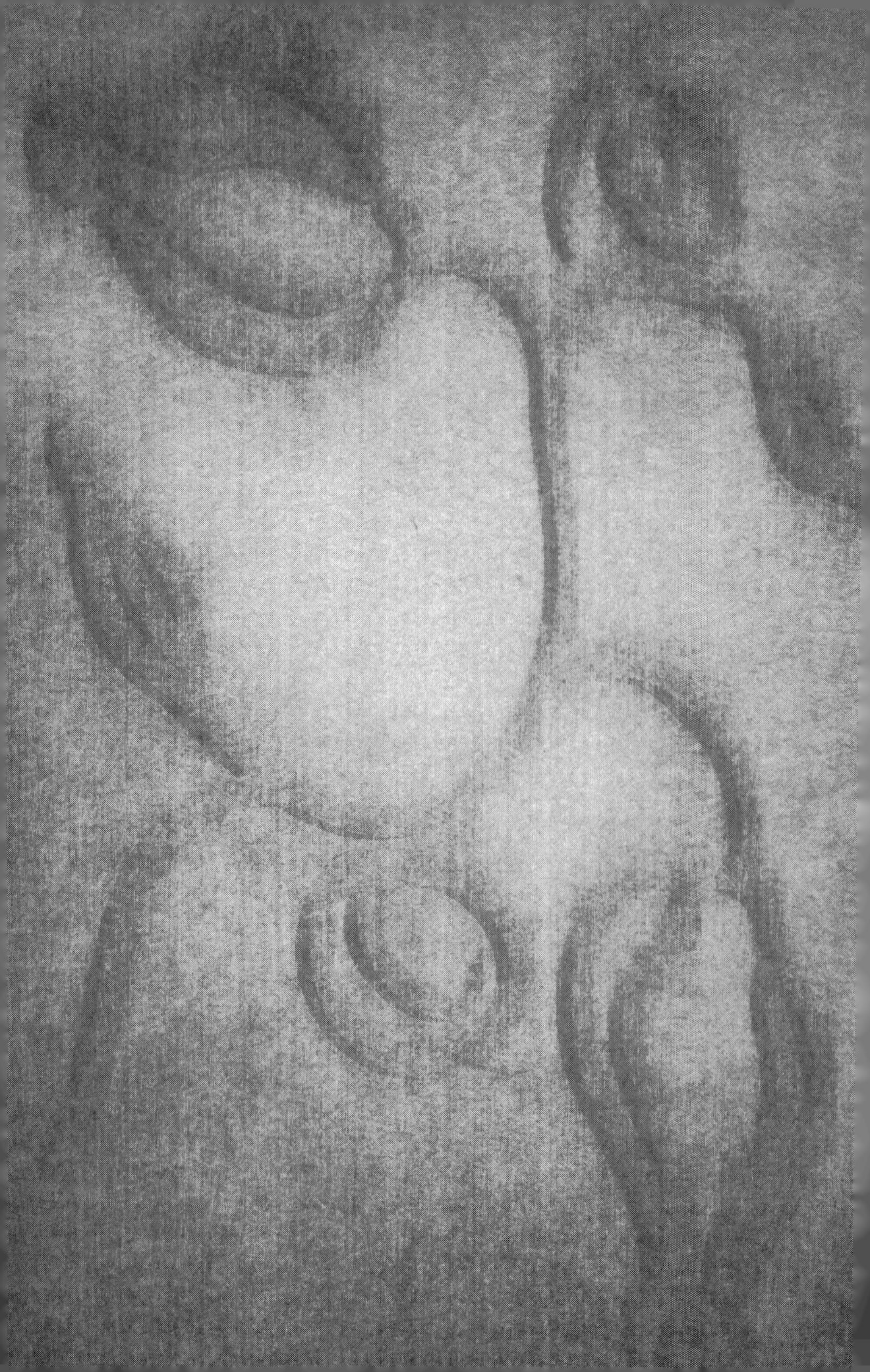

5

Telling Secrets

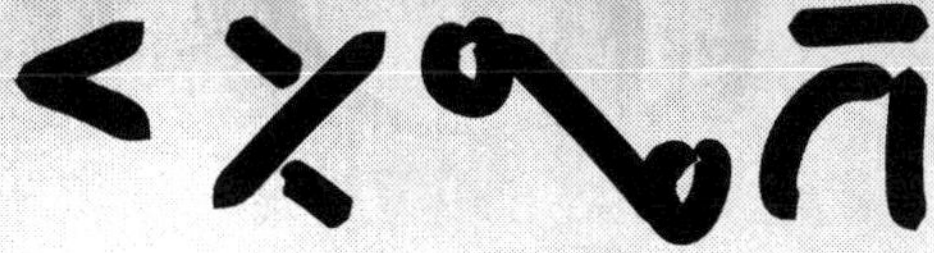

Beem lay in his hammock, wide-awake. He couldn't stop thinking about overthrowing the Keeon, bringing freedom to his people, and the strange picture of Lyndal. The stories his mother and Lyndal told him seemed worlds apart. But if somehow they were true, it would be too fantastic.

Beem's body finally relaxed enough to fall asleep just as the sun's rays found their way through the gaps in his curtains. Morning had arrived. Sleep would have to wait . . . again.

He was proud of how hard he worked the previous day. He was also thrilled with the new level of trust he and his mother now shared. He felt confident he would be able to get away from the house for a few hours.

It was critical for him to talk with the other children. There was so much to discuss and there were decisions to be made.

Beem washed up, changed into clean clothes and made his way into the kitchen.

"What gets you up so early?" his father asked.

"Oh, I don't know," Beem yawned, "Just a good night's sleep, I guess."

Beem was, indeed, excited for the new day, but his body was struggling to keep up.

"I want you to help out again today," his father instructed, "You did a great job yesterday, but there are a few things I need you to do in the back."

Beem could tell by his father's serious expression there was no getting out of it.

"Yes sir," he moaned.

Beem's enthusiasm crumbled. His plans for the day seemed impossible. He hung his head and began to play with the bowl of noodles his mother had set in front of him.

"Well it's time for me to get going," his father announced.

He patted Beem on the shoulder.

"You behave yourself today and you can go play with your friends tomorrow."

He kissed his wife, grabbed the bundle of flatbread and meat on the counter and left the house.

"Do I have to work in the yard today?" Beem whined.

"Of course you do. Just because we were up late telling stories doesn't mean you didn't break the house rules. Your punishment for coming home late still stands."

"But I need to talk with everyone . . . today. Tomorrow will be too late."

"That means you'll have to get everything done before lunch."

"Why? What happens at lunch?"

"That's when your friends are coming over," she revealed with a smile.

She bent down and whispered, "I'm going to arrange everything. You'd better be about it. You don't have much time."

She removed her apron and walked out of the kitchen.

Beem felt his excitement returning, until he saw the list of chores lying in front of him.

1) Mend the hole in the fence
2) Water the garden
3) Stack the wood next to the house
4) Clean and organize the shed

There were only a few hours to get it done. Beem's lack of sleep robbed him of any remaining motivation. He slouched over the bowl of noodles and began to slurp.

Clomp, clomp, clomp came the sound of his mother descending the stairs.

"What are you still doing there?" she scolded, "Get a move on!"

She pulled on her cloak and draped her satchel over her shoulder, pausing at the front door.

"I'm heading to Stalwart's house first and then . . ."

Beem's senses awakened with a rush of energy. The Wisdom cautioned him about Wort's mother.

"I'm not sure it's a good idea to invite Wort," he interrupted.

"Well, he was with you wasn't he?

"Yes, but . . ."

"If he was there and knows the story you told me last night, then he needs to be included."

Before Beem could say another word, she was gone.

"Oh, bother!" he blurted out in frustration.

Beem didn't waste any more time. He headed outside to the shed, grabbed some tools and went to repair the damaged fence. As he worked, his mood improved. To his surprise, things were progressing better than he could have imagined. He still had second thoughts about Wort, but he was excited to see his friends. Before he knew it, the first three tasks were complete.

He was almost finished sweeping out the shed when he heard a familiar voice.

"Ho! What are you doing in there?"

Beem poked his head through the cloud of dust billowing from the shed.

"Ho yourself!" he coughed, stepping out for some fresh air.

Jinx stood before him laughing.

"It looks like you used your face as the broom."

"Very funny . . . here, hold these tools while I finish sweeping. We can't do anything until I'm done."

Out through the back door stepped Pria.

"Doesn't this look like fun?" she teased.

"Loads," answered Beem sarcastically.

He stepped back inside to finish sweeping.

Jinx turned to Pria.

"Did you get in trouble?"

"Didn't we all? I've been working non-stop since we got back. I think this is the first break I've had, other than meals and sleep."

"My mom came down pretty hard on me too," said Jinx, "But somehow Spinny was able to make up a story. I don't think he even missed a meal."

Pria became irritated.

"I just passed him in the kitchen and he was sneaking bites of cake."

They looked over to see Spinny waving through the rear window with a mischievous grin.

"I don't think so!" steamed Jinx as he took off running, "He's going to help!"

He swung open the back door, grabbed his brother's arm and dragged him into the yard. Spinny knew exactly what they were thinking, but the smirk never left his face.

"So . . . what are you guys doing?" he asked.

"Oh, come on!" scolded Pria, and she smacked him on the back of the head.

Spinny giggled as he rubbed the spot.

Soon the shed was clean and Beem's list of chores was complete. The four of them went inside to find a house full of women catching up on the latest gossip.

Beem approached his mother who was arranging food on a serving platter.

"Why did you invite the mothers?" he whispered.

"Lucas, you know very well you are all still in trouble. You need to trust me. I know what I'm doing. You'll see. Why don't you and your friends go set up a table in the backyard and I'll bring out the food."

Moments later the children were outside, devouring the rich meal of sliced meats and flatbread slathered with spicy green chutney.

"This is great," Beem said.

"What is?" asked Jinx.

"Everything . . . you know, being together and laughing . . . and eating really good food. I didn't think we'd be able to see each other for days."

Beem kept looking at the house and when he could no longer see anyone through the windows, he stood and announced, "We need to make a decision today. I met with The Ancient yesterday and he wants to know if we would be willing to fight the Keeon."

There was a lengthy pause as the children looked up from their plates in disbelief. Spinny began to snicker.

"Is this for real, or is this another adventure you're dreaming up?"

"This is real! The Ancient, Lyndal that is, met with me and told me the real history of our world and our people. The way we live now is not the way we are supposed to live. He told me we were once equal with the Keeon and lived in freedom. He said we could be free again. He wants to train us as freedom fighters!"

"That's ridiculous!" retorted Pria, "Why would we even consider such a thing? We aren't at war. Besides, how could a bunch of kids fight an army?"

"But we are at war . . . as long as we remain under Keeon rule. We have settled for slavery but in our hearts, we know we are meant to be free. Lyndal is offering to restore our freedom, but we will have to fight for it."

"I'll fight!" exclaimed Jinx, leaping to his feet in agreement.

"You don't know what you're talking about," argued Spinny, "Sit down!"

"No! I won't sit down!" insisted Jinx, crossing his arms in defiance, "I know this sounds strange, but what Beem's talking about has me all stirred up inside. I think this is the right thing to do . . . even if it looks impossible."

"You're crazier than he is," added Trince.

"Crazy?" snapped Jinx, "Watch this . . . Come whisper something in my ear."

She sat unmoved, glaring at him.

"Come on!" he insisted.

Trince hesitantly whispered something and sat down. Jinx turned to Beem and took his hand.

With a confused look, Beem blurted, "Goo goo nanie noomie muchie mush?"

Meekus giggled. The rest of the children looked very confused, except for Trince whose eyes were wide with astonishment.

"How did you do that?!" she yelled, "That's exactly what I whispered to Jinx."

"I can talk to Beem by touching his hand," explained Jinx, "and I can see in the dark, and I can transport to other places and be healed of any wounds. Look at this . . ."

He rolled up the sleeve of his tunic.

"Remember the scar where that branch almost took my arm off? It isn't there anymore . . . and look at this . . ."

Jinx pulled the side of his mouth back and pointed to one of his teeth.

"This tooth fell out last week. Now it's back! If stuff

like this can happen, then I say we can do just about anything, no matter how young or how few we are! If Lyndal thinks we can do it then so do I."

Jinx's demonstration and his newly found confidence were both amazing and convincing.

"Trince?" asked Beem, "What do you think? Are you in?"

"I don't know, Beem, this seems wrong. I love a good adventure, but taking on the Keeon . . . ? They wouldn't hesitate to kill us right now if they heard what we're talking about. I'm going to have to give this more thought."

"What about you, Spinny?"

"I'm in!" he announced jumping to his feet, "What have I got to lose? I'm not running from a good fight! Besides, I want to be able to do all the great stuff you guys can do."

"There is something else," added Beem.

He leaned in and looked intently at each of his friends.

"Either we're all in or everything is off. If one of us backs out, Lyndal will pack up and move on."

"What about our parents; won't they get suspicious?" asked Trince.

"Good question," said Beem, "That's something I'll have to ask him. If this is going to take us away from our families, then I'm going to tell him no. And you, Meekus . . . if you don't want to do this, we'll stop right now."

Meekus looked at Beem and the twins.

"If you're going then I'm going!" he announced with a decisive nod.

"Stand up, then," encouraged Trince.

She lifted him on his chair so he was standing at eye-level with the others.

"I'm in too," she said, "I can't let Meekus have all the fun."

"What about you Wort?" asked Beem, "Do you think we should do this?"

Wort didn't like the idea of more danger. Falling in the hole was enough trauma for a lifetime. Now they were talking about fighting the Keeon. Why couldn't they go back to the way things were before? As he looked around the table, everyone was standing except Pria.

Maybe she doesn't want to go either. If she says no, then I won't have to.

"Come on, Wort!" yelled Spinny, "Get on with it."

"It's all right," reassured Beem, "You can take all the time you need."

Wort remained seated.

"I'm going to do whatever Pria does!"

Pria was horrified.

"That's not fair! I'm not making the decision for both of us. What if something were to happen to you, Wort? I couldn't bear that sort of responsibility. You have to choose for yourself."

"I don't care. Whatever you choose is what I'm going to choose."

"Don't worry, Pria," Beem interjected, "Your decision is your own, regardless of what Wort does."

She was torn.

"You will hate me if I don't go along."

"Not true!" assured Beem, "I swear, if you choose not to do this, we will be as we have always been . . . best friends to the end. I would rather forget the whole idea, than leave someone behind."

"I agree!" said Trince as she slapped the bench with her hand.

"Me too!" said Jinx slapping his hand down in agreement.

The others followed suit and their thunderous support reverberated through the backyard.

Pria was moved by their demonstration of love and loyalty.

She stood up and announced, "I guess I'm in too!"

She was laughing and crying at the same time. Trince gave her a hug.

"It'll be great, I promise," she whispered.

"Wort?" said Beem, "That leaves you. What's your decision now?"

Wort squirmed, but his pride left him no other option.

He climbed on his chair like Meekus, and muttered, "All right, I'm in."

"Yay!" yelled Spinny, raising his hands in the air.

"Woohoo!" cried Meekus.

He began dancing and spinning on his chair. Soon they were all jumping up and down, hands in the air, cheering at the thought of the very real adventure that lay ahead.

Pria's mother poked her head out the back door.

"What's all this about? Are you playing a game?"

"No Mrs. Limm," Beem said, "this is no game."

The children looked at each other and giggled as she approached the table.

"Let's get this cleaned up. There's cake for you in the kitchen."

"Yay!!" they shouted all together.

The excitement of overthrowing an army was quickly overshadowed by the promise of cake. They gathered up the dirty dishes and filed into the kitchen.

"Lucas?" whispered Mrs. Limm, pulling him aside, "I need to ask you something."

"Sure, what is it? If it's about the other day . . ."

"No, no. It's not about coming home late. That's all over with now. What I need to know is . . ."

She paused, struggling to find the right words.

"Well," she continued, "I'm just going to say it."

Beem's heart began to flutter, fearing he might be in trouble.

"I need to know if . . . if I can touch-talk with you."

Beem was stunned. How could she have

known about touch-talk? Was she listening in on their conversation?

"What are you talking about?"

"Don't worry, Lucas. Your mother told us everything – about you and Jinx, and The Ancient you met."

Beem swallowed hard. His mind began to race.

"But the thing is," she continued, "I'm not like the other women. I mean . . . I do believe The Legends are true. They're not just stories. Because . . . well . . . because I can see in the dark, just like you. I've been able to do it since I was a little girl. But that's all I know. Do you think I have the other powers . . . like touch-talk?"

Beem was confounded. Why would his mother disclose what he had shared in confidence? And now, Pria's mother claimed to have the powers.

"I'm not sure I understand what you're asking," said Beem.

Mrs. Limm took Beem by the shoulders, sat him down and looked earnestly into his eyes.

"Listen to me, Lucas. The reason we let you kids play together, away from the village, is so we can talk about The Legends without being interrupted. We read stories from the little book your mother keeps in the blue box."

"So what you're saying is you have secret meetings while we're out playing?"

"That's it," she said with a smile, "No one knows

about it. Not even our husbands. It's too risky. When Illie told us the story about what happened to you, I couldn't sit around and do nothing. Something is happening here."

"So you can see in the dark. Like during the black?"

"Yes! It's so beautiful to walk at night when the mist is shimmering in the air. It's like the night is alive!"

"I've seen it too!" exclaimed Beem, "I saw it last night when I met with The Ancient."

"So it *is* true! It's not just a story your mother made up. You have the powers."

"Yes," he confessed, "But what does this have to do with you touch-talking?"

"Don't you see? Until now, I've been the only one. None of the other women have the powers. I'm not sure they believe me anyway. Now, with you and Jinx, I'm not alone. If I can touch-talk, then I'll know it's all true."

"There's one way to find out," said Beem as he offered his hand, "Hold on and let's see."

She took his hand, wondering what she would have to do to make it work.

Beem: *Do you know about The Wisdom?*

She continued looking at Beem for instruction, but after a few seconds realized he was already communicating with her.

"I can't do it can I?" she sighed in disappointment.

"But you can see in the dark," said Beem, pondering the discrepancy, "That's strange. I'm going to have to ask Lyndal about this."

"You mean The Ancient? Are you going to be talking with him again?"

"I have to. I need to tell him . . ."

The Wisdom cautioned him not to divulge too much information.

". . . tell him . . . he needs to stay here, because he's going to leave Maidenton. Oh! I think I see my Mom. We should get inside before they miss us."

Beem ran to the house, leaving Alma Limm sitting alone and a bit discouraged.

Inside, everyone was eating cake and thoroughly enjoying themselves. Instead of rigid mothers and restrained children, the house was buzzing with lively conversation.

"Oh, here you are," Beem's mother declared.

She clapped her hands and announced, "It's time to quiet down and settle in for our special meeting."

The women sat in chairs and the children plopped down on the floor wondering what 'meeting' she was talking about.

"This has been quite an exciting couple of days. I know it has been difficult, but in light of what we've all learned, I think we will find we have a lot in common."

She clapped her hands softly with delight. The children looked at Beem to see if he knew what she was talking about. He was just as bewildered and shrugged his shoulders.

"To open the meeting," she continued, "I would like Lateen to read a short paragraph from the book."

This confused the children even more. What book was she talking about? Illie handed the little book from the blue box to Meekus' mother. She flipped through it to find a certain portion of text.

"This is from page fifty-seven, the second paragraph," she said.

The women whispered their approval to one another. This was one of their favorite parts. As she began to read, a hush fell on the room. Some of the ladies even closed their eyes.

"When adversity comes," Lateen began, "or when everything is good, The Wisdom will be there for you. It is the voice of understanding. It is knowledge where there once was ignorance. Life without The Wisdom is to fall back to the old ways of thinking. This is a place you should never go again."

Lateen held the book to her heart for a moment before closing it and placing it on her lap.

"Very nice!" gushed Illie, "I couldn't have chosen a better portion of text to fit our current situation."

She motioned to her son.

"At this time I would like Lucas to share a few thoughts."

All eyes focused on Beem. He shot his mother a horrified glance.

"What did you want me to talk about?" he asked hesitantly.

"Oh come on, Lucas," she urged, "Tell us the story you told me last night, about you and Jinx – and The Ancient."

The children's faces paled. Their sacred trust had been violated. Spinny slammed his fist to the floor.

"Now hold on a minute," Beem cried, desperately trying to re-establish his credibility. "I just found out from Mrs. Limm you've been secretly meeting and studying The Ancients. I want you to understand, I had no idea this was going to happen. I'm not sure *what* to say."

"Go on, Lucas," his mother pushed, "Tell us more of the story you told me."

Beem was paralyzed. He had a million thoughts running through his mind. He tried to listen to The Wisdom, but confusion drowned it out.

"Beem," encouraged Jinx, "I think it will be all right. In fact, I know it."

Jinx's words resonated within him. Confidence began to return. He still wasn't sure how much to share, but he opened his mouth and started to speak.

"As you all know by now . . . I think. All of us kids ended up inside a hole . . ."

Spinny slapped the floor again.

"Beeeeeeem!" he growled through clenched teeth.

"There, there, Mylan," said Mrs. Spin, patting him on the head, "We know all about your little adventure in the underground building."

"Go on, Lucas," she said.

"I–I don't know what my mother told you, but when we were down there, Jinx was badly hurt and he was rescued by a mysterious man."

"The Ancient," his mother added with reverence.

"Yes, an Ancient," said Beem, "Anyway, this man, I mean The Ancient, saved Jinx's life by giving him certain powers. I got the powers too. Then we got home late and we all got in trouble."

The mothers smiled knowingly at each other.

"That was a very intriguing story," said Mrs. Tummins.

"Of course it is," his mother interjected, "So what I was thinking is – we should continue to meet every week, but now include the children."

The women began discussing the idea and quickly came to a consensus.

"Well then," said Illie, "I propose we all meet at the Tummin's home next week. Will that work for you, Liana?"

"That would be lovely," she replied, "I'll get back with you on the time and what you should bring."

"Good," Illie continued, "Let's pass the image and we can dismiss."

She pulled the picture of Lyndal from the box and handed it to Liana. She solemnly studied the image before offering it to the next person in the circle.

"Wow!" said Meekus, startled by the realism.

"Shhhh!" warned his mother, "This is not the time for such an outburst. Now pass it to Jinx."

Jinx immediately recognized the face of Lyndal. He looked at Beem who confirmed his discovery.

When the picture had completed its circuit, Beem's mother kissed the frame and placed it back in the box. She closed the lid, and said with reverence, "Until we see The Ancients."

The women echoed in a monotone drone, "Until we see The Ancients."

She slid the box under her chair and instructed the children to go outside and play. The kids stampeded through the house and out the back door. As soon as Beem stepped outside, he was bombarded with accusations.

"What was that about!?" demanded Spinny.

"Are you crazy!" added Trince, "I can't believe you told your mother . . . and she told MY mother!"

"Don't blame me!" Beem yelled, "I'm just as confused as you are."

"Really?" said Pria, "None of us told our parents anything."

"Hold on," retorted Beem, "Your mother told me she can see in the dark and apparently they've been meeting like this for years. *We* are the newcomers here."

Pria was stunned by Beem's disclosure.

"I don't want to be a newcomer!" yelled Spinny.

Jinx jumped between Beem and the others.

"Stop! This is *not* Beem's fault. He didn't know this would happen. Couldn't you see he was just as shocked as we were?"

"Does this mean we're not going to fight the Keeon?" interjected Wort, secretly hoping to wriggle out of his previous decision.

Beem sighed and sat down, head in hands. He felt baffled and embarrassed.

"I don't know what to think anymore," he confessed.

"How much *do* they know?" inquired Pria.

Her voice softened.

"Did you tell your mom everything . . . about us being trained to fight?"

"No, absolutely not."

"Then we're still fine," said Trince with relief, "They don't know about it."

"And they never will! Right Beem?" added Spinny.

"Never! Whatever happens, this will remain our secret. We are the only ones who can ever know what Lyndal intends to do."

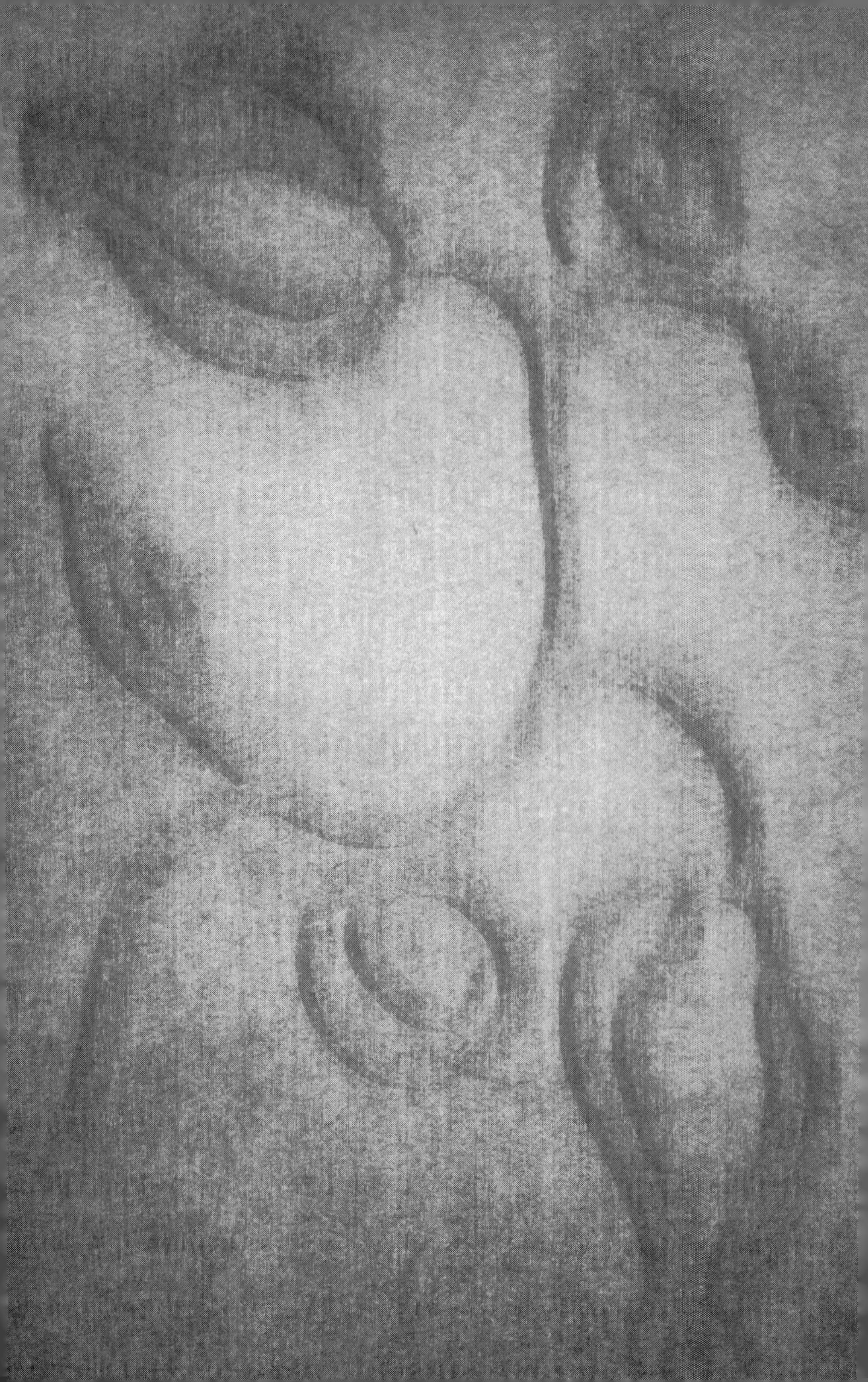

6

A Family Reunion

Beem decided he and Jinx would meet with Lyndal—alone. For now, this was the best way to prevent a reoccurrence of the previous day's chaos. He was relieved his mother didn't know about the meeting. He imagined her smothering Lyndal with unnatural affection. Somehow, the man in the picture, who was indeed Lyndal Froam, had become like a god in her eyes.

As Beem hurried to the center square, a realization hit him. He and his friends had been given the opportunity to change the world. The predictable life of a fieldworker suddenly had an alternate course. For the first time, Beem felt like he had a future and a hope for a better life.

So this is what freedom feels like.

The plaza was crowded with harvesters gathering for lunch, but Beem easily spotted Jinx sitting on top of the best table in the marketplace. It was the perfect vantage point to scan the area for Lyndal.

"I hope we're not too late," Beem said as he studied the faces of passing shoppers.

"What if he doesn't show up?" responded Jinx, "What if he's already left Maidenton?"

Beem sat down and let out a heavy sigh. Even though they had only been there a few minutes, both of them were getting anxious.

"Hey!" Beem said, fiddling with something on his hand, "Did you get a chance to see the ring?"

"You mean the one in the box?"

"Yeah."

"How could I? Your mom kept all that stuff under her chair."

"Take a look at this."

Beem held out his hand. The ring hung loosely from his middle finger.

"Did you steal it?" he whispered.

"I took it from the box while my parents were sleeping. It belongs to Lyndal, so I'm not sure if it's stealing."

"Let me see it."

He handed it to Jinx. The band was dazzling white and seemed to emit its own light. In the center was a small glass orb filled with deep red liquid. Suspended inside was a tiny seed.

"Did you read the inscription?" asked Jinx.

"I didn't know there was one."

Jinx turned the ring to read what was on the inside.

"This is amazing! It's all in symbols, but I know what it says."

"Isn't that strange? What does it say?"

"You were right. It *does* belong to Lyndal. Listen to this, 'Lyndal my love – forever in my heart – Meerin.' It must be the name of his wife or something."

Their conversation was interrupted when a small wooden ball rolled in front of them, bumping into Beem's foot. Close behind was a young boy running to retrieve it. He smiled at Beem as he reached to pick it up, but Beem paid no attention. Instead, he kicked the ball in the opposite direction, sending the boy back into the crowd.

"This waiting is starting to bother me," said Jinx.

"Me too. Maybe something happened, or perhaps he changed his mind."

Beem turned to see the boy with the ball standing next to him again.

"Come play with me," the boy said.

"Get out of here!" ordered Beem, "Can't you see we're busy?"

He reached over and gave the boy a nudge on the shoulder to encourage him to leave.

"Please?" the boy insisted.

"No! I said we're busy."

"Wait," said Jinx.

He lowered his voice to a whisper.

"The Wisdom is telling me to play with this kid."

"Are you crazy? We have to stay put so Lyndal can find us."

Beem leaned down to shove the boy aside, only this time their eyes locked. His eyes sparkled with a familiar light.

"Oh my!" exclaimed Beem, "I – I guess we can play with you for a while."

The Wisdom confirmed his discovery. The youngster tugged at Beem's tunic, urging him forward.

"Come on, follow me!"

Beem tossed the ball to Jinx and grabbed the boy's hand.

Beem:	*I know it's you, Lyndal.*
Lyndal:	*Very good, Beem.*

The boy led them to the edge of the village. Jinx kept looking behind them to see if he could spot Lyndal.

"Are you sure it's a good idea to leave the square?"

"What do you think?" Beem asked the boy.

"Oh yes," he replied, "We need to play where we won't be bothered by anyone."

"What about Lyndal?" whispered Jinx.

The boy looked up at him and smiled.

"Things aren't always as they seem."

Jinx still didn't make the connection.

"Look at his eyes," Beem insisted.

Jinx gazed in awe at the shimmering light dancing in the boy's eyes.

"Is this . . . ?"

Beem nodded.

Lyndal:	*He can hear The Wisdom as clear as a bell, but he's not very imaginative is he?*
Beem:	*Jinx is amazing once you get to know him. Give him a chance. He'll catch on.*

They passed the last row of houses and crossed into the field between Maidenton and Broadside Hill. The tall grasses stood motionless, blanketing the countryside in all directions. A narrow path cut a small ribbon through the stalks, leading toward the mountains.

Lyndal:	*Meet me in the middle of those trees. I'll open the door from the inside.*

At the far side of the field was a cluster of trees. Their white trunks stood like sentinels guarding the slopes of Broadside. The boy released Beem's hand and ran straight for them.

"Throw me the ball!" he yelled.

Jinx lobbed the ball, and as usual, missed his intended target. The boy tried to catch it, but it flew over his head. He dove into the grass, leaving a small cloud of dust behind him. Beem and Jinx ran to the spot expecting to find Lyndal grazed and bruised. Instead, all they found was the ball, nestled in the flattened grass. Lyndal had vanished.

"It's all right," said Beem, "Grab the ball and let's get going."

"Where do you suppose he is?" asked Jinx.

"I'm not sure. He said something about opening a door somewhere in these trees."

Standing in front of them was the wall of massive tree trunks. At their base, a thick layer of underbrush covered the ground. The sharp branches presented an unpleasant obstacle to walk through, but they cautiously navigated the briars with only a few scratches.

In the middle of the grove was a small clearing where the bushes gave way to a patch of grass. The only view not obscured was a glimpse of sky directly above them. It was framed on all sides by the canopy of large flat leaves.

"Psssst!"

Both boys jumped back, startled by the sound

coming from near their feet. Creeping along amongst the dried leaves was a chunk of turf. Upon closer inspection, they could see an arm pushing it away from a newly formed opening in the dirt.

"Down here," said a familiar voice.

Lyndal's silhouette was dimly outlined in the space beneath them.

"When you're sure no one can see you, come down."

The boys quickly scanned the area. The tree trunks and bushes formed an impenetrable wall, shielding them from view.

Beem squatted next to the opening.

"You first, Jinx."

Beem was having second thoughts about going underground again. Jinx, on the other hand, wasted no time. He flipped his legs into the hole, and lowered himself down. Beem had no choice but to follow.

The boys descended into the hole and activated their night-vision while Lyndal pulled the lid of the underground chamber into place. Although this was Beem's third venture into a hole, he was still afraid that it might cave in and bury them alive. The trauma of his first underground encounter was still fresh in his mind. But Jinx was full of excitement. He and Lyndal seemed to be quite comfortable in this subterranean world. Lyndal squeezed past and took the lead.

Beem inhaled deeply and whispered to himself, "Let's be about it."

The twisty corridor was so low they were forced to stoop as they made their way downhill. Beem's only view was of Lyndal and Jinx's back ends. It wasn't the greatest thing to look at, but having them close by put him more at ease. The passage made a couple of sharp turns guiding them to an even deeper hole.

"Does everything you do happen underground?" Beem teased, "It seems like you're part rodent or something."

"Sometimes I feel like it," chuckled Lyndal as he climbed down a ladder, "I would prefer to be outside, but these buildings are much safer. No one can see us or hear us down here."

The boys followed Lyndal as he disappeared into the opening. At the bottom was another room like the ones they had been in a few days earlier. The floor and walls were polished stone and everything was coated in dust.

"What are these places?" asked Beem.

"This is part of the same building where I first met you. These rooms all connect and end up inside Broadside Hill where you and your friends fell in."

"But why are they here, and what are they for?" asked Jinx.

Lyndal motioned for them to follow as he crossed the room into a corridor.

"Well," answered Lyndal, "They weren't always underground. This used to be part of the great

Paddoran city of Stacia. After The Ancients left, the Keeon took over and attempted to destroy all evidence of our existence, including where we lived. When they discovered the buildings were too difficult to tear down, they buried them instead. Broadside Hill isn't really a hill at all. It's a mound of rocks and dirt on top of a city."

"So that's why holes are evil and against the law!" deduced Beem, "To keep us from knowing the truth."

"Very good!" said Lyndal, "If the Keeon can keep everyone fearful of going underground, no one will discover what really happened. Their greatest advantage is keeping you ignorant. Remember, the best lie is one that is mostly truth. The Keeon are experts at this kind of deception."

Lyndal turned a corner and entered a small room. Attached to the wall was a large metal box with several handles, wheels and knobs, identical to the one they had seen a few days before.

"What is this?" asked Beem.

"This is a machine that lights up the walls."

Lyndal pointed to a large handle.

"Grab onto this and push it to the far end of the slot."

The boys pushed the handle across the length of the box until it jerked into place. They looked at Lyndal wondering what might happen next.

"Now Beem," instructed Lyndal, "Twist this knob and watch . . ."

Beem took hold of the knob, looked at Jinx, and smiled. Jinx nodded in approval. Beem slowly turned the knob to one side. In an instant, an incredible buzz came from inside the box. Both boys jumped and then burst into laughter when they saw the surprise on the other's face.

They watched in fascination as the lever vibrated along the slot toward its original position.

"Cover your ears!" yelled Lyndal.

There was a huge CRACK, followed by a flash of intense light. The boys ducked down and closed their eyes. Moments later, a gentle hum began emanating from the box.

They looked around cautiously and stood up in amazement. The walls were beginning to glow . . . pink at first, then transforming to a soft white. They deactivated their night-vision and stood in awe.

"Light!" announced Lyndal with a sweeping gesture.

The boys were drawn to the walls and rubbed their surface in wonder. Not only did the stone emit light but it was warm to the touch.

"We sure don't know very much about anything do we?" stated Beem.

The moment was interrupted by something crashing to the floor in the next room.

"Stay here!" ordered Lyndal as he ran for the door.

He turned a knob on the box and everything became dark in an instant. CRASH! Lyndal dashed out of the

room leaving the boys behind. Beem reactivated his night-vision and slid behind the large machine. His mind began to race. What if the Keeon discovered them? It would be a death sentence for sure, but then he thought there might be something worse . . . like a dangerous underground creature. In either case, he didn't like any of the possible outcomes. He fought the instinct to panic and turned to see if Jinx was all right. To his surprise, his friend didn't seem bothered at all. Beem reached for his hand to touch-talk.

Beem:	*Aren't you scared?*
Jinx:	*Not anymore. Normally I would be, but The Wisdom is telling me not to be afraid. We're safe.*

Beem had forgotten about The Wisdom. He let go of Jinx's hand and began to concentrate on the unfamiliar voice inside him. He pushed his fears aside to listen more closely. Gradually, a sense of peace flowed over his mind and emotions like warm honey. Tension melted away and he began to relax. He smiled at Jinx, no longer fearful of the unknown on the other side of the door. It was now an adventure.

After a few moments of silence, they heard a very familiar sound.

"Aauuooohh!" someone yelled.

"Put the lights on!" shouted Lyndal.

The boys followed his orders but this time they left the room and closed the door. Seconds later, the walls began to glow.

“We’re in here!” Lyndal announced.

The boys ran down the hall to the large room. On the far side of the space, Lyndal was pulling someone from behind a pile of dusty furniture. They soon discovered he had Spinny by the ear. He was squirming and struggling to break free of Lyndal’s firm grasp.

“Jinx, could this possibly be your brother?” asked Lyndal.

Both boys began laughing.

“I’ve never seen him before,” teased Jinx as he elbowed Beem.

“He’s a stranger to me too,” added Beem trying to regain his composure.

Lyndal twisted Spinny’s ear a little tighter.

“Oww!” he yelled, “Come on you guys. Tell him you know me.”

“Why should we?” retorted Beem, “. . . and how did you get in here?”

Lyndal gave his ear another turn.

“Ahhh! That hurts mister! I – I followed you to see where you were going.”

“Is there anyone else?” Lyndal asked.

“No. Ahhhh!” he cried out again as Lyndal applied more pressure, “I mean, yes . . . yes.”

Lyndal eased up a little.

"Trince is outside."

"Is that everyone?"

"Yes! I swear it!" pleaded Spinny fearing the worst for his throbbing ear.

Lyndal looked sternly at Beem.

"Go get her, and bring her straight down."

"I'm sorry, Lyndal. I thought I looked everywhere to make sure we weren't followed."

"You didn't look good enough!" retorted Spinny.

Lyndal released Spinny's ear with a final yank.

Spinny winced and stepped away to give his ear a good rub.

"I'll be right back," Beem said as he climbed the ladder.

"Make sure there isn't anyone else," Lyndal reminded him, "Pay attention to The Wisdom this time, not just your eyes."

Beem navigated the narrow passageway until he could see Trince through the opening. She leaned into the hole.

"Spinny. Where'd you go?"

"Trince! It's me, Beem. I need you to come down here right now!"

Trince was shocked and then a little embarrassed by Beem's discovery of her. She made no argument or excuses and hastily descended through the opening. She stood in the dark and waited for a reprimand from

Beem. He said nothing as he pushed past her to scan the area above them. This time he focused on The Wisdom. When he was sure everything was secure, he pulled the plug of dirt firmly into the opening.

"Where are you?" asked Trince.

"I'm right here."

Beem wrapped his arm around her shoulder.

"Stay close to me and you'll be all right."

Trince liked the feel of Beem's arm holding her securely. Ever since he rescued her from falling down the hole, her feelings of friendship had been changing into something new.

Beem guided her through the narrow tunnel until they could see the glow from the room below. They climbed down the ladder to where the others were waiting.

"Is this everyone?" Lyndal inquired.

"Don't let him near your ear!" warned Spinny, who was keeping his distance.

"Yes sir," she replied, "Spinny and I are the only ones who followed. The others don't even know about it."

She felt remorseful for what she and Spinny had done. She was also fearful about being punished. She recognized The Ancient and wasn't sure what this stranger might do. Lyndal bent down and looked into Trince's frightened eyes. He could see she was upset.

"Weren't you the one who saw Jinx and I transport?"

"Yes," she said, ". . . and Spinny saw it too."

She clung even tighter to Beem's arm.

"That was the scariest thing I've ever seen in my life."

"Everything's going to be fine now," he assured her, "I promise."

Lyndal sat at one of the large tables where he was joined by the children. Spinny, however, remained on the far side of the room.

"Do all of you know why I asked Beem to meet with me today?"

Jinx slapped the top of the bench and blurted, "Beem said you wanted to train us to fight the Keeon!"

Lyndal was surprised by his enthusiastic response. He smiled at Jinx's passion.

"I don't know if I would say it quite like that. Maybe a better way to put it would be to *displace* them. If we are wise and careful, fighting may never be necessary."

Lyndal turned to Beem.

"Did you make a decision?"

Even though everyone at the table was a friend, Beem tried his best to look grown up and important as he stood and addressed them.

"We discussed it as a group, we decided as a group, and as a group we accept your offer."

Lyndal looked at the children with concern.

"Listen to me. This is no small undertaking. Have you seriously considered all the possible outcomes? This could be very dangerous."

"This *could* be dangerous?" declared Trince mustering some boldness, "Haven't we already been discussing a revolt? Aren't we hiding in an underground room, talking with an *Ancient*? You see sir, it already *is* dangerous."

Lyndal was impressed with Trince's sudden transformation from intimidated girl to bold young woman. Faith began to grow in his heart as he considered the courage and willingness of these children. In all his years of seeking committed followers, he had never conceived of working with anyone so young. Now, sitting before him, was the hope and future of Beniwan.

"Here!" said Beem digging into his pocket, "I give you this as our pledge."

Beem opened his hand to reveal the white ring. Lyndal was stunned. He took the ring from Beem's hand, studied it for a moment and slipped it on his index finger.

"I can't believe it . . . my old ring. Where did you find it?"

"There's more," continued Beem, "I know who Meerin is."

An explosion of distant memories and conflicting thoughts inundated Lyndal's mind. The ring was his, but he had lost track of it more than three hundred years earlier, in a village on the far side of the mountains. What Beem was claiming to know was impossible.

"How could you know who Meerin is?" Lyndal exclaimed.

"Because," responded Beem, "She is my great, great, great, great, great grandmother!"

Lyndal stared at him, completely baffled.

"That's nonsense! You have no idea what you're talking about!"

Lyndal knew he was getting too emotional. He let out a heavy sigh before beginning again in a more controlled tone.

"I hate to disappoint you, Beem, but regardless of what you think you might know about me, she is not your grandmother, or anyone else's for that matter. What would make you say a thing like that?"

Beem humbled himself after seeing Lyndal's reaction and sat down in his chair.

"Because," he replied, "this ring was in a box of things my mother said belonged to her great, great, great, great, great grandfather. Then she showed me a picture of him . . . and it was a picture of you."

Silence filled the room. Trince scooted her chair away from him, thinking he might be lying in order to win favor with Lyndal.

"Well that's perplexing isn't it?" said Lyndal.

He frowned and sat quietly. Could there be any truth to this claim?

"I don't see how it could be possible. What else was in the box?"

Beem thought back to the night he and his mother sat on the floor telling secrets. He tried hard to remember the scene.

"There was a little book about The Legends and The Wisdom, and the ring of course. I think I saw a map, but I didn't get a good look at it. It was folded up. And, there was some fabric or a sash or something."

"What did the sash look like?" Lyndal asked with interest.

"It was red with purple trim and had some fancy stitching all over it, just like the pattern on the inside of the box."

Lyndal stared off into space with a hint of a smile.

"Will someone tell me what's going on?" asked Spinny who was now quite frustrated, "What are the two of you going on about?"

"It's all right," explained Lyndal. "I can explain everything . . . I think. This ring and all the items in that box were the property of the most beautiful woman on Beniwan. Her name was Meerin." His voice was thick with emotion as he gently held the lost relic. "She lived in a small village on the far side of the Dulman Mountains. She was . . . my wife. Though our time together was brief, it was the happiest season of my life."

The children listened solemnly as Lyndal recalled bittersweet memories.

I met Meerin a very long time ago at a harvest

celebration. I was passing through town but when I saw her, I was immediately captivated by her beauty and grace. I simply had to stay and get to know her. We fell in love instantly and were married a few weeks later. We had been together for only a month when the town's people accused me of being a sorcerer. They became afraid when they saw fire in my eyes. The men of the village conspired together, captured me and planned to execute me in the public square. As the executioner's sword came down on my neck, I had no choice but to vanish . . . right before their eyes. To them, my disappearance only confirmed their accusations against me. That night, before I could return for my beloved Meerin, her father stole her away to a secret location. I was devastated. I searched for forty years, but never found her.

Lyndal paused for a moment as his eyes filled with tears. He quickly wiped them away to hide his emotions.

"I'm sorry to disappoint you, Beem," he continued, "But we never had any children. So you see, we can't be related."

Beem hung his head.

"I suppose it is possible she remarried and had a family with someone else. It was a very long time ago."

"But my mom said *you* were my great, great, great, great, great grandfather. The box held *your* picture, not her's."

Lyndal suddenly had a spark of inspiration.

"There is a way to find out for sure."

He looked at the children with a funny grin. They couldn't help but lean in to hear what he had to say.

"All of the Froams have an identical birthmark."

Lyndal turned his head to one side and pulled his right ear forward, revealing a small purple spot, the shape of a footprint.

Trince gasped and covered her mouth in shock. She stood straight up from the table, sending her chair flying backward to the floor.

"What's your problem?" asked Spinny, "It's not that big a deal."

Beem grabbed his own ear and pulled it forward for everyone to see.

"What about me?"

They all gathered around to take a look.

"Ahhh!" Trince yelled.

"Wow!" said Jinx, "They're the same! Beem's mom was right. You *are* his great, great however-many grandfather."

"Really?" asked Beem, "Do I really have the same mark as Lyndal?"

Lyndal reached across to examine the mark. It didn't make sense, but there it was. The evidence was undeniable. Beem was of the Froam lineage.

"It seems your mother is right," he conceded, "This sure has been an interesting day."

"So it's true!" Beem shouted with excitement, "I'm an Ancient just like you."

"That's not how it works," stated Lyndal.

He took Beem by the shoulders and looked him in the eye.

"The only way you could be an Ancient is if *both* your parents are. The woman who owned the box with this ring was not an Ancient, she was a Kinsmen, just like you. If you are truly my descendant, it would explain why you were able to receive the powers so quickly."

"That reminds me," interupted Spinny, "Are you going to give us the powers, like you did with Beem and Jinx?"

"Yes!" Lyndal announced with a smile, "I *am* going to give you the powers. But I need to know how many there are of you. Trince mentioned 'some others' and Beem said his mother knows about all of this. Correct?"

"That's an interesting question," Beem said, "Until yesterday there were just the seven of us. Then we discovered our mothers have been meeting secretly and reciting stuff from your journal."

"Yeah, they read from the book, then rub your picture. It's kind of weird." explained Spinny.

Lyndal looked a little confused.

"What about your fathers?"

"They don't know a thing. They would kill us if they

found out," replied Jinx.

"So there are seven children and seven mothers?"

"Six mothers." explained Beem, "As you already know, Jinx and Spinny are brothers. That reminds me, Trince's mom says she can see in the dark, but when I tried to touch-talk her, she couldn't do it. Is that possible?"

"That's not unusual at all. I'm surprised some of you can't see in the dark. Is Beem the only one who breathed in the smoke?"

"I breathed in a little bit," interjected Spinny, "and so did Trince, but Beem is the only one who breathed it in deep."

"You know, it doesn't take much to activate the night-vision," said Lyndal, directing his comment to Spinny, "You might have the ability already and not even know it."

"Really?" yelled Spinny.

He ran around the table to Lyndal who pretended not to notice him.

"How can I tell? What do I do?"

Spinny was shaking like an excited puppy. Lyndal smiled.

"Run down the hall to a dark room and touch your eyes."

Before Lyndal had even finished his instructions, Spinny was racing toward the hall.

"Come on, Trince!"

He didn't wait for a response, and spun around the corner out of view.

"You go on and let me know what happens," she muttered.

Trince seemed unusually quiet and preoccupied with something.

"What's wrong, Trince?" asked Beem. "You don't seem yourself."

"WOOOHOOOO!"

The sounds of joy echoed through the corridor. Spinny had discovered his new power.

"This is GREAT!" he panted as he ran back into the room, "I can see in the dark. It's just like it was day. I could see everything!"

He ran to Trince, grabbed her arm and tried to pull her up.

"Come on! You've got to try this, it's so fantastic!"

"Stop!" she yelled, yanking her arm away.

All eyes were on Trince who was now visibly upset.

"I'm confused about something. You're saying that because Beem has the same birthmark, he's your relative?"

"That's the only explanation I can think of. I wouldn't have believed it if I hadn't seen it for myself. He has the family mark. I must have been a papa and didn't know it."

"So what you're saying is *anyone* who has that stupid mark on their ear is related to you?"

Lyndal thought about it.

"The possibility of someone else having the birthmark would be practically impossible."

"That's what scares me."

Trince's voice was trembling.

"My father has the mark behind *his* ear. I've seen it."

Beem began to understand. "I w o n d e r . . ."

The children ran to Trince and she pulled her ear forward.

"Well, what's there?" she cried.

"Woah!" said Spinny.

Jinx reached up and grabbed his brother's ear.

"OWWW!"

Spinny was still smarting from his encounter with Lyndal.

"Unthinkable," remarked Lyndal.

Jinx turned around and pulled his own ear forward.

"What about me, what about me?"

It was soon discovered that every child in the room possessed the same birthmark in the same place. Lyndal began to chuckle.

"It appears the impossible is possible, after all. Maidenton must have been where Meerin's family took her and apparently, where our child was born. Now, here I am, sitting with the family I never knew I had."

Over the next several weeks, Lyndal trained the seven in the use of their new powers. Soon they were all able to touch-talk, see in the dark, log and transfer memories, and listen to The Wisdom as if they had been doing it all their lives. As their training progressed, a transformation took place. The children were becoming increasingly confident in the way they approached life. They were more mature somehow, but at the same time, completely childlike. Trince and Spinny fought a little less over trivial issues, and the younger ones shed fewer tears from hurt feelings. Lyndal was overwhelmed with love for his newly discovered family.

When they weren't busy training, he would show them around the complex of underground buildings, explaining the use of the Paddoran machines. The children were fascinated by them, but only a few were still in working order. Everyone's favorite was the communication portal. Lyndal insisted it wasn't a machine, but the children couldn't see the difference. A portal could transfer and retrieve information just as they had learned to do with each other. Lyndal described how to activate it by inserting their arms into the entry holes. He told them how the sphere inside would glow when it was touched. It all sounded so interesting. They would discover one every now and then as they explored the underground world, but could never get one to work.

The Stone Room became their home away from home and while no one remembered who first came up with the name, they began to refer to themselves as 'The Following.'

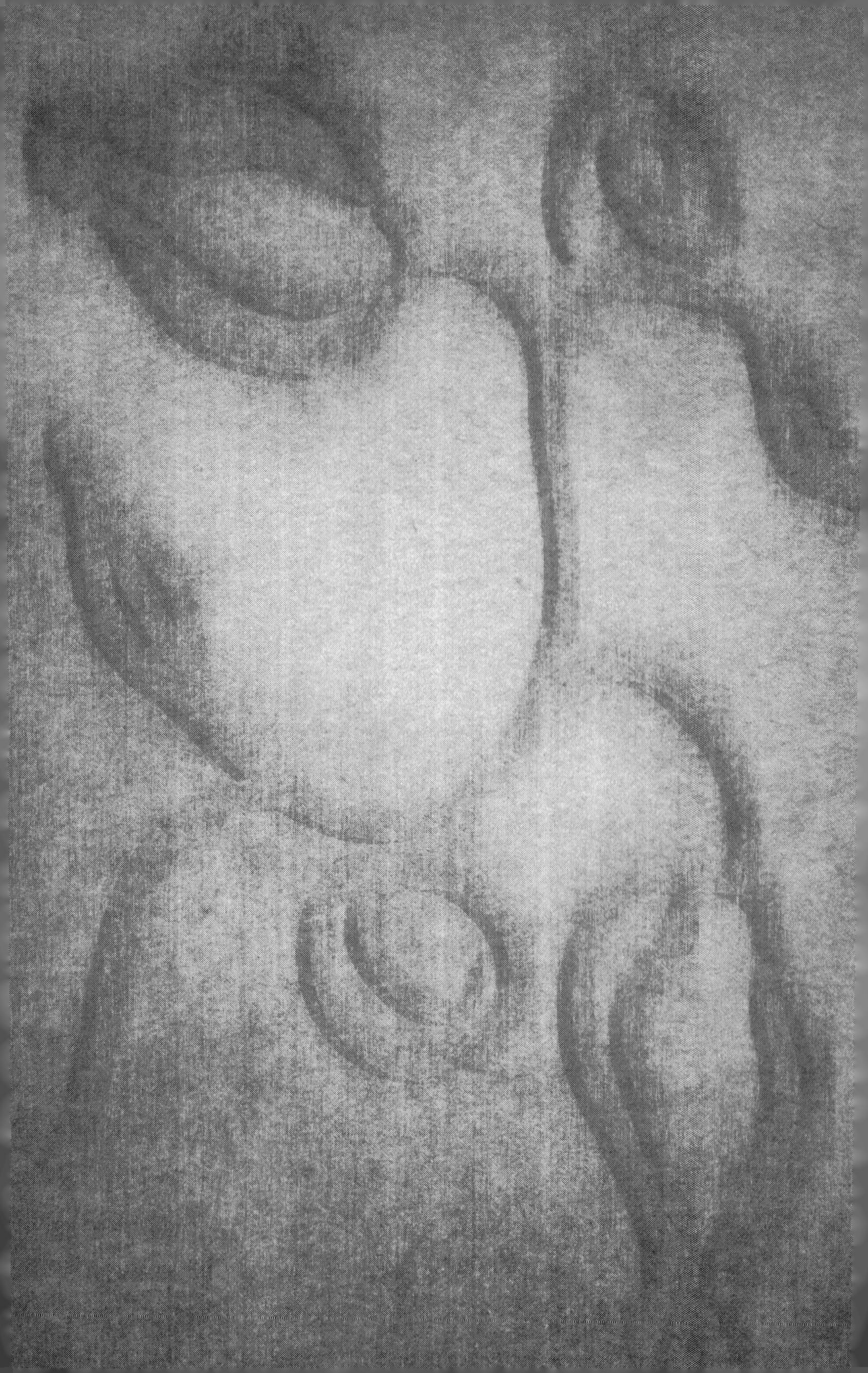

7

A Disappearing Act

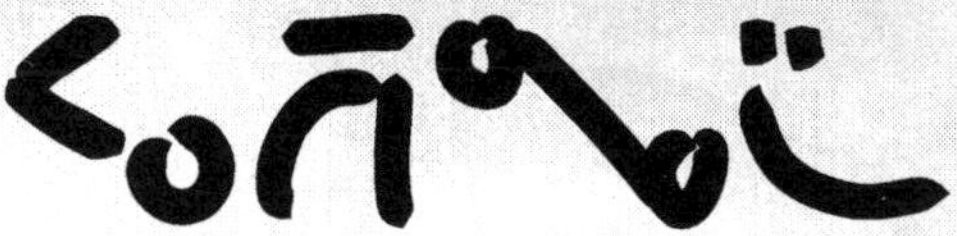

Beem reached under the floorboards and pulled the rough cloth bag from its hiding place. Tucked inside, was the blue metal box containing the 'sacred relics.' His stomach fluttered with excitement as he quietly rehearsed what he was about to say.

The Beeman's fancy chairs, the ones with the embroidered backs, were arranged in a semicircle in the middle of the room. The mothers were seated, chatting away while the children sat cross-legged on the floor awaiting Beem's announcement. When he entered the room, the women burst into quiet applause. They were always thrilled to read from the book.

It had been three months since Lyndal started training the children. Today was the day the mothers would be introduced to The Ancient for the first time. Beem thought it best not to give them advance warning. He would simply introduce Lyndal, and let their reaction determine the next step.

"Can I have everyone's attention please?"

The room quieted as all of them focused on Beem. He smiled nervously and after a brief pause, hesitantly announced, "I have a surprise for you today."

The children squirmed with excitement anticipating Lyndal's appearance.

"Today, instead of just *talking* about the powers and looking at an *image* of the man in the picture, I thought we should experience the real thing."

He could tell by their blank expressions they didn't understand.

"Lucas," his mother interrupted, "Are you saying the items in the box aren't real?"

"No, not at all. I know the book and the other objects are real things – but it seems like you enjoy talking *about* the words in the book more than trying to understand what the *words are talking about.* So, I thought it was time for you to see and touch instead of just . . . hope and dream."

The room erupted in a flurry of heated discussion as the women struggled to make sense of his words.

"Hold on," Beem said with a sigh, "Let me try this again. You remember the story of when we met The Ancient . . . the day we fell in the hole?"

"Yes," gushed Mrs. Spin, "That's one of our favorite stories. We love the way you tell that one."

Beem fought to restrain his frustration.

"That's just it. It isn't a story! It was . . . I mean, it is, all REAL."

"Of course it is, Lucas," said his mother, trying to calm him down, "That's why we like to hear it so often."

"Hold on, Illie," interrupted Alma Limm, "I think I know what you're talking about, Lucas. I've been trying to explain night-vision to them for years."

"Ooo, I like that story too," said Mrs. Tivley.

Exasperated with the way things were going, Beem jumped in, "Enough about stories and introductions. Let's just get on with it." He shifted his attention to the reason they were all gathered, "Jinx, can you pull the curtain across the back window?"

Jinx did as he asked, signaling to Lyndal it was time.

"How wonderful." said Mrs. Tivley, "He's creating a mood this time. Should we light a candle?"

"No," interjected Beem as the room darkened, "You don't need to . . ."

In the blink of an eye, Lyndal Froam appeared in the center of the room. Some women screamed while others gasped in awe. Esta Cromwell leapt to her feet and began hurling anything she could find at the strange man.

"Keep him away! Keep him away!" she shrieked, "He's EVIL!"

Illie and Liana ran to her side and attempted to comfort her.

"Shhhhh," whispered Alma, gently patting her hand, "Someone outside might hear you. You need to be quiet."

"This is no time to be quiet!" she snapped.

Her arms flailed, forcing her friends to back away. She grabbed Illie by the shoulders and shook her. There was terror in her eyes as she struggled to speak.

"I – I thought this was a *nice* meeting – where we could do *nice* things with each other. But this is going too far!"

She snatched up her satchel, grabbed Wort's hand and fled to the front door.

"Oh please, Esta," Illie pleaded, "Don't go. There's nothing evil going on."

Mrs. Cromwell paid no attention. She swung the door open with a bang and marched down the front walk. Wort resisted her pull, begging to go back, but she yanked him along as she stormed toward the village square. Alma closed the door and approached Lyndal.

"I'm honored to meet you, sir. Please forgive Esta's behavior. I'm worried about what she might do. I wouldn't be surprised if she reports this to the committee."

As soon as the words left her mouth, the mood in

the room changed from concern to outright fear.

"It could be worse," added Mrs. Spin, "She might tell her husband."

"I'm so sorry everyone," Beem said, "I had no idea this would cause such a problem."

He turned to Lyndal and whispered, "What should we do?"

Lyndal paused and listened to The Wisdom.

"Nothing," he responded.

"Ladies," he continued, "How *you* choose to react could be just as compromising as your friend telling the committee, or her husband. Until we know for certain what she does, you should go about your business as if this never happened."

Lyndal pulled Beem aside.

"It's no longer safe for me to be here. My presence will put everyone at risk."

They walked to the back of the house.

"Find out how the other women react, and listen to The Wisdom as you do. We need to know who we can trust."

Beem hated that everything had backfired. He blamed himself for Mrs. Cromwell's reaction.

"I'm sorry about all of this," he said, "I had no idea . . ."

Lyndal smiled and placed his hand on Beem's shoulder.

"It's all right, Beem. Everything will come right in the end. You'll see. Keep hope alive."

Then he vanished from the room.

Beem returned to the front of the house where everyone was quietly gathering their things to leave. Instead of the usual lively conversation, the women spoke in hushed tones, exchanging apologies. His mother handed him the box and motioned for him to put it away. He could see from her expression his big surprise had been a complete disaster.

Beem crawled under the kitchen counter and returned the box to its hiding place. As he released the bag, a tremor shook his body. It came from inside and was so strong he had to steady himself to keep from falling over.

That was strange.

He glanced down at the opening in the floor and it happened again, this time even stronger. It was like nothing he had ever felt before and it frightened him. He fought the urge to tell his mother. Instead, he focused on The Wisdom.

What's going on?

As quickly as the question formed in his mind, he knew the answer. He didn't have to think about it or conjure up a response; he just knew. This was no longer a safe place for the box. In fact, he knew he had to get it out of the house.

Where can I hide it? Whom can I give it to? Everyone is probably gone by now.

"Trince," he loudly whispered, trying to get her attention.

Perplexed at his secretive behavior, Trince walked into the kitchen to figure out why he was beckoning her in such a manner.

"What do you want?"

Beem positioned himself close to Trince, hiding the bag between them. His actions surprised her at first but she enjoyed being close to him.

"I need your help," he quietly explained.

He glanced over her shoulder, making sure no one was watching. Then in a swift move, he pulled the box from the bag and shoved it in her satchel.

"Take this home and hide it. Better yet, bury it somewhere, where nobody can find it."

"Why are you . . . ?"

"Trincy – come on. It's time to go," interrupted her mother.

Trince was conflicted. She didn't want to disappoint Beem but hated the thought of taking something that wasn't hers. Before she could react, her mother took her arm and led her toward the door.

What should I do?

"Hide the box," said the voice inside her.

The Wisdom confirmed what Beem didn't have time to explain.

As soon as it was safe, Beem grabbed a few sweet cakes from the cupboard. He shoved them in the bag and slipped it under the floor before joining his mother in the other room.

"What do you think Mrs. Cromwell will do?"

"I don't know," she said matter-of-factly, "Esta can be pretty contrary at times. I think she had quite a scare."

"What about the others? Do you think everyone else is all right with what happened?"

"They'll do fine."

"Do you think Mrs. Cromwell will report us?"

She paused.

"It's one thing to have a disagreement, even a harsh one, but none of us would ever turn in a fellow Kinsman to the Keeon."

Beem stopped what he was doing and sat in one of the chairs.

"What about you? How did it feel to actually meet the man from your picture?"

Beem's mother turned to him with a look of confusion.

"What are you talking about?"

"Lyndal . . . The Ancient . . . the man from the picture in the box."

Mrs. Beeman put her hands on her hips and glared at him.

"Are you telling me you think that friend of yours is the same man from the picture in the box?"

"Of course. Didn't you recognize him?"

"You've got quite an imagination young man."

She rolled her eyes and returned to the sink of dirty dishes.

"I was impressed he could come and go so quickly, but really Beem . . ."

She shook her head and chuckled.

"But didn't you see his eyes?"

"I'm sure he has nice eyes," she answered, "and so do you. But you need to understand something, Lucas. The man in the picture is something special. He's no ordinary man. If *he* were to show up in my house, we would know it. You know, we would feel it inside, like when we look at his picture. Besides, it would be impossible. The man in the picture would be hundreds of years old by now."

Beem could tell he wasn't getting anywhere with her. Then he remembered the ring.

"Lyndal IS the man!" he argued, "He confirmed it when I gave him the ring."

"You did WHAT?" she exclaimed.

She dropped what she was doing and stared wide eyed, in shock at Beem. She looked as if she could burst into tears.

"How could you do such a thing?" she scolded, "You know that's one of the sacred objects. You've violated my trust!"

"I thought it would be best for him to have his own ring back," he attempted to explain.

“I can’t believe this! He’s probably down at the square right now trying to sell it. I bet this Lyndal fellow is nothing but a liar and a thief. Did you see how quickly he left the house? Oh, Lucas, what have you done?”

She wiped the tears from her eyes and returned to the washbasin. Beem knew it was pointless to continue arguing.

“I’m sorry,” he said quietly.

He hung his head and went to his room to sort things out.

Beem spent the rest of the afternoon in his room wondering how to make things right. He was racked with guilt, feeling responsible for the afternoon’s upheaval . . . and he knew it could get worse.

He climbed onto his windowsill and stared out across the rooftops of Maidenton. If he thought hard enough, maybe some sort of solution would come to mind. But the more he pondered, the more discouraged he became. This was not how things were supposed to turn out.

Hours passed, and the shadow of the neighbor’s tree slowly crept across the main path and up the side of the house. Then, like clockwork, small plumes of smoke began rising from the nearby chimneys.

Is it dinnertime already?

The quiet was suddenly interrupted by a commotion coming from outside. Beem could see his father returning from the fields, only he wasn't alone. Mr. and Mrs. Cromwell were right next to him walking at a brisk pace. His father's face was red with frustration. He said nothing as Mrs. Cromwell waved her hands about, chattering on and on. Mr. Cromwell was trying to calm his wife but she shoved him aside, continuing her rant.

"This can't be good," Beem said aloud.

His stomach began to churn as they approached the front gate.

His father pushed open the front door and bellowed, "Illie!"

He heard the pitter patter of his mother's footsteps pass by his door.

"Get the boy and come down here!" his father barked.

Beem cracked his door and peered into the hall. His mother motioned for him to join her.

"Come on," she whispered, "We might as well get this over with."

Esta Cromwell was still jabbering away, trying to make some point about conjuring up evil spirits as Beem joined them in the front room.

"There he is," she said, pointing her pudgy finger in his direction, "He's the one who's responsible."

Beem looked innocently at his father who paid no attention.

"Well Lucas? What's this all about?"

Illie could see by the desperate look on her son's face that he was about to reveal too much.

"So . . ." Beem began, "we were all . . ."

"Let me tell it," his mother interrupted, "I am the one who is responsible, not the boy."

Beem was relieved to let his mother take over.

"Well?" his father prodded.

She fidgeted a bit, took a deep breath and began.

"You know I get together with the girls every week, right? So today was our weekly meeting and we decided we should include the children this time. I made a beautiful salad and Marlyne made this wonderful loaf of . . ."

"Get to the point, Illie!" Beem's father demanded.

"All right," she said, "Anyway . . . today Beem decided it would be fun if one of his friends magically appeared in the room . . . you know . . . as a joke. So when this fellow suddenly became visible, everyone was amazed. Nobody could figure out how he did it, but Esta left the house before we had a chance to explain."

"It wasn't a trick!" Esta argued, "It was real! It's all part of a secret religion your wife has been leading for years."

"What?" Mr. Beeman yelled.

His glare intensified.

"That's right," Mrs. Cromwell continued, savoring her accusations, "She and all of her friends get together and worship a picture of an Ancient and read about the powers."

An understanding smile spread across Mr. Beeman's face.

"You mean The Legends?" he snickered.

"OF COURSE I mean The Legends!" Esta snapped, stomping her foot on the floor.

Beem's dad leaned over to Harlin Cromwell.

"Women . . . and their silly superstitions!"

Harlin smiled back, nodded and then turned to his wife who was now fuming. His countenance immediately changed back to its former expression.

"Now – now see here, Mark . . ." he began.

"You can't be taking this seriously can you?" Mr. Beeman interrupted.

"You'd better believe we're serious," spewed Mrs. Cromwell, "And I'll prove it to you. I know where Illie keeps the picture."

Esta Cromwell paraded herself into the kitchen and pointed to the spot on the floor next to the tall cupboard.

"Right there, underneath the floor, is where she keeps the box. I've seen the boy put it there many times."

She stood, arms folded, tapping her foot impatiently. Nobody said a word.

"Oh this is ridiculous!" Mark exclaimed, "But if it's that important to you, feel free to take a look."
Esta glared at Illie, relishing her impending exposure. Illie remained deadpan, refusing to budge.

Esta let out a huff and crouched down on her hands and knees to find the evidence. She was a short, plump woman, well known throughout Maidenton for baking delicious desserts. She greatly enjoyed her own cooking, which was the cause of her rather generous proportions. Her ample backside protruded into the air and jiggled back and forth, as she struggled to wedge herself under the counter. Harlin flushed with embarrassment.

"Oh my," Illie exclaimed as she covered Beem's eyes.

"Really, Esta!" Harlin complained, "Is all of this necessary?"

"Ah hah!" she cried with delight as she discovered the loose board.

She pulled it up and slid it across the kitchen floor. Beem's father looked at his wife with great concern.

"Here it is!" she announced wiggling out from beneath the counter. She stood up, holding the bag in the air like a trophy. Then she untied it and tipped the contents on to the table.

"See for yourself!" she gloated.

The sweet cakes came tumbling out. Esta Cromwell was dumbfounded.

"Beem!" his mother shouted in astonishment.

She quickly regained her composure.

"I – I'm surprised at you!" she scolded, trying to conceal her relief, "Hiding food like that. Don't I give you enough to eat at meal times? You go to your room immediately!"

Beem walked out of the kitchen, partway up the stairs and stopped, continuing to listen in on the conversation. Mark picked up one of the cakes and examined it.

"This little guy doesn't look like an Ancient to me," he mocked.

"Ooof!" Esta blurted.

She slapped the muffin from his hand sending it flying across the room. Her face was boiling with anger. Everyone could see the pressure building as she tried to think of what to do next.

She clenched her fists and yelled, "I'm telling you there is something evil . . . ," and she burst into tears.

Her breakdown was met with blank stares.

"There, there, Esta," said Harlin, "I think it's time for us to be going."

He wrapped his arm around her shoulder and walked her to the door.

"But . . . but," she stuttered.

"We'll see you in the morning, Mark," he said as he led her down the front path.

"Tomorrow then," Mr. Beeman replied.

As soon as the door closed, Mark turned to face his wife.

"Calm down, dear," she said as she nervously backed into the kitchen.

He pursued her step for step.

"You're having those meetings again, aren't you?"

She bumped into the eating bench and stumbled backward onto a chair. She could think of nothing to say, so she smiled nervously, hoping to appease him.

"It's this sort of thing that will get us in trouble with the Keeon." he lectured, "You're not only risking your own life but the lives of your friends – and now the children! Illie, this has to STOP!"

"Lucas!" he yelled.

Beem poked his head around the corner.

"Sir?"

"Where is the box?"

Beem swallowed hard.

"I don't have it. I – I gave it to Trince. I told her to bury it."

Upon hearing this, Mr. Beeman's expression changed from anger to relief. "Now that's the smartest thing I've heard all day!"

He pulled Beem by the arm and stood him next to

his mother. They stared at him, wide-eyed.

"I want you to forget all about this nonsense. Do you understand?"

"Yes sir," Beem said.

Illie nodded in agreement.

"It does nothing but cause problems. We're lucky she didn't report this to the committee!"

"Now," he said calmly, "What's for dinner? All this excitement has given me quite an appetite."

He looked down at his son and smiled. Beem smiled back but wondered what had happened to cause such a sudden change of mood.

They ate in silence, cleaned the dishes and turned in for the night. Beem was exhausted. He was anxious to put the events of the day behind him.

Before sliding into his hammock, he looked out the window. The second moon hung low in the sky. Its dim glow peered through the gathering clouds. He could smell the humidity in the air. It was later than he realized.

Beem was amazed at how much his life had changed in the last few months. Every day was a new adventure; only now he didn't get to choose how things turned out. It was a far cry from the days of pretending with his friends on Broadside Hill. As he nestled into bed, he decided to log the events of the day into his memory.

>Memory Log 7.20.2026.23.5

>Today was a close call. We decided to introduce Lyndal to our moms. But when he appeared, they got scared – especially Wort's mom, Esta Cromwell. She ran out of the house, told her husband and my dad, who came back to our house and began asking questions. Mom covered for me though. Thanks to The Wisdom, the only proof of the accusation was a bag of sweet cakes under the floorboards. I gave Trince the box and told her to bury it. As long as nobody comes after her, we should be safe.

>I did tell my parents I gave the box to Trince, which made my Dad really happy.

>It was strange my Dad was so nice to me after I told him. I wonder if . . .

>Oh no. I hope I didn't compromise Trince.

>End

Beem's eyes popped open. He jumped up, cracked opened his door, and looked down the hall. There was light coming from under his parent's door. He could hear them arguing.

He changed out of his nightclothes, stuffed them with pillows and covered them with his blanket. He grabbed his cloak and snuck into the hall. When he was halfway down the stairs, he heard a door open. He turned to see his dad backing out of their room.

"I'll only be gone a little while, and then this will be over – forever," he said.

I've got to get to Trince fast, before my father does!

He slipped out the back door and activated his night-vision. As he cleared the back fence, he could see his father through the rear window. He was putting on his cloak.

It was now total black and Beem's ability to see in the dark gave him a great advantage. His father would have to use a lantern, which would slow his progress. As Beem approached the main path, he heard a voice within him.

"Hide! Now!"

He dove into the bushes.

Marching toward him, with torches blazing, was a small group of Keeon guards. Beem had never witnessed anything like this. Lying motionless in the grass, he waited for them to pass. Instead of staying on the main path, he watched in horror as they turned down the lane to his house.

This is worse than I thought. She must have turned us in.

Beem gathered himself and took off running. He vaulted over the Tummins' back fence and climbed the large tree next to the house as he had done a hundred times before. He shimmied along the branch next to Trince's window and tapped the glass lightly. Her face appeared on the other side and she quietly

slid the window open. She was startled by the terror in his eyes. He reached through the opening and clutched her hand.

Beem:	*Hurry and gather your things. We have to leave. Now!*
Trince:	*What happened?*
Beem:	*There are Keeon at my house and my parents know I gave you the box.*
Trince:	*I never had a chance to bury it. It's still in my satchel.*
Beem:	*Good! Bring it with you.*
Trince:	*I can't just . . .*

The sound of barking dogs broke the silence of the night. It came from the direction of Beem's house and spread throughout the village. They watched the windows of neighboring houses light up one by one.

Beem:	*We don't have much time. We need to get the others.*

Trince threw on some clothes, slung her satchel over her shoulder and climbed out the window. When they had cleared the back fence, Beem stopped and grabbed her hand again. Trince's heart was pounding. She had never done anything like this before.

Beem:	*You get the twins and Pria and I'll get Meekus and Wort.*
Trince:	*All right.*
Beem:	*Then bring everyone to the Stone Room.*

Trince felt safe as she held Beem's hand. A surge of excitement coursed through her as she looked into Beem's eyes.

"Be careful," he whispered.

He released her hand and the two set out to fulfill their mission.

"Who could be calling at such an absurd hour!" grumbled Mr. Beeman.

As soon as he unlatched the door, it flung open knocking him to the floor. Keeon guards filled the front room, their faces cold and expressionless.

"Are you Markus Beeman?" the chief demanded as he referenced some papers in his hand.

"Yes," responded Mark, "that's my name. What's all this about?"

"Are you the husband of Illian Beeman and the father of Lucas Beeman?"

The realization of what was happening gripped him and the color drained from his face.

"Yes," Mr. Beeman responded, "but you know all of this. We're registered in the village records. We've lived in Maidenton all our lives."

Mark's mind raced to devise a plan to protect his family. He had to figure out a way to keep them safe.

The chief turned and addressed two of his guards.

"Attend to this man. The rest of you – bring the woman and the boy to me."

When they had left the room, Mark bolted toward the kitchen in a desperate attempt to find a makeshift weapon. The remaining guards tackled him, strapping ties around his neck and wrists to restrain him. He struggled to get free, but it was no use. Then he heard the sickening sound of Illie's screams as the guards dragged her down the hall.

"Where is your son?" ordered one of the Keeon.

"He's in there," she whimpered, trembling in terror, "But he didn't do anything. Please don't . . ."

"The brat is gone!" he bellowed angrily.

They forced Illie down the stairs and stood her in front of the chief like a prize. Tears streamed down her cheeks, as she looked frantically about the room for her family.

"Here's the woman," the guard reported, "but the boy is missing. We found these."

He clutched Beem's nightclothes in his grubby hand.

"They were wrapped around some pillows to make it look like he was asleep."

"So it's true. We do have a little troublemaker at work here," sneered the chief.

The allegations had been confirmed.

He turned to his guards and snarled, "Take them to Punishment House. Find the boy. I want to know how he spends his days, where he likes to go, and who his friends are."

"Why are you doing this?" Illie cried, struggling against her captors, "We haven't done anything wrong."

Mark was jerked to his feet and dragged out the front door. He struggled at first, but after a couple of jabs to the back with the blunt end of a spear, he fell into line. He was tortured by the pitiful sobs of his wife who followed close behind.

Beem ran as fast as he could toward the grove of trees at the far end of the open field. He plunged into the claw-like underbrush giving no thought to the outcome. The jumble of branches snagged his clothing and scratched his legs but he paid no attention as he pushed forward. Behind him, the village of Maidenton was wide-awake. The torchlight reflected off the low hanging clouds, creating an eerie glow over the rooftops. Beem made no attempt to be quiet, as twigs snapped loudly beneath his feet. No one in the village would be able to hear them over the incessant barking. He entered the clearing, took a quick look around and pulled the clay plug from its pocket in the ground. He slipped inside the opening; then closed the lid over his head. Instantly the noise from the outside world disappeared. Beem moved through the tunnel with only the sound of his breathing and the muffled pounding of his heart. There was no light coming from the Stone Room below as he tapped the ladder three times with a small rock. He quickly descended into the familiar chamber.

Waiting at the bottom were Pria and Meekus. They were disheveled and half-asleep with moisture dripping from their clothing. Beem stepped off the ladder and was bombarded with questions. They demanded to know what was happening and why they were forced to leave their homes at such an hour.

"I'll explain everything as soon as we're all here," Beem panted, struggling to catch his breath.

"Where's Trince?"

"She went to get the twins," explained Pria, "They're probably right behind you."

"Where's Wort?" asked Meekus, "I thought you were going to get him?"

Beem examined their fearful faces. He could see

that their hope and trust in him were still alive. He didn't want to do anything to disappoint them.

"I did go to Wort's house," Beem explained, "but there was light coming from inside. When I looked . . ."

They were interrupted by the sound of three taps overhead.

"That must be Trince," whispered Pria.

Trince started down the ladder, followed by Jinx and Spinny.

"Is everyone here?" she asked as she removed her hood and wiped the night mist from her face.

"Everyone but Wort," said Meekus.

Trince turned to Beem with an inquiring look.

"Let's get a fire started," he said, "We can talk while we dry off."

The children removed their dripping cloaks and proceeded into the kitchen. They huddled around the cooking hearth while Jinx stacked wood on top of a wad of wooly-grass. Spinny leaned in and soon a small spark leapt from his flint, igniting the grass. They sat shivering as the fire came to life.

"Mind if I join you?" said a man's voice from the far side of the room.

The older boys spun around and moved swiftly into a defensive stance to protect the group. Pria instinctively tucked Meekus under her arm.

"It's me," Lyndal reassured them as he walked into the flickering light. He was impressed by their well-executed response to his sudden appearance.

Relief replaced vigilance and soon everyone was feeling more relaxed as they warmed themselves around the crackling fire.

"So what's going on?" he asked, "The whole village is in an uproar – something about missing children?"

"Am I ever glad to see you!" Beem exclaimed, "We're in a lot of trouble."

Lyndal removed his cloak and sat down on the hearth amongst his young followers. He listened to The Wisdom and he chose his words carefully. He could sense a wide range of emotions stirring within the children.

"Trouble doesn't begin to describe the situation," he replied, "but, this is what we've been preparing for. Don't let fear block your ability to hear The Wisdom. Stay focused and you will be victorious in the end."

Lyndal paused.

"I only count six of you. Where's Wort?"

"I was in the middle of telling everyone," said Beem, "I went to get him but there was light coming from inside his house. When I looked through the window, I saw his parents talking with Keeon guards – and Wort was sitting on his mother's lap. I didn't think it would be a good idea to wait around, so I came here as fast as I could."

"Did the Keeon come to everyone's homes?" Lyndal asked.

The children all shook their heads.

"Just so you know," Lyndal continued, "I checked around the village before coming here, and the Keeon were tearing Beem's house apart."

"Really?! I had no idea it had gone this far," said Beem anxiously, "Did you see if my parents were all right?"

"No, but The Wisdom told me not to worry."

Beem paused and listened. Immediately peace calmed his fears.

"I think the soldiers were looking for something," continued Lyndal.

Trince picked up her satchel.

"It was probably this."

She reached inside and pulled out the box.

"I believe this is yours . . . with all of your things in it," she explained.

"May I?" asked Lyndal.

Beem took the box from Trince and handed it to Lyndal. The blue metal came alive as it reflected the firelight. He placed it in his lap and carefully lifted the lid. The children watched with curiosity as he studied each item. His seriousness melted into delight.

"Just look at all these marvelous things," he sighed, "The last time I saw these, was when Meerin and I were still together . . . right before I transported."

Spinny interrupted Lyndal, barely able to contain his impatience, "What are we supposed to do now? We can't go back home. Is it time to fight?"

"And what about our parents?" inquired Pria, "What's going to happen to them?"

Lyndal reluctantly set his box of treasures aside as a stream of questions assailed him. The children were frightened and they needed answers.

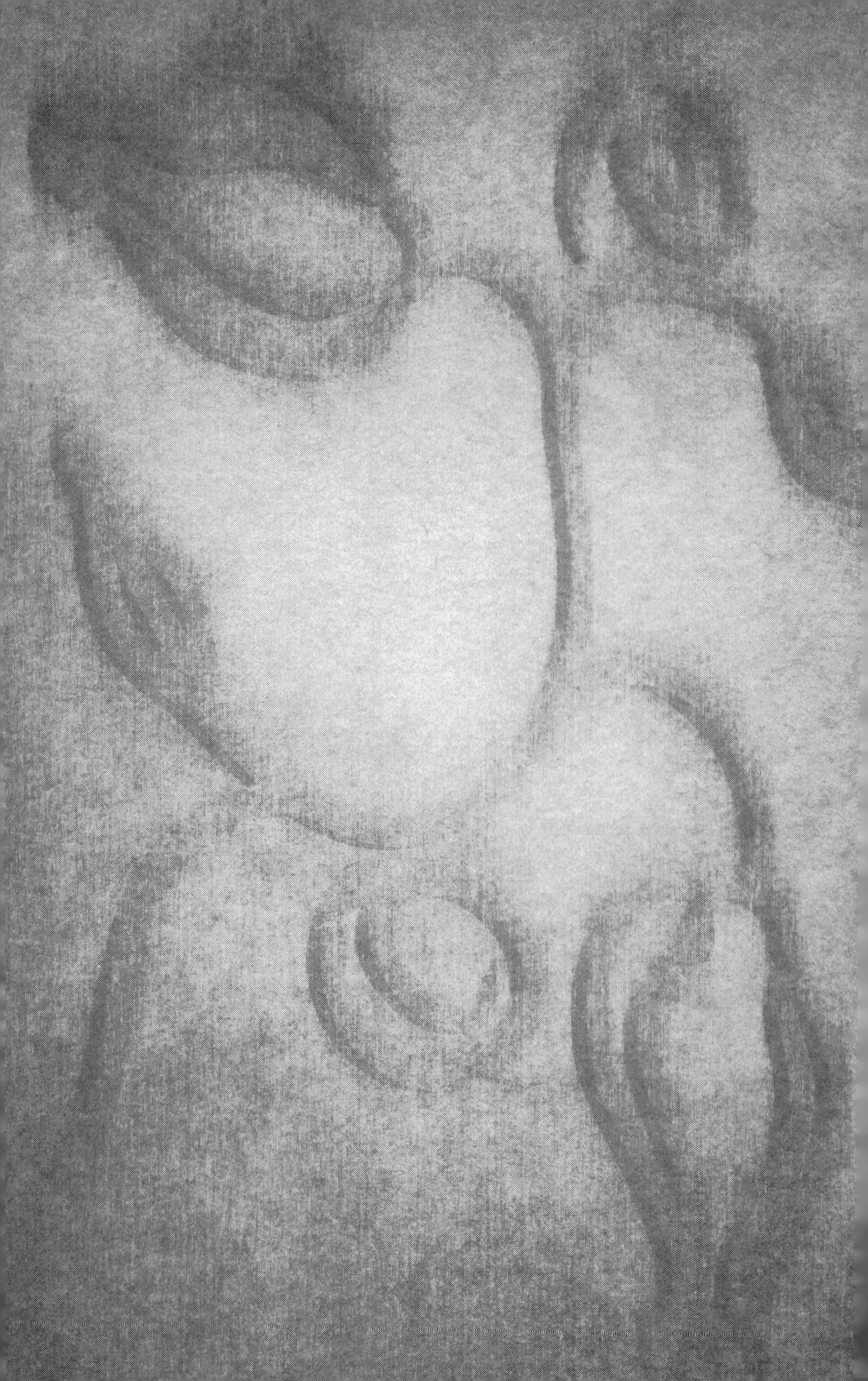

8

PUNISHMENT HOUSE

Pria and the twins were preparing breakfast while the rest of the children slept. Beem was awakened by the inviting aroma of the simmering meat. He stumbled from his pile of pillows into the kitchen, rubbing the sleep from his eyes. Spinny and Jinx sat next to the hearth poking sticks into the fire while Pria placed bowls and spoons around the table. Without windows, it was impossible to tell what time it was, but Beem knew the sun was up in the outside world.

"Am I the last one up?" he yawned.

"No, Trince and Meekus are still sleeping," said Pria as she sprinkled some spices into a bubbling pot.

"Lyndal's awake too," added Spinny, looking up from the fire, "He got up early and went into the village to listen to the gossip. He said it was the best way to get information without being too obvious."

Beem wondered what Lyndal might discover from his reconnaissance, but his growling stomach kept him distracted. He was more interested in what was simmering in the pot. The smell was mouthwatering.

"What are you cooking?"

He leaned over the fire for a closer look.

"Just some noodles," replied Pria, "Go sit down."

She pushed him out of the way and emptied a pan of sizzling meat into the boiling pasta. She swirled the mixture around and ladled some into a bowl.

"Here," she said handing it to him, "It's pretty tasty."

Beem leaned over the bowl, and carefully slurped the near-boiling contents. The fragrant steam of the extra-spicy noodles quickly cleared his nose and revived his tired brain.

Trince and Meekus joined the others and noodles were passed around. Soon everyone was back to normal, arguing about what to do next. Spinny was convinced he should sneak into the village and gather supplies.

"This is no time for running off and doing something stupid," said Beem, "Don't you remember what we discussed last night? We need to stay right here until Lyndal returns. He will tell us what to do."

Spinny began pacing the room like a caged animal. Nothing Beem said seemed to make any difference.

"But, don't you think he should be back by now?"

he snapped, "Maybe I should check if he's been captured or something."

"He's not captured!" insisted Beem, "You need to wait it out like the rest of us. Lyndal can take care of himself."

Pria sat across from Beem fighting back tears.

"What do you think happened to our parents? I'm scared they're in trouble."

"And what about Wort?" added Meekus.

The children became quiet at the mention of his name.

"Wort presents a problem, doesn't he?" Beem stated, "Mrs. Cromwell must be behind this mess we're in and Wort is stuck right in the middle. We need to find a way to rescue him."

"I don't think so!" interjected Spinny, "Wort isn't one of us anymore."

Beem was shocked by Spinny's confession. He wondered if anyone else felt the same way.

"I agree," said Trince, "In fact, we're probably not safe down here. Wort could be leading the Keeon to us, right now."

A huge debate erupted on whether Wort had the right to remain in The Following.

Without their knowledge, Lyndal quietly appeared on the far side of the room. For a few moments, he listened and watched the mayhem. One by one, they realized he was there. The noise subsided and they stood, embarrassed by their outburst.

"Well, this is disappointing, isn't it?" Lyndal began, "I leave for a couple of hours and you fall apart! If we're to be successful in rescuing your parents, we must be united."

"What did you mean when you said 'rescue our parents'?" asked Pria.

"First, let's clear up this argument you were having about Wort. I don't like what I was hearing. Didn't I teach you to listen to The Wisdom? You need to remember what's important – especially when things aren't going well."

Lyndal focused intently on each child.

"You must get this established in your minds – better yet – in your hearts. This is NOT a club . . . or a business. You can't just kick people out because you don't think they fit in, or get rid of them because they're not doing what you want."

Spinny and Trince hung their heads, embarrassed by what they had just said about Wort.

"Do you understand why *you're* sitting in this room, and the people you live with day-to-day aren't?"

He paused but no one said a word.

"I'll tell you why. You're here because you chose to be. It's that simple. When I revealed the truth – about The Ancients, your culture and who you are, you chose to believe it. Nobody forced you. It was a decision each of you made in your hearts."

"But what about the smoke . . . and the powers?" asked Spinny.

"The smoke only revealed what you already believed in your heart. It was the same for all of you . . . Wort included. Again, this is NOT a club. It's your identity and when we come together, we're a family. Do you understand?"

Spinny was quick to repent.

"We need to save Wort, don't we?"

"Yes," said Lyndal calmly, "But he's not the only one who needs our help. All of your parents, including the Cromwells, have been arrested and are locked inside Punishment House."

The children were stunned.

"Oh!" exclaimed Pria, "This is awful. What are we going to do?"

"We're going to rescue them!" announced Lyndal with a smile, "We're going to walk right in to Punishment House and set them free."

As soon as Lyndal said 'rescue' the boys got excited. Finally, they would be able to use their powers for something other than training. Pria, however, was very concerned about the safety of their parents. It was widely known that prisoners entering Punishment House were rarely seen again. And there had never been a successful escape from this Keeon stronghold.

Lyndal's plan was wonderfully simple and became the model for every difficult situation they would face throughout their lives. It went like this: First things first, then wait for instructions – which meant, listen to The Wisdom for the next step. So far, the only thing Lyndal knew for certain was he needed to get inside Punishment House. That was enough. Once inside, he would listen to The Wisdom for the next thing to do. By listening and obeying, he would be able to master every new situation as it arose. This real-time strategy would give him a huge advantage.

"What do *we* get to do?" asked Jinx who was eager to get going.

"Stay put," Lyndal stated, "None of you can afford to be seen right now. The Keeon know you're hiding somewhere and they're searching for you in earnest. You will have to be patient and wait until the sun goes down."

Lyndal turned his gaze to Spinny, knowing that he would have the biggest challenge following his instructions.

"I get it," Spinny acknowledged.

"Now, let's talk about what to do if you get captured," he continued.

Up to this point, the children had been running on adrenalin, but the sobering possibility of being apprehended by the Keeon immediately refocused them.

An unusual stirring swept through the circle.

"Did anyone else feel that?" asked Trince.

They all nodded in astonishment and waited for an explanation from Lyndal.

"This must be important," he responded, "The Wisdom is warning all of us. Now listen . . . if you are caught, don't resist. Understand? Simply go along with whatever they want, but tell them nothing. Be careful to conceal your powers. They think you're normal children, so act like it. Remember, the Keeon have a deep-rooted fear of anything associated with The Legends, especially The Ancients. Exposing your identity could be life-threatening."

The Wisdom shook them a second time.

"I'm scared," said Meekus.

He ran to Pria and crawled up into her lap. She wrapped her arm around him and looked to Lyndal with concern.

"What does this mean?"

"I'm not sure. I've never felt a shaking like this before."

Lyndal faltered for a moment.

"Perhaps it was a bad idea to involve you children in something so dangerous."

Beem leapt to his feet. A surge of boldness swept through him. He slapped the top of the bench with a loud smack.

"No!" he yelled, "This is not a time for us to back away. Not now! Lyndal, you prepared us yourself, and we're ready. The Wisdom is present in all of us – as you just witnessed. It's as powerful in Meekus as it is in you. You're the one who taught us that. We knew the dangers and risks when we joined you. Now our parents are in trouble and *we* are equipped to rescue them. If you don't believe we can save them from a few Keeon guards, then we have no business trying to liberate an entire world . . . right?"

Beem sat down . . . startled by his own speech.

Lyndal was moved by Beem's passion. The truth of his words reminded him of what he already knew.

"You're right. You *are* the ones. There is nobody better suited for this adventure than the seven of you."

"But what do we do if it becomes life-threatening?" asked Pria.

"If the situation becomes desperate and you're facing death, you must transport – as far away from Maidenton as possible."

"To where?" asked Jinx.

"The Wisdom will take you to a place of safety."

Beem thought about it for a moment.

"But wouldn't that mean . . ."

"Yes," interrupted Lyndal, "It would be a one-way trip. You'd be unable to return for a long time."

It had never occurred to them that this situation might prevent them from ever returning to Maidenton.

"Wherever you transport will be your new home," Lyndal explained, "Remember, you will have to act the age you become. If anyone should get suspicious about you, you won't be able to transport very far."

"So when *should* we come home?" asked Spinny.

"Listen carefully," cautioned Lyndal, "If the Keeon are about to kill you, it is imperative for you NOT to return until you are old enough to transport away again – they might still be waiting for you." Beem worked some quick calculations in his head.

"Our parents would be dead by then," he announced.

Lyndal was immediately inundated with an onslaught of questions and concerns.

"Quiet down!" shouted Beem above the commotion.

He slapped the bench to get their attention.

"This is not going to happen. The worst they might do is lock us up for a few months for practicing a forbidden religion, or banish us from Maidenton, but they would never kill a bunch of kids!"

"Beem is right," added Lyndal, "Things are not that desperate. We need to turn our attention back to the situation at hand – the rescue of your parents. Think about the celebration you will have when you are all happily reunited again!"

Lyndal's words broke the heaviness that had gripped them. A sense of hope and excitement returned. He watched serious expressions turn to smiles. Soon the room was filled with the sound of happy children.

All at once, Lyndal felt The Wisdom.

"It's time for me to leave – right now," he announced.

He gathered a few items from a shelf nearby and stuffed them into his satchel.

"I'll be back before you know it. Keep hope alive!"
Then he vanished from the room.

The mothers, along with Wort, were being held in a large communal cell inside Punishment House. It was constructed of huge vertical logs fastened together from the outside. The timbers had been stripped and polished, resulting in a smooth surface impossible to climb. The ceiling rose twenty feet above their heads, making the room very dark. The only light came from three small windows at the top of the walls. As the morning sun rose, thin bands of light trickled in, illuminating the filthy dirt floors.

The Keeon made no distinction between the Cromwells and the other families, even though Mrs. Cromwell was the one to report the incident. She was as guilty as everyone else was, as far as they were concerned. The only person receiving any special attention was Wort. Every hour, a guard would escort him to a special room that looked more like a palace than the inside of a prison.

The first time Wort stepped inside, The Wisdom warned him he was entering enemy territory. He was amazed at his willpower. The room was filled with all sorts of distractions, but he remained focused and demanded to be returned to the others. The guard didn't hesitate. He brought him back to his cell, but like clockwork, the guard would take him away again an hour later.

During Wort's second visit to the room, he decided to take a quick look around before he asked to leave. What harm could it do?

The walls were covered with lush, richly colored tapestries depicting exotic and faraway places. Soft animal furs overlaid the floors and at the far end of the room was an ornately carved table, gilded with what looked like real gold. Spread out on top was a feast of roasted fowl, sliced meats, rich sweet cakes and other delicacies. Off to the side was another beautiful table with cages containing small animals and birds. He heard The Wisdom warning him to stay on his guard, but Wort couldn't see anything wrong with admiring these nice things. He took one last look and asked to be taken back.

After trip number five, Wort began to look forward to these brief visits. He would poke his fingers into some of the cages and let the animals nuzzle and lick them. The tickling sensation made him giggle. He had never seen anything like the tapestries. The scene of a giant city beneath a crisscrossed sky was captivating.

By his eighth visit, the smell of the food was almost too much to bear. He had never stayed up so late, nor had he ever gone so long without his mother's delicious cooking. He found himself staring at the food, his mouth watering and stomach growling. He glanced over at the guard who was posted by the door. He knew the right thing to do was to leave.

"Go on then," the guard urged, "It ain't gonna kill ya."

Wort stared at him in torment, struggling to resist the temptation.

Finally, the guard approached the table, squatted down in front of him and asked, "Which one looks the best?"

Wort hesitated. Then he pointed to a tray of meat slices tucked inside delicate golden pancakes. The savory rolls were artfully arranged on a silver platter and topped with a drizzle of rich red gravy. The guard grabbed one and popped the whole thing in his mouth. Wort watched with great interest as a small stream of sauce dribbled down his chin.

"Tasty," the guard declared licking his lips.

He returned to his post.

"I want to go back, now!" Wort hollered.

"Suit yourself then."

He unlocked the door and led Wort down the cellblock. As they rounded the final corner of the corridor, three guards were just leaving the cell. One of them was carrying a stack of empty bowls caked with bits of putrid smelling gruel. Mealtime for the others had just ended. Wort stepped inside as the door slammed behind him. He squatted in the dirt next to his mother. No one spoke a word to them. He closed his eyes and tried to imagine something good and noble, but all he could envision was the amazing room down the hall, filled with delicious food.

I should have eaten. They fed everyone else. Who cares if it's a different type of food? It's just food.

Wort's mind soon became fixated on eating, and his stomach started rumbling again.

"Didn't they feed you?" his mother whispered.

"The food was still on the table. But I didn't think it was right to eat it."

"But you have to eat something. You haven't had a meal since yesterday. When you go there again, you should have some."

A war was now raging in Wort's mind. The voice of The Wisdom cautioned him, but the voice of his stomach was drowning it out.

I'm going to eat, as soon as I go back.

He leaned against the cold, hard wall and fixated on the cell door.

He should be here by now. It's been far too long. What's happening out there?

He listened desperately for the sound of footsteps in the corridor, but nothing! The longer he waited the more agitated he became.

"Try to get some sleep son," urged his mother.

Wort closed his eyes but his mind and stomach were in knots.

Where's that stupid guard?

After what seemed like ages, he heard the familiar creak of the lock. Wort jumped to his feet and ran to the door. As soon as it opened, he hurried into the corridor. He looked up at the guard, smiling from ear to ear.

A sense of euphoria washed over Wort as they entered the room. He wasted no time devouring a pastry filled with custard and berries. It was marvelous! Next, he tackled a leg of roasted foul smothered in a glistening yellow glaze. He moved from dish to dish sampling the exotic fare. Never in his life had he tasted such wondrous flavors. He ended the feast with a handful of sugar drops that melted away on his tongue.

When he was done gorging himself, he collapsed into a pile of pillows on the floor. He smiled at the guard and belched.

"That was great!"

The guard said nothing, but Wort didn't care. His belly was full and the pillows were very comfortable.

"Stalwart . . ."

The Wisdom was stirring inside him. Wort tried his best to pay attention, but his eyelids were heavy.

"Stalwart . . . stay alert!"

The voice seemed distant and muddled as Wort was overcome with exhaustion. His mind eventually drifted off to the place where conscience thoughts fade away and dreams come to life.

He found himself in the middle of a great adventure. All of his friends were with him and Lyndal was there too. He could see everyone, even himself, from a great distance. They were climbing a huge mountain dotted with gnarled trees. There were sheer drop-offs on all sides and a massive waterfall cascading for miles below them. Suddenly, Wort realized he was clinging to the face of the cliff. Before him was a rock wall with small fissures and cold ledges barely large enough to hold onto. He realized he was stuck, unable to climb up or down. The other children were above him, ascending higher and higher. Below him was an immense void, so vast he couldn't see the bottom. He could hear Beem calling for him to catch up, but he was paralyzed with fear. He started to cry.

Then, he noticed a man standing next to him. He didn't recognize him and wondered how he kept from falling. He was emanating light. It was so radiant it was difficult to see his face. The man gently placed his hand on Wort's shoulder.

"Why are you crying?"

"I can't climb any higher and my friends are leaving me behind."

The man reached down and took Wort by the hand.

"Follow me," he said.

Wort was no longer afraid and let go of the cliff.

Instantly, he was walking with the radiant man through a forest. The path they were on was lined with beautiful flowers. Enormous trees formed a canopy of green overhead. As they walked, the man explained many things to Wort – about courage, patience and hope.

They came to a place where the path forked. To his right he could see his friends running toward the sun, calling for him to join them. He was excited to see them again and tried to catch up – but after a few steps, he was distracted by a horrible sound coming from the other direction. He turned to see what was making the noise. This path was very different. It was a jumble of twisted trees and thorny underbrush. In the distance, he could barely make out the shape of something moving. He focused in and discovered it was his beloved dog caught in the jaws of a large metal trap. His pitiful howls tugged at Wort's heart. He looked down the beautiful path again and saw his friends getting farther and farther away. He knew if he didn't follow right away he would never be able to catch up. Then he heard the voice of the man.

"You will have to make a choice."

He touched Wort's shoulder again. The next thing he knew, he was high above the forest looking down. He saw himself standing at the fork trying to decide which way to go. They rose even higher until he could see the paths carved into the landscape below.

The man pointed down and said, "All will be well, my stalwart one. When you emerge, you will no longer be the same. Look! The paths reunite in the end."

They flew higher and higher until the landscape disappeared into the mist. He could still feel the man's hand on his shoulder and a sense of peace enveloped him. Then the hand began to shake him – and shake him . . .

Wort's eyes flew open. The Keeon guard was standing over him shaking him by the shoulder. It startled him so much he crawled backward up the pillows and bumped his head on the wall.

"What?!" he yelled in confusion.

Satisfied he was awake, the guard returned to his position next to the door. For a moment, Wort was stuck between the dream world and reality. The images, still fresh in his mind, seemed so lifelike. He looked out the window to get his bearings. The sun was almost overhead. He had been sleeping for hours. He stretched, rubbed his eyes and began to think about food again.

As soon as the thought of breakfast entered his mind, he noticed the most delectable aromas in the air. They were coming from a freshly prepared selection of food that had been carefully laid out for him just minutes before. The table was arrayed with sweet and savory porridges, grilled vegetables with fruit chutney, and at the far end, a platter piled high with spiced sweet cakes. Steam was still rising from the serving bowls. Wort's stomach began rumbling even though it had been filled to the brim only a few hours earlier. He bounded over to the table and filled his plate to overflowing.

"Do you like the food?" said a voice behind him.

"Yes, very much, thank you. Are you going to have some?"

He heard footsteps approaching behind him and turned to greet the guard. Instead, a strange man was standing there.

"I don't think so," the man said, "I ate on my way to Maidenton this morning. May I introduce myself? My name is Scullins . . . Martin Scullins."

"Hello, Mr. Scullins," Wort said through a mouthful of sweet cake. Crumbs spewed out, speckling the front of the man's black tunic.

Scullins was a tall, bony man with a pinched face and course black hair. His dark grey eyes were deep set, giving him the look of someone near death. As he addressed Wort, his thin lips twisted into a contorted smile.

"And what is your name, son?"

"Stalwart, but all my friends call me Wort."

"Do you miss your friends?"

"I guess so," Wort replied as he nibbled on a handful of purple berries.

"Would you like me to take you back to the cell to be with your friends?"

"Oh . . . they aren't . . ."

Wort stopped mid-sentence. The Wisdom erupted in his mind with a strong caution.

He looked at Scullins' face again but this time he could discern his sinister heart lurking behind the polite mask. His stomach began to turn as he realized how close he had come to confiding in this man. Wort set down his food. He had lost his appetite.

"You were saying?" Scullins pried.

Wort looked blankly at Scullins and said nothing. Instead, he fixed his thoughts on what Lyndal had taught them. Soon a flood of knowledge came pouring from his memory logs, giving him the focus and confidence he needed to resist Scullins' devious tactics.

"I said, 'Wouldn't you like to be with your friends?' and then you said ' They aren't,' " Scullins reiterated. "They aren't what?"

A surge of strength and self-control filled Wort's mind. The Wisdom instructed him to remain silent.

"How are we supposed to get to know one another if you don't talk to me?" Scullins asked in a bewitching tone, "I just want to know a little bit about you, like where you live and what sort of things you like to do. That's all."

"I live in Maidenton and I like to play with my building blocks and go on adventures. Where do *you* live?"

Scullins was startled by Wort's pointed response.

He composed himself and forced a smile that looked more like a smirk.

"I live in a village called Sandy Point on the edge of the great sea of sand. It's a village very much like Maidenton."

"And what do *you* like to do?" Wort continued.

"I am one of only four Kinsmen representatives to the grand council," he boasted.

He strutted pompously across the room and pointed to part of one of the paintings on the wall.

"I have a house not far from this place . . ."

"Well . . . you don't look like a Kinsman to me," Wort said bluntly, "You look more like a skinny Keeon."

"You are a cute boy, aren't you?" Scullins retorted sarcastically.

He glanced over to the guard in frustration.

"Bring the boy's mother to me – NOW!" he ordered.

The guard obeyed, leaving the two of them alone. Flustered, Scullins gathered himself and tried a new approach to his line of questioning.

"So tell me about the adventures you go on, Wort. Are they real or make-believe?"

"I want to go back with the others now."

Wort started walking to the door.

"Not so fast," Scullins crooned stepping in front of Wort. "I just sent the guard to get your mother. You don't want to leave so soon. This is a much nicer room than that old nasty cell."

"I don't know about that. This is still a cell isn't it?"

"I wonder what's keeping them," Scullins muttered under his breath.

"If this *isn't* a cell, am I free to go home?"

"Wouldn't you rather stay here with your mommy than go home to an empty house?"

"I can manage."

Wort maneuvered closer to the door.

"So can I go?"

Scullins blocked his path. His pasty white cheeks flushed with frustration. He could no longer mask his rising irritation. *"Impudent little brat,"* he murmured.

"You're quite the . . . Oh . . . finally – here they are."

Està Cromwell was escorted into the room. Scullins snatched the guard's keys from his hand and locked the door from the inside. He dangled them in front of Wort with a conniving grin.

Esta paid no attention to Wort or Scullins and skipped over to the table of food, clapping her hands with glee.

"Go right ahead," urged Scullins with a wave of his arm, "Have as much as you want."

"Mother, wait!" interrupted Wort, trying to get her attention.

She glanced at her son and smiled, but wasted no time circling the table, eagerly examining each dish.

"This man would like to talk to us," Wort reiterated,

hoping to distract her, "Don't you think it would be rude to eat and talk at the same time?"

She was so overcome by the tantalizing sights and smells that she was deaf to her son's pleas.

"No, no. Don't be silly," chuckled Scullins in a sickly sweet tone, "Feel free to eat while we talk. It doesn't bother me in the slightest."

Scullins slipped between Wort and his mother, pushing him aside in the process. Esta Cromwell dove into the platter of spiced sweet cakes, shoving them by the handful into her mouth.

"Mmmm," she mumbled, "Ths ss rlly gd."

"Mom!" Wort growled as he stomped his foot, "Mr. Scullins is going to let us GO HOME!"

She stopped chewing for a moment and looked at him in unbelief.

"No, no, no, no, no," Scullins corrected, trying to draw Mrs. Cromwell's attention away from Wort, "That's not quite right. I just want to ask you some questions. I have no idea when you will be able to go back to your home."

Wort stepped in front of Scullins.

"Then take us back to the cell!" he demanded.

"Stalwart!" his mother scolded, "What a rude thing to say. This gentleman is our host. It would be dishonoring to leave so soon."

She turned back to the table, dipped her fingers into a bowl of sweet porridge and then sucked them clean.

"Tell me Mrs. Cromwell," Scullins said, "How long have you been meeting with those other women?"

The Wisdom was stirring inside of Wort.

"You don't have to answer if you don't want to."

"Don't be silly, Stalwart. I have nothing to hide from this nice man."

She looked up at Scullins and smiled, almost flirting.

"How could you possibly know if he's nice?!" Wort yelled, "You don't know anything about him. All you care about is this stupid food."

Wort grabbed the end of the table and lifted it, causing the glorious feast to come crashing to the floor.

"Nooo!" cried Esta, desperately trying to rescue a dish of custard. Bowls and platters shattered, splattering their contents all over the tapestries, furs and Mr. Scullins.

"Stalwart – Alec – Cromwell!" she screamed, "What has gotten into you!"

She looked sheepishly at Scullins who was wiping bits of food from his clothing.

"I'm so sorry, sir. I swear he's not like this at home. He's really a nice boy."

She reached down, grabbed Wort's arm and dragged him to the far side of the room, out of earshot from Scullins.

"Now you listen to me, young man," she whispered through clenched teeth, "The only way we're going to get out of this mess is if we tell this Scullins fellow what he wants to hear. So whatever it is you're trying to do – stop it, this instant!"

"But Mom . . ."

She yanked him up until his feet left the floor and smacked his backside with a hard wallop.

"Do you understand me?"

"Yes ma'am."

Wort's eyes welled up with tears while he rubbed the welt forming on his bottom.

"Now go back and apologize!"

She marched him across the room.

"What do you have to say?" she snapped.

"I'm sorry."

"We would be happy to answer your questions," she conceded, "with or without the food."

Scullins motioned to the guard.

"Take the boy back to *his* cell. I'll be there shortly. I have what I'm looking for – right here."

Scullins directed his attention to Mrs. Cromwell with an entrancing smile. Wort shot a final desperate glance at his mother, but she turned away, giving Scullins her full attention.

Wort felt the guard's rough hand clamping the back of his neck as he was led into the corridor. The door slammed behind them, but he could still hear Scullin's muffled voice.

"Now, you seem like an intelligent woman . . ."

Wort struggled to break free, but the guard's grip

tightened. He pulled him down the passageway, past the cell he had been in previously.

"Excuse me, sir. I think you missed the door."

The guard laughed and continued forward until they reached an isolated hallway.

"In ya go, boy," the guard said as he tossed him into an empty chamber.

Wort stumbled forward, landing on his hands and knees. He was enveloped in darkness as the lock slid into place. Then . . . silence. He was utterly alone. His knees were bleeding and burning with pain. He began to sob.

Once Esta Cromwell was removed from the cell, the other women were able to speak freely.

"What do you think they're doing?" Illie asked as she pressed her ear against the cell door.

"Probably bribing her with food like they did with the boy," declared Liana.

"Or maybe they set them free," added Lateen, "Esta probably told them everything."

"I doubt it," said Alma.

She stood and brushed the dirt from her clothes.

"They won't let any of us go. It's too risky for them to allow us back into society. The best we can hope for is to be banished to a correctional colony across The Sands. I just hope the children are all right. I can't bear the thought of never seeing them again."

Tears began to flow. They did their best to comfort one another. In their hearts, they knew Alma was right.

"I wonder what will become of our husbands?" asked Illie.

No one had wanted to bring up the subject because it was well known that the Keeon punished men more severely than women. It wasn't uncommon for men to be executed for capital crimes like conspiracy – which was what they had been charged with.

Their conversation was interrupted by the turning of the lock. They expected to see Wort or Esta. Instead, a guard, in an ill-fitting uniform, stepped inside.

"Which one of you is Alma Limm?" he asked gruffly.

The women offered no answer but some of them unconsciously looked in her direction. Alma mustered her courage and stepped forward on her own.

"I'm Alma Limm," she said in a trembling voice.

She took one last look at her dearest friends as the guard jerked her into the corridor. Alma's terror gave way to tears but the guard was unmoved and completely focused on his task. She watched in horror as he poked the end of a small stick into one of the torches secured to the wall. Her stomach turned at the thought of being tortured and burned. She braced herself, expecting the worst, but was surprised as he lowered the stick and held it behind his back.

"Don't be afraid, Alma," Lyndal whispered, "I'm here to help you escape."

Peace flooded her emotions as she recognized the voice. Relief displaced dread. All at once, the adrenalin drained from her, leaving her weak and wobbly. She reached to steady herself against the wall.

"You're The Ancient we met at the Beeman's yesterday!"

Lyndal pulled the smoldering twig from behind his back and smiled as he handed it to her.

"Breathe in the smoke as we walk," he whispered, "and don't say a word."

He led her down a maze of corridors until he found an empty cell. He looked both ways, and pulled her inside, out of sight.

"Give me the stick."

She handed it to him, and he held it before her eyes, revealing the familiar sparkle and fire of The Wisdom's presence.

"Excellent," declared Lyndal, "We don't have much time. I'm going to transfer some information to you. If we get caught, act like you're my prisoner."

She nodded and smiled, eager to begin. Lyndal placed his hands on her temples. Their heads tilted back as the knowledge and understanding of the powers was imparted to her. When the transfer was complete, Lyndal took her hand and led her back to the cell.

Lyndal:	*Can you hear me?*
Alma:	*Yes – this is amazing*
Lyndal:	*Where are the Cromwells being held?*
Alma:	*They've been taken away and we don't know where they are.*
Lyndal:	*What about the men?*
Alma:	*We haven't seen them since we arrived. Please tell me the children are safe.*
Lyndal:	*They're fine. You will see them tonight. We are planning an escape. The details of the rescue are already logged in your memory.*
Alma:	*You're right. That's amazing.*
Lyndal:	*Pay close attention – once you are free of Punishment House you must leave Maidenton – all of you. Do you understand?*
Alma:	*We can never return, can we?*
Lyndal:	*I'm afraid not. You will need to start a new life somewhere else. Each family must relocate to a different village, far from Maidenton. They will always be looking for you here.*

They stopped in front of the women's cell.

Lyndal: *Don't worry; I'm confident in our escape plan. I have a secret weapon.*

He smiled and jangled the keys in front of her. He closed the door and set out to find the men.

"Ho there!"

Lyndal turned around to see a guard approaching.

"Are you going on break?" he asked.

"No," Lyndal replied, "I'm trying to locate a prisoner – a man who was brought here last night. He's with a group."

"Oh them," the guard said matter-of-factly, "More than likely they were transferred to the labor camp and executed first thing this morning."

Lyndal was shocked by his words. He struggled to regain his composure. The guard noticed his expression and laughed.

"You're new here, aren't you?"

"Y-Yes," Lyndal replied, "I just arrived today."

"You must have come with the ambassador from the domes."

Lyndal felt a warning from The Wisdom. This information might affect their rescue plans. He continued to play along.

"Yes. I just arrived. It's good to be away from The Sands."

“Ugh,” the guard said dramatically, “You won’t catch me crossing them again. Now that I’m on this side of the sand, I don’t ever want to go back.”

“I know what you mean,” Lyndal agreed, “Well, I must be going, good talking to you.”

Lyndal walked down the corridor, turned a corner and transported away.

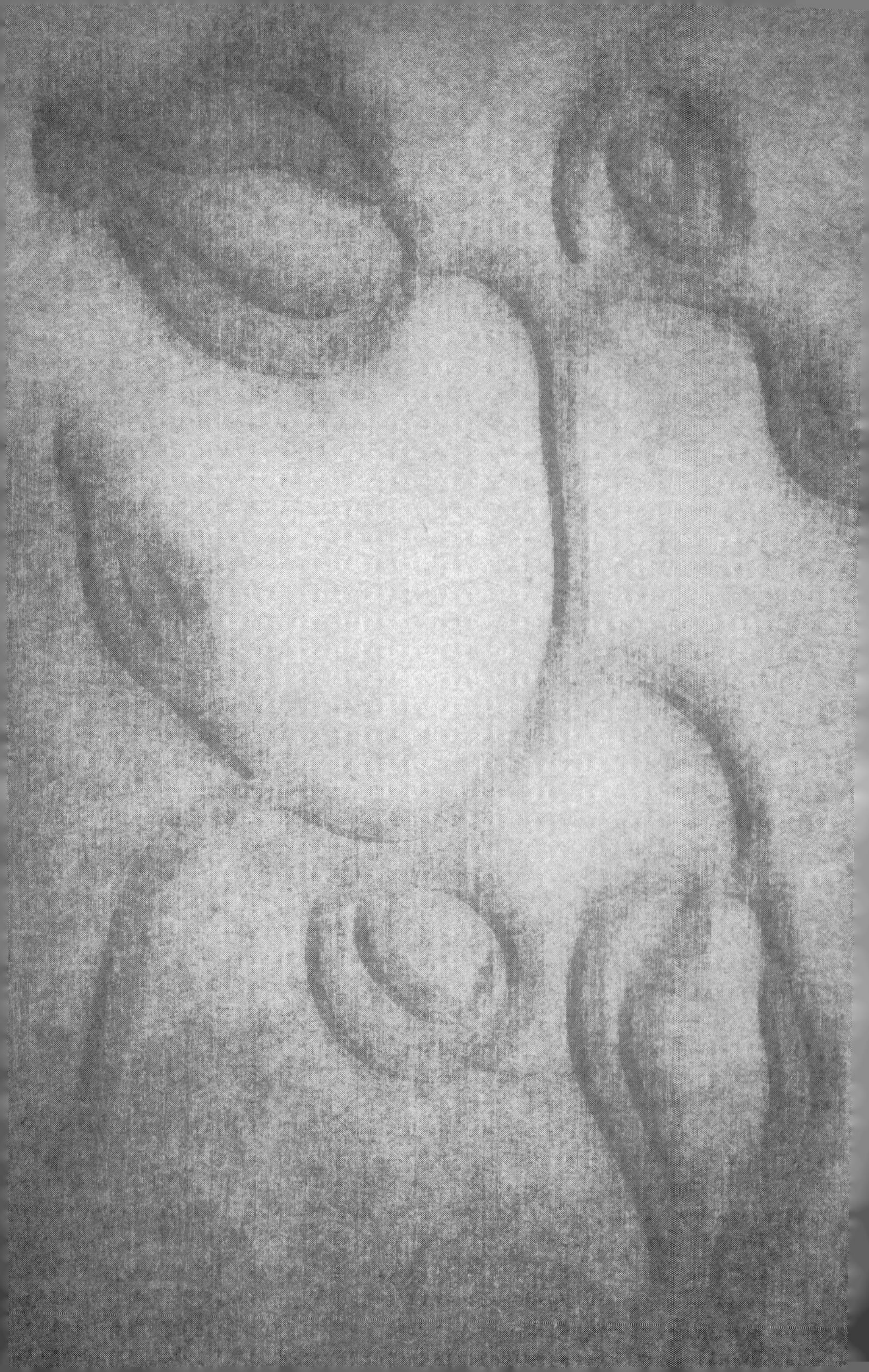

9

The Waiting Game

"I'm sick of this stupid hole!" yelled Spinny as he kicked the bottom rung of the ladder, "I'll go crazy if I don't get out of here soon."

"Calm down!" Beem scolded. "Having a fit won't accomplish anything."

"Kinsmen weren't designed to live underground," Spinny argued, "We need to be out in the fresh air with the birds and the trees and the sun. This place is suffocating me!"

Spinny wasn't the only one feeling claustrophobic. Waiting for Lyndal to bring news about their parents had them all on edge. They tried their best not to make a fuss, but it was too much for Spinny.

"It will all be over soon," Trince reassured him,

"Anyway, where's your sense of adventure?"

"What do you know about it?!" he snapped.

"A lot more than you!" she yelled.

"Quiet you two!" ordered Beem, stepping between them, "Better yet . . . why don't you find Jinx and do a little exploring? See if you can find another tunnel connecting to the main complex."

Beem's suggestion immediately caught their attention. Spinny and Trince couldn't resist the opportunity for an excursion. There was still so much to discover in the underground city. Their argument now forgotten, they began scurrying around the room, gathering supplies.

Pria glanced at Beem with concern.

"Didn't Lyndal tell us to stay put?"

"Yes . . . but they won't be going outside – and they can't get very far."

Pria let out a sigh.

Beem watched as Spinny filled his water skin.

"Whatever you do, don't get lost . . . and be back within the hour."

Spinny secured the stopper and hung the skin across his shoulder. Trince smiled enthusiastically.

"Shall we be about it then?"

He nodded in agreement and they raced down the hall.

"Hurry up Jinx!" yelled Spinny as they disappeared from sight.

"You know they'll get in trouble," stated Pria, "They always do."

"They'll be fine," Beem countered. "They just need to get rid of some energy."

It was too late to change his mind so Pria headed to the kitchen to begin dinner preparations. Beem began to have second thoughts but pushed them aside, hoping to prove Pria wrong this time. At least he didn't have to hear Spinny's complaining any longer.

Trince sprinted down the main corridor leading away from the Stone Room. She was two full strides ahead of Spinny. When she reached the end of the hall, she slapped her hand to the wall and slid down its smooth surface to the floor.

"I win!" she panted.

"That's not fair," Spinny gasped, "You didn't give me a chance."

"That's no excuse. You should always be ready. Don't you remember what Lyndal taught us?"

Jinx had no interest in racing. Instead, he systematically poked his head into each of the rooms along the way to see what was inside. He eventually caught up and pulled them to their feet. They walked together for a short distance and discovered the hall branched in two directions.

"Which way do we go?" asked Jinx.

"It doesn't matter," answered Trince, "We haven't explored either one."

"Stay to the right!" said Spinny, "If we always stay to the right we'll never get lost."

The unfamiliar hallway was long, straight and featureless. It seemed to go on forever. The only thing that kept them from turning back, was knowing it took them farther inside Broadside Hill.

The passageway finally ended at the mouth of a vertical shaft. Below them, it was jammed with rocks and dirt. Above them, it rose for more than fifty feet. Off to one side was a door that concealed a flight of stairs. In the other direction, another corridor headed off into the distance.

"Which way now?" asked Jinx.

Before Trince could respond, Spinny pushed past them and began running up the stairs.

"Wait a minute!" ordered Trince, "We don't want to get separated."

"You can't lose me, Silly" taunted Spinny, "Just follow my footprints."

He kicked a cloud of dust in Trince's direction and continued climbing.

"Come on," he yelled, "Let's see how high this goes."

The sound of his feet on the metal stairs echoed off the walls.

"He never listens," Trince complained. "He's such a boy!"

"And what am I?" asked Jinx.

"Oh – you know what I mean," she said.

"Wait for me!" she shouted.

Trince dashed up the steps, taking two at a time, determined to catch up. Jinx plodded along behind them.

"Why does everything have to be a competition?" he muttered.

The children reached a place where they could go no higher. The stairwell above them was clogged with debris from a cave-in. The decision was made to go back and explore the next level down.

They shoved open the heavy door, and stepped into an enormous chamber. They stood in awe for a moment trying to take it all in. The ceiling towered above them and was adorned with colorful murals depicting people and places they had heard about in The Legends. Farther down, it was connected to similar rooms, all supported by a series of archways and ornately carved columns. The children were awestruck by the magnificence of the structure. Even the thick layer of dust could not diminish its beauty.

They went from chamber to chamber, speaking only in hushed tones as if they were on sacred ground. Everywhere they turned a new discovery delighted their senses. In the far corner of a large open area, they discovered scores of chairs and tables, stacked high against the walls.

"I wonder what this place was used for?" whispered Spinny.

"It looks like a community gathering place," said Trince.

"Like the square in Maidenton," added Jinx, "Only inside."

"And look at these old banners on the walls," said Spinny.

The wall hangings were as tall as the room. They craned their necks to examine the unusual symbols and shapes covering their surfaces. Jinx ran his finger along the soft fabric, causing a shower of dust to spill to the floor.

"Take a look at these paintings," Trince announced, "Everyone has glowing eyes – they must be Ancients."

"Can you imagine how much trouble we would be in if we took one of these back to the village?" laughed Jinx.

"Hey! What are these?" asked Spinny.

He had discovered an extraordinary cabinet. Covering its doors were detailed paintings in vivid colors. The scenes depicted people moving in ways the children had never seen before. Some were bent in strange contortions while others were leaping in the air. On the inside were peculiar objects displayed on shelves and hanging from hooks. There were wooden bowls with long handles, and clear crystal tubes with holes running along their length.

"This one looks like the thing on the door," said Jinx, pointing to one of the painted images, "See – the old man is holding it in his mouth."

Jinx placed the end of the glass tube to his lips and sucked in. Nothing happened. Then he blew out hard, releasing a piercing, high-pitched squeal.

"Stop!" exclaimed Spinny, "That's horrible. Give me that. I'm going to break it."

"No you don't!" yelled Trince, snatching it from Jinx's hand. She slid it safely inside her cloak.

"I want it – I think it's pretty."

Spinny rolled his eyes.

"You're such a girl!" he mocked.

"Hey! Come over here!" shouted Jinx, "I think I see daylight!"

"At last!" yelled Spinny.

At the far end of the gallery, a large section of wall had caved in. Jinx was perched on the rubble examining the opening near the ceiling. Spinny deactivated his night-vision, clearly revealing a shaft of sunlight filtering in through the fissure. He scrambled up the blocks of loose stone, pushed aside a mass of roots and peered through the breach. He grabbed the sides of the opening and pulled up until his head poked into some thick underbrush on the outside.

"We're on the back side of Broadside," he yelled down to the others, "I can see the woods above where Lyndal lives."

Trince and Jinx climbed up to where Spinny was struggling to keep his footing.

Without warning, Spinny yelled with all his might, "Yeeeeaaaaahhhh!"

Jinx grabbed his brother by the ankles, and jerked him down from the opening, causing a small landslide. The three of them tumbled down the debris to the floor.

Jinx backhanded his brother across his shoulder.

"What was that?" he demanded, "What were you thinking?"

Realizing his mistake, Spinny tried to make up an excuse.

"It-it was the sunshine. I had to yell. I couldn't help it."

"That's the stupidest thing I've ever heard," scolded Trince, "Somebody could have heard you."

"Are you kidding," he said with a smug little laugh, "Nobody comes to the back of Broadside. You're just paranoid."

They glared angrily at him and said nothing for a long time.

Jinx finally took Trince's hand, helping her to her feet.

"We'd better get going. It's been more than an hour since we left. We'll be in trouble when we get back."

They hung their heads and walked silently toward the stairwell.

"Mark this spot!" the Keeon guard said to his comrade, "There's something strange going on here. I've never heard an animal make a sound like that. We need to report this."

His partner gathered some sticks and shoved them into the ground. He tied a piece of bright red fabric to the top, constructing a small flag.

"That'll do," he said.

"I hope you're not too tired," the first guard continued, "I have a feeling we'll be climbing back up here first thing in the morning."

The two men looked down at Maidenton. The village looked small from the grassy ridge of Broadside's summit. The sun was already setting, making the hill difficult to navigate. They would have to hurry to get back before the black.

Pria finished grilling vegetable slices and was layering them on top of the crust she had made. The only thing left to do was to pour on the sauce. She couldn't delay the meal any longer. Dinner would have to be served.

"The food will get cold if we wait for them!" she complained, "Where are they?"

She turned to Beem.

"I told you something would happen."

Beem was confident their friends were all right. He figured they had been distracted by some new discovery. He concentrated on The Wisdom for a moment but didn't sense anything unusual.

"Let's eat," he replied, "I'm sure they'll be back soon."

Beem and Meekus joined Pria at the table where she was placing bowls of food. Beem pulled a hunk of bread from the freshly baked loaf, dipped it in the sauce and took a bite.

"Wow, Pria! This is fantastic," he announced.

Pria smiled. "Thanks for trying to get my mind off worrying."

The three of them dove into the sumptuous meal. The savory flavors and delicate textures took their minds off the tension of the day. Their feasting, however, was interrupted by the sound of footsteps coming from the next room.

"That must be them," said Beem.

"We're in here . . . and you're late for dinner!" he hollered.

Pria looked up expecting to see her friends. Instead, the color drained from her face. She gripped the edge of the table and let out a shriek.

"Aaahhhhhhhhh!"

A Keeon guard had stepped through the doorway. She shot up from her chair, backing away like a trapped animal. The table tipped forward, spilling a hot bowl of food into Beem's lap. He jumped to his feet, dancing in pain and turned to face the intruder. Meekus assumed the defensive stance he learned from Lyndal and prepared to protect himself.

"I am rather hungry," the guard said, laughing.

"Lyndal!!" Pria shouted.

She stomped her foot and hurled the serving spoon at him.

Lyndal ducked to avoid the flying utensil and laughed even harder.

"Well, it *was* a good meal," Beem growled as he wiped vegetable bits from his clothing.

Lyndal removed the Keeon cloak and sat at the bench.

"Where's everyone else?"

"We're right here!" exclaimed Spinny, bursting into the room. Trince and Jinx followed close behind, trying to catch their breath.

"What's all the excitement?" panted Trince, "We heard Pria scream."

Pria's face was flushed and she was still shaking in the aftermath of Lyndal's joke.

"This crazy man scared me half to death!" she exclaimed, slapping his arm.

"He was wearing that stupid cloak . . . and I thought . . . well . . . Oh, never mind."

Everyone started laughing. Moments later, Pria began to giggle. It felt good to be silly.

Pria's cooking was delicious and they were all ravenous. They devoured the food as if they hadn't eaten in days. By the time they finished, every plate had been licked clean and there wasn't a morsel left on the serving platters. Lyndal wiped his mouth on his sleeve, leaned back in his chair, and let out a sigh of satisfaction.

"That was delightful!"

The others chimed in with their accolades, except for Meekus, who let out a small burp.

"It's time to get down to business," Lyndal announced, "The rescue must happen tonight, during the black."

A mix of excitement and nervousness swept through the group. Spinny was thrilled that he would finally be allowed to sneak around Maidenton using his night-vision. Beem thought of the months of preparation that had led to this moment. Pria squeezed Meekus who was sitting on her lap. She looked forward to being reunited with her parents.

"We're going to move in fast and leave even faster," he explained, "By the time the Keeon discover your parents are missing, you will be halfway to the Dolman Mountains."

Lyndal described the layout of Punishment House: where the guards were posted, where the exits were and most importantly, where their mothers were being held.

"But you didn't say where they put our fathers," said Beem.

Lyndal paused, struggling with how to respond.

"Don't you know where they are?" asked Pria.

"I'm not sure," Lyndal confessed, "I wasn't able to find them."

"But they're safe . . . right?" she pleaded.

"I trust they are still inside Punishment House. We will carry out the plan with that assumption. Once we are on the inside, listen to The Wisdom. Remember – 'First things first, then wait for instructions,' Once your parents are safely out of Punishment House, you must leave the village *immediately*. No one is to return to their home for any reason – understand – not even for your pets or your favorite book. It's just too dangerous. You already know the Keeon are fearful of high places, so head to the mountains – the steeper the better – and stay away from The Sands. Chances are they won't venture beyond the backside of Broadside Hill. Once your parents are safely hidden away, meet me back here for final instructions. Make sure you arrive before sunrise. Tomorrow night, we will say our final goodbyes, and each of you will begin a new life far away from Maidenton."

The mood became solemn as they realized they would no longer be together. They had all grown up in Maidenton and the bond between them was more like family than friends. A deep sadness filled the children and no one could bring themselves to talk about the separation.

"One last thing," added Lyndal, "Pria and Meekus will stay here during the rescue. Meekus is too young for this sort of thing."

"That's not fair. I want to go," begged Pria, "Besides, who is going to guide my parents in the dark?"

"I gave your mother all of the powers," Lyndal replied, "She is now fully-equipped to get safely out of Maidenton. You will rendezvous above the old stone quarry up Dry Creek canyon. Jinx – you will go with Meekus' parents."

The only thing left to do was to pack and prepare for the rescue. As Trince was filling her satchel, the glass tube she had taken fell out of her cloak. It hit the floor with a loud clatter. Lyndal bent down and picked it up.

"I haven't seen one of these in hundreds of years," he said with a smile. Where did you get this?"

Trince hesitated. She felt awkward about leaving the Stone Room while he was gone. Sensing her apprehension, Beem came to her rescue.

"I told them they could go explore," he said nervously, "It was only for a little while . . . and nothing happened."

"It's all right, Beem," Lyndal reassured him.

He turned to Trince and urged her to continue.

"So, while we were exploring today, Spinny found a beautiful cabinet, and this was inside."

"Do you know what it is?"

Trince shook her head. The others gathered around, intrigued by the crystal tube in his hand.

"Listen . . ."

Lyndal pressed it to his lips.

Trince and the twins braced themselves, clapping their hands over their ears awaiting the shrill, painful sound they had heard in the gallery. Instead, a sweet, mournful melody flowed out of the little pipe. They sat, entranced as the music wrapped around them like a soft, peaceful blanket. Meekus crawled onto Lyndal's lap and studied it, trying to discover where the sound came from. Lyndal stopped.

"You've never heard music before, have you?"

"Is that a 'music'?" asked Meekus, pointing to the pipe.

"No," Lyndal said with a chuckle, "This is a flute. The sound it makes is called music. Would you like to hear some more?"

"Yes, very much, thank you," exclaimed Pria, smiling from ear to ear.

They all agreed. Lyndal began to play again. The sounds moved them greatly, filling them with indescribable joy.

Trince leaned against a wall, eyes closed, caught up in the beauty of the song. The gentle pulses of the tune stirred her deeply and she began to sway back and forth to the rhythm. A marvelous sensation of delight and pleasure filled her. Without thinking, her feet, then her arms, began to move. All at once, she was gliding gracefully about the room, her steps moving in perfect unison with the melody coming from the flute.

The children watched and listened for a long time, amazed at what was happening to them. When Lyndal played the final notes of the song, Trince stopped her movements and opened her eyes. Her face was radiant. For a minute, she was unaware of anything around her. Then she noticed the bewildered expressions of her friends. Self-consciousness gripped her and she immediately felt the urge to hide.

Meekus looked up at Lyndal.

"Did the flute make her do that?"

"No. Well . . . maybe. What do *you* think, Trince?"

Everyone was still staring at her. She blushed with embarrassment, covered her face with her hands and ran out of the room.

"Why did she move like that?" Beem asked.

"Did you enjoy it?" responded Lyndal.

"Yes. I've never seen anything like it before."

"It's called a dance. It's a natural response to music. The sounds on the pipe can move you on the inside. Some people are moved so strongly that it moves them on the outside too."

"I liked it," Pria sighed. "It was lovely to watch."

Lyndal handed her the flute and went after Trince.

He found her sitting on a pile of pillows, crying.

"You dance beautifully," he said softly, "There's nothing to be ashamed of."

"I don't know why I did that," she sniffed, "I couldn't help it."

She thought for a moment.

"That's not true. I could have stopped, but I didn't want to. Once I started, it was so wonderful. Then I had to move. But now I feel stupid."

Meekus had followed Lyndal and was standing behind him.

"Can you teach me how to do it, Trincie?" he asked.

"We all thought it was great," added Beem as he poked his head in the room.

Trince smiled and wiped away her tears.

"You're all very nice."

Meekus gave her a big hug.

"It's almost time for us to leave," reminded Lyndal, "Finish packing and we'll meet in the kitchen."

"Tell me again what you heard on your patrol of Broadside Hill," demanded Scullins, as he continued his interrogation of the guards.

"At first, we heard a screeching sound, but it

wasn't like any animal I've ever heard," the first guard explained.

"And then we heard a woman's voice . . . yelling," said the other.

Scullins thought for a moment and then stood up from his chair.

"Could it have been the voice of a child?"

"I suppose so."

The guard scratched his head.

"Sure – it could have been a child. But we never saw any kids. The sound came from nowhere."

Scullins began pacing the room, deep in thought. After a couple of laps he stopped, midstride.

"Or out of the ground!" he exclaimed as the revelation exploded in his mind, "They're underground you idiots! Didn't you find any holes?"

"We weren't looking for holes. We were looking for children – like you ordered."

"We marked the spot though," said the other guard, "We can take you there first thing in the morning."

"You will take me there immediately!" Scullins ordered, "Morning will be too late! Gather a dozen guards. NOW! Meet me out front in ten minutes . . . and bring shovels. One more thing . . . Fetch me that little Kinsman brat! He may be of some use after all."

The guards left the room in haste, leaving Scullins alone with Mrs. Cromwell.

"It seems your stories may be true after all," he

crooned, "They've been playing in holes just like you said."

"No, no." she clarified, "Not holes. They called it a stone room – with smooth rock walls – and furniture and all sorts of peculiar things."

Esta's disclosure proved that the children were more deeply involved than he first thought. He stepped out of the room and motioned to the guard posted by the door.

"Take the woman back to the others and lock her up. I want you to make preparations to have them terminated – first thing in the morning. They have become a threat to the very fabric of our society."

"Yes sir."

The guard collected Mrs. Cromwell from the room, and led her down the corridor. Scullins headed for the front of the building.

"This is worse than I imagined."

His pace quickened.

"I must lance this boil before the infection begins to spread."

He yanked his cloak from its hook, threw open the front doors, and marched out of Punishment House. Awaiting him at the end of the portico was a company of Keeon guards. They were a bit disheveled and their formation was untidy, but Scullins was pleased to see so many. They were each equipped with a torch and a shovel. There was some confusion among them as to why they would be digging at such a late hour.

The door swung open. Wort – weary, filthy and bruised – was brought out and paraded before his captors. His hands were tied and he was being led by a long tether secured around his neck. Scullins looked down at Wort and with a wicked smirk, jerked hard on the leash, forcing Wort to his knees. Tears streamed down his dirty face.

"You said you wanted to leave, so I decided it was time to take you for a walk. Isn't this going to be fun!" he sneered sarcastically.

He motioned to the chief.

"Lead on. There is no time to lose."

The guards lined up and began marching into the darkness toward Broadside Hill.

Lyndal and the children arrived at Punishment House and found it virtually deserted. The exterior torches were blazing, but only one guard was posted at the entrance and the two guards who usually patrolled the perimeter were absent. Lyndal turned to the children, astonished.

"This might be easier than I thought," he whispered.

They were positioned behind the bushes in the ravine next to the main bridge.

"Stay here until I signal you," he said.

He pulled on his Keeon cloak and walked calmly to the front of the building.

"Ho there," he said as he approached the guard.

The Keeon sentry lowered his spear defensively but relaxed once he recognized the uniform.

"You gave me quite a scare. Where did you come from?" he asked, confused by Lyndal's sudden appearance.

"I just need to get some things," Lyndal replied, moving closer to him.

"How did you get here in the dark like that?" he asked, "You don't have a torch."

Lyndal's pace quickened.

"Oh it's a little trick I learned. Here, let me show you."

Before the guard could react, Lyndal took hold of his arm. The man fell limp, his spear clattering to the floor. The children watched in amazement at this new display of The Wisdom's power. Lyndal nodded for them to approach.

They scrambled up the slope, keeping to the shadows as they neared the entrance. Each one knew their assignment by heart and took their positions. Beem undid the keys from the guard's belt and tossed them to Jinx, who unlocked the doors. Lyndal and Beem dragged the unconscious guard inside. Spinny snatched up his spear and backed through the doors as soon as everyone was inside. Within seconds, the front of the building was quiet. Trince locked the door from the inside making sure no one could gain entrance.

They waited in the foyer while Lyndal locked the unconscious guard in an empty cell. Beem and Jinx began extinguishing the torches along the hall. Soon the front of the building was dark. Everything was proceeding as planned. Lyndal signaled for them to follow him down the corridor.

"Is that you Kyle?"

A guard stuck his head around the corner. The team continued forward without slowing their pace.

"You're not Kyle." he exclaimed, "Who are you?"

"I'm a replacement," responded Lyndal as he advanced.

The guard was bewildered and began to back away.

"Are these the brats we've been looking for?" he asked.

"Yes, and they would like to see their parents."

Lyndal was now within reaching distance.

"But why is that young fellow carrying a spear, and . . . and why are your eyes . . . ?"

The guard backed into a wall. He looked around, desperately seeking a way of escape but before he could bolt, Lyndal grabbed him by the throat. He covered his mouth with his free hand. Spinny ran up and touched the tip of the spear to the man's chest.

"Listen carefully," ordered Lyndal, "This can be easy or hard. All you have to do is give us the information we need. If you cooperate, no harm will come to you. Understand?"

The terrified guard nodded his head in agreement.

"Where are the rest of the guards?"

Lyndal uncovered his mouth.

"Only Kyle and I stayed behind," he gasped in a quivering voice, "Everyone else went to go look for these nice children here."

He smiled nervously, glancing down at Spinny.

"And . . . and they took that other nice boy with them." he continued.

"They have Wort," said Beem.

The news about Wort caused a fierce sense of resolve to surge inside the children's hearts. They closed in on their captive while Spinny applied extra pressure to the spear.

"When did they leave?" Lyndal demanded.

"About an hour ago," he whimpered.

"And when will they return?"

"They didn't say."

The guard broke down and began trembling uncontrollably. Lyndal loosened his grip.

"Thank you," he said, "that's all we need to know."

The guard, fearful of what might happen next, shouted, "Wait! Don't kill me. I can help you."

"What could you possibly have to offer me at this point?" declared Lyndal.

"I . . . I can take you to . . . ah . . . these children's mothers."

"Too late," Lyndal replied, "I already know where the women are being held."

The guard struggled to come up with something else to bargain with.

"I also know where they're holding the men!" he blurted.

"You mean they're still here?"

The children turned to Lyndal, baffled by his response.

"Yes," the guard said with relief, "They're holding them down below. I can take you to them."

The small band, guard in tow, followed Lyndal through the corridor until he reached a particular cell. As soon as the door opened, the courageous young freedom fighters became children again. They ran into the arms of their mothers where they were greeted with hugs, kisses and tears. The whole room buzzed with excitement, except for Esta Cromwell, who sat unmoved and alone in the corner.

"I told you they would come for us!" declared Alma excitedly.

"I am so sorry I doubted you," confessed Illie.

A chorus of apologies broke out around her.

"I need your attention," announced Lyndal.

The room quieted.

“Everyone stay right here until I get back. Spinny, get your spear and come with me.”

The two of them followed the guard to the end of the corridor.

“This is the one,” he said, pointing to a nondescript cell.

“Unlock it!” Lyndal ordered.

“Oh, it’s not locked.”

The guard nudged the door open to reveal an empty cell.

“If this is some kind of joke . . . !” Lyndal threatened, tightening his grip on the man’s arm.

Spinny pressed the spear against his back.

“Below . . . below!” the guard groaned, “They’re underneath.”

He pointed to a place on the floor with the toe of his boot.

“Pry it open boy,” he pleaded, “Right here in this gap.”

Spinny wedged the spear into the opening and pulled down, revealing a trapdoor in the floorboards. He lifted it open.

“Dad?” he yelled into the dark.

“Mylan – Is that you?” answered a welcome voice.

“Yes! We’ve come to rescue you! Hold on,” called Spinny.

He hurried into the hall, grabbed a torch and lowered it into the hole.

"We can't reach it son," exclaimed Mr. Beeman, "We're chained to the wall."

Spinny turned to Lyndal with a look of desperation.

"Where's the key?" Lyndal demanded, seizing the guard by the throat.

"Kyle has it," the guard gasped, "He keeps it in his boot as a safeguard."

"I think I'll toss *you* down there when this is over," said Lyndal, noticeably irritated.

"Please, sir," the man pleaded, "I've told you everything you wanted to know."

Lyndal conceded. He gagged the guard and shoved him in the empty cell across the corridor.

"I'll be right back," he said.

Then he vanished.

Spinny took the torch and climbed carefully into the dark dungeon. As his eyes adjusted to the dim light cast by the torch, he was immediately horrified by what he saw. The place was unspeakably filthy and the stench made him gag. The men were hunched over, sitting in what looked and smelled like sewage. Their hands were tied behind them, attached to a heavy chain running the circumference of the wall. Spinny caught sight of his father. His face was bruised and bloody and his left eye was swollen shut. He could see the rest of the men suffered from similar wounds.

"Are you all right?" he asked his father.

"I'm feeling much better *now*."

A few chuckles broke out and Spinny felt hope begin to replace the desperation that had been there moments before.

"Do you know where your mother is?" Mr. Spin asked.

"She's with the other women and everyone is fine."

Overcome with relief, some of the men broke into tears while others laughed aloud.

"Now listen carefully," Spinny explained, "What I'm about to tell you is of extreme importance. Lyndal will return shortly, so we don't have much time."

The men were astonished. The young boy they thought they knew was addressing them with such confidence and authority.

"We are going to free you from these chains and meet up with the others. Once we are out of Punishment House, each family must head for the mountains – as far away from Maidenton as possible. It's no longer safe for us to remain here, and we will never be able to return. And, there's one more thing."

Spinny paused, carefully choosing his words.

"The Legends are true. The man who was just with me . . . is an Ancient. His name is Lyndal. He gave us kids the ability to see in the dark. You're going to need to trust us completely so we can get everyone out of the village safely."

The men sat speechless for a few moments. Then Markus Beeman spoke up.

"This is a lot to take in right now, but we'll do whatever you say. If your friend is here to free us, then who are we to argue."

The rest of them agreed.

Then, right before their eyes, Lyndal appeared, holding the key to their shackles. Everyone stared in amazement at the man with the shimmering eyes.

Spinny's father turned to him, gulped and whispered, "I believe you, son."

In that moment, something amazing happened between Spinny and his father. The love and respect they felt for each other was worth everything they had suffered.

Within minutes, the men were evacuated from the hole. Waiting to greet them were their families who had just arrived. Hugs were shared, kisses exchanged and tears of joy flowed freely.

Harlin Cromwell searched frantically among the faces for his wife and son.

"Where's Esta?" he asked anxiously, ". . . and Stalwart?"

Lyndal pulled Mr. Cromwell aside.

"I am sorry to tell you that your son has been taken by the Keeon," he explained, "They're trying to get information from him, but don't be afraid. He'll be all right. He has the ability to escape at any time. Your wife's whereabouts, on the other hand, are a mystery. She must have slipped out when no one was looking.

This puts us all in a very delicate position. She could, without realizing it, be jeopardizing our efforts to escape. I think it would be best if you went with the Limms and let me attend to your family."

Mr. Cromwell understood all too well the unpredictable nature of his wife. He nodded his head in consent, trusting Lyndal to do what was best. Lyndal called everyone to attention.

"You know what to do, so let's be about it."

With Punishment House safely in the distance, each family said their goodbyes and broke off from the group, heading in different directions. The children led their parents carefully through the black, moving slowly at first to maintain complete silence. When they had gone far enough to avoid discovery, they lit torches and advanced into the hills with greater speed.

Beem took his parents through the valley north of the village. They scrambled up a steep slope until they found a rocky outcropping undetectable from below.

"This will be a good place for you to hide," Beem explained, "I'll meet you here tomorrow night, before the sun rises. If I am unable to make it, wait one more day. If I fail to return, it means something went wrong and I had to transport. The Keeon will be scouring the hills by then so you will have to run – as fast and as far you can *without me*. Do you understand? Whatever happens, be assured – I will be safe."

Beem looked into his parents' faces. Tears streamed down their cheeks. He fought hard to stay focused on the task before him.

"I love you both," he said.

The three of them embraced in a hug that no one wanted to end. He kissed his mother one more time and set off down the mountain.

"I love you, Lucas," she sobbed.

Illie and Markus Beeman held hands and watched their son walk away, slowly disappearing into the black.

10

Going in Circles

Scullins had slipped in the mud again. He cursed under his breath as he wiped the dirt from his legs.

"Aren't we there yet?" he yelled.

His smooth-soled shoes made it hard going on the damp slopes of Broadside Hill. Every time he stepped onto a smooth rock or a patch of grass, his feet would slide out from under him, slamming his knees into the ground. Wort thought it was hilarious. It took everything he had not to burst out laughing. It also kept his mind off his horrid situation.

"Just about there, sir." said one of the guards who had crested the steepest part of the hill.

They arrived at the top and scanned the summit in the dim torchlight.

"We were standing on the far side of the hill," explained the guard, "I could see down the backside into the valley."

After a small hike, the search party stopped in front of a pyramid of sticks tied together with a red flag.

"This is it!" exclaimed the guard, "This is where we were standing when we heard the sounds."

Scullins straightened his grimy, disheveled jacket, slicked back his hair and thrust out his pointy chin. He began to strut pompously in front of the guards.

"Very well then. Spread out in all directions. Probe the ground for any kind of hole. If you find *anything*, I want to know about it immediately."

The guards were hesitant to follow his orders. The Keeon, like the Kinsmen, had always been told that holes were evil. While they couldn't recall why they believed this, they had never questioned the law – they followed it religiously. Scullins grew furious at their reluctance.

"Get going!" he bellowed, hitting one of the guards with the flat end of the shovel.

They began slowly moving away, holding their torches and nervously poking the ground with their shovels. Scullins turned his attention to Wort.

"So," he sneered, "How does it feel to be so close to your little Stone Room, or whatever you call it?"

"I have no idea what you're talking about," replied

Wort calmly. "I've never been here before in my life. My house is in Maidenton . . . but you already know that."

Scullins hated to think this venture might be for nothing. He was also infuriated by Wort's confidence. He poked his bony finger in his face.

"We'll see about that, won't we?!"

As Scullins began pacing, Wort sat on the ground and watched the torches move slowly across the top of the hill. When they were at quite a distance, he noticed one particular torch suddenly vanish from sight.

One of the guards must have slipped just like stupid old Scullins did climbing the hill.

He waited for the torch to reappear, but it never did. He looked to see if anyone else had witnessed the mishap, but the rest of the searchers continued on, unaware. Wort chuckled to himself.

"What's so funny?" Scullins asked.

"Nothing," Wort said, "I was just clearing my throat."

After a couple of hours of finding nothing, the guards began to lose interest. Scullins became enraged when he noticed their inactivity.

"Come back you lazy idiots!" he shouted into the darkness.

The torches began moving in their direction. After a few minutes, the guards had gathered in a circle around Scullins.

"Well?" he shouted, "Haven't you found anything?"

They stared blankly at him, saying nothing. Wort watched his mounting rage with great amusement and wondered if he might explode.

"Nothing?" he shrieked.

Finally, a short, stout guard stepped forward.

"I found this . . ."

He reached into his pocket.

"Let me see that," Scullins demanded.

The guard handed him a small, prickly ball. It unrolled, revealing a long snout and pointed ears. It took a nip from his finger.

"Disgusting vermin, just bit me!" he screamed, throwing the terrified animal to the ground.

"You imbeciles; we are looking for a HOLE. How hard can that be?!"

"Well, its dark out here," explained one of the guards, "and it's not easy to tell where you've been."

"Hey everyone," interrupted another guard, "Where's Leffin?"

They scanned the circle, but he wasn't there. Then they began searching the perimeter for his torch, but found no sign of him. "What do you think happened to him," asked the guard, "He was between Glimm and me when we started."

Fear swept through the search party and they were soon convinced something evil had happened to Leffin. Scullins could see he was losing control.

"All right, all right! Everyone stop. You two . . . go

look for this Leffin fellow. The rest of us are going to try something different."

The two guards hurried off to where Leffin was last seen while Scullins attempted to reorganize the search. He was still struggling to explain the plan when one of the guards raced back to the group.

"We found a hole!" panted Glimm, trying to catch his breath, "with Leffin lying at the bottom."

"I knew it!" Scullins announced triumphantly, "Now we're getting somewhere!"

He swaggered over to Wort and stood over him, gloating.

"I think it's time to pay your friends a visit."

He grabbed the tether and yanked him in the direction of the new discovery.

When they arrived, Glimm cautiously lowered his torch to the opening, hoping to find a way to his friend, Leffin. Scullins snatched the torch from his hand.

"Give me that!" he snarled.

He threw the torch into the hole where it landed a few feet from the lifeless body. The sound of gasps and cries of surprise could be heard as the subterranean room was illuminated beneath their feet.

"Look!" screamed Scullins with delight pointing to the floor, "Footprints! Ha! I knew it!"

He grabbed Wort by the collar and yanked him up next to his face.

"They're mine now," he hissed, showering Wort with spit.

His foul-smelling breath turned Wort's stomach. He could do nothing but stare back at his twisted face. For the first time, he felt the gravity of his circumstances.

Neither Pria nor Meekus could sleep. Pria kept going over every detail of the rescue in her mind. They snuggled up and talked quietly, wondering how their friends were getting along.

"Are you hungry?" she asked.

"A little."

Pria sat up in bed and began brushing her hair.

"I'm sure everyone is going to be starved when they get back. Why don't we fix them a meal?"

Meekus jumped up and bounced over to Pria's back. She stood, with him attached, and they raced into the kitchen. Giggles and squeals of delight echoed through the room. It wasn't long before the coals were glowing and the kitchen was filled with the aroma of sizzling meat and her delectable noodle soup.

"When do you think they'll be back?" asked Meekus.

"Soon, I hope. It's getting close to first light. Lyndal said they would return before the sun comes up."

As they set the table, Pria started to hum the song Lyndal had played on the flute. Meekus danced around the table and set a cup at each place in between pirouettes. They sang and twirled about, caught up in the joy of the moment.

Their celebration was interrupted by the sound of footsteps in the other room.

"They're back!" Meekus yelled, running to greet them.

Instead of finding his friends, a man in a Keeon uniform entered through the doorway.

Pria let out a half-hearted scream, then giggled and returned to her cooking.

"You're not going to fool me again Lyndal! Go put on some normal clothes."

"These be the only clothes I got, Miss," said the guard.

Horrified by the stranger's intrusion, Pria ran to Meekus and tucked him behind her.

"They're in here!" bellowed the guard.

Scullins led the way with Wort in tow. Soon the room was overflowing with Keeon guards.

Shocked by the sight of Wort with the enemy, Pria hung her head in disappointment. Tears rolled down her cheeks and dropped to the stone floor.

Oh Wort, how could you do it – how could you betray us?

"Pria," Wort cried, but she refused to acknowledge him.

Scullins traversed the room like a snake. He lifted Pria's chin and forced her to look into Wort's pleading eyes.

"Isn't it a shame? You can't even trust your friends."

"Please listen," Wort pleaded, "I didn't . . ."

Smack! Scullin's struck Wort across the face, sending him reeling to the floor. He grabbed the back of his cloak and dragged him to a nearby guard.

"Gag him – and keep him away from these two!"

Wort hated being thought a traitor. He burst into tears. The guard was noticeably disturbed by such harsh treatment of a child, but fear compelled him to carry out his orders.

Tap, tap, tap. The sound reverberated through the chamber.

"Silence everyone!" Scullins hissed.

He scooted behind the doorjamb.

"If any of these brats makes a sound," he whispered to the chief, "kill them."

Soon, a pair of legs descended the ladder into the outer room.

"Something sure smells good!" Spinny shouted.

He skipped the last two rungs and jumped to the floor. Without warning, he was seized by two Keeon soldiers. They had his hands tied before he could figure out what had happened.

"This is easier than I thought," Scullins quipped,

"I'll simply wait at the bottom of this ladder and see who else drops into my trap."

One-by-one the children returned, and one-by-one they were captured. Scullins turned the kitchen into a makeshift holding tank where the children were lined up against the wall with knives held to their throats. They stood, pale and trembling, each one face-to-face with a guard.

Beem was the next to be added to the lineup. The only one missing was Jinx.

"Well, well," crooned Scullins. "Isn't this a pretty picture? Six criminal families locked up in cells, and six nasty brats without their mommies and daddies. I think it's time we had a family reunion."

Scullins turned and addressed the chief guard.

"Make sure none of them escape. I plan to squelch this rebellion swiftly, without any more incidents. Now let's get moving."

Jinx had taken special care delivering Meekus' parents to a safe hiding place. He took his responsibility very seriously. As a result, it took additional time to select the perfect spot. He knew he was running late, but was confident he could make it back before first light.

As he made his way down the final stretch of path near the village, he looked across the field. He was astonished to see Lyndal standing by the stream. He picked up a stick and threw it at him to get his attention. Lyndal turned to see Jinx waving. Instantly he was standing in front of him.

"Why aren't you at the Stone Room?" he asked, "It's almost sunrise."

Jinx was panting and trembling with excitement.

"I can still get there in time," he said, grinning from ear to ear, "but I saw you standing there so I thought I'd stop"

Lyndal smiled.

"I've got a great idea. Stay right here."

Suddenly he vanished. Jinx watched him materialize alongside the stream, pulling something from the water. Then Lyndal was standing by his side again holding a dripping stringer of fish.

"Here," Lyndal laughed, "Take these to Pria. Ask her to cook them up for a special treat."

Jinx was puzzled.

"Wouldn't it be simpler if you took them?"

"I was going to, but now that you're here I can look for Mrs. Cromwell who has gone missing. I'm concerned she is in deeper trouble than we thought. I'll meet you at the Stone Room in a couple of hours."

"See you then."

Jinx set off, taking special care not to drop or damage the fish. He laughed to himself. In all his life, he couldn't remember being so happy. What a fantastic adventure it was turning out to be! He skipped along, lost in his thoughts until he came to the turn on the trail leading into the clearing. He immediately noticed something was wrong. He ducked into the bushes and crept forward, hiding behind trees until the woods ended. He could see torches burning in the grove surrounding the entrance to the Stone Room. He hung the fish on a broken limb and climbed to a better vantage point.

"No!" he whispered in shock.

A dozen Keeon guards emerged from the trees pulling his friends, bound in tethers, after them. The soldiers marched them to the village leaving two of their company behind to guard the area. Jinx remained in the tree for some time, paralyzed by what he had witnessed.

"How could this have happened? Somebody must have betrayed us. It was probably Wort. This is bad, really bad!"

His thoughts began to race. He scrambled down the tree and took off running as fast as he could toward Lyndal's house.

"What am I doing?" he said aloud.

He realized Lyndal was somewhere near

Punishment House by now, looking for Mrs. Cromwell. He stopped in his tracks and stood motionless, alone and confused in the middle of an unfamiliar forest.

"What should I do?"

He plopped down on an old log. To his surprise, he felt The Wisdom begin to speak.

I almost forgot about The Wisdom. What do you think I should do?

As he sat and listened, the light of the sun broke through the branches, stirring the forest to life all around him. Without another thought, peace welled up inside. His mind became clear again.

"Go to the square – speak the truth."

At first, he didn't think he was hearing correctly. He thought the voice in his head was his own.

That doesn't make sense. Why would I go to the square? That's the last place I want to go. I think I should hide out and wait for Lyndal.

"Go to the square – speak the truth," the small voice repeated.

"What truth?" he spoke aloud, "I have no idea what to say."

"Say what you hear me say," The Wisdom responded.

Jinx realized they were having a conversation. He *could* discern his own thoughts from those of The Wisdom.

"I understand now. It doesn't make sense, but

I'm going to obey what you say . . . and trust that you're right."

He stood up and headed for Maidenton.

An old and wrinkly Lyndal sat in the village center sipping a hot cup of morning brew, on the watch for anything unusual. Only two merchants had opened this early. Slowly, the other shop owners filtered into the square to set up their displays.

The quiet of the morning was rudely interrupted by a piercing shriek. He turned in the direction of the noise. Mrs. Cromwell stumbled onto the entryway of Punishment House as the doors slammed behind her. Her hair was tangled and matted and her shredded clothing was filthy.

"They're all gone!" she screamed through her sobs, "They've all escaped! . . . and they've taken my husband with them."

She crumpled to the ground, wailing.

At the same time, the Keeon search party, led by a tall and twisted looking man, entered the marketplace with the children tethered behind them.

Two of the guards ran across the square, snatched up Mrs. Cromwell and dragged her back inside the prison. Without hesitation, Lyndal jumped up and set out to intercept them. He reached inside his cloak and pulled something out.

Scullins yanked the arm of the guard marching next to him and pointed at Lyndal.

"Keep that old man away from us."

Beem recognized Lyndal as the guard attempted to block his approach.

"Grampa!" he shouted.

Beem lunged forward but fell to the ground as the wrist strap yanked him back. Lyndal dove behind the guard and managed to grab Beem's hands.

Lyndal:	*I'll come for you tonight*
Beem:	*We'll be ready and waiting*
Lyndal:	*Transport if your life is in danger*

Lyndal slipped a small cloth bundle into Beem's hands just as the guard jerked him up by the scruff of his neck. He turned and kicked Lyndal in the ribs. He dropped to his knees, struggling to catch his breath. He watched the guards hurry the children inside just as a crowd of curious Kinsmen began to gather.

Beem knew he didn't have much time to come up with a backup plan in the event they were forced to transport. He closed his eyes and tried to concentrate. He began working some quick calculations in his head.

2111 – We can all remember that. In eighty-five years, these people will be long gone – then we can return to Maidenton.

Once inside Punishment House, Scullins began barking orders.

"You and you – go find the sentries who are supposed to be posted here and bring them to me at once!"

"And you!" he yelled to another, "Take this woman. Lock her in the cell with the others – and find out how she escaped. The rest of you, don't let these rodents out of your sight. I don't want to go looking for them again."

While Scullins strutted around, distracted by his own importance, Beem slid over to Trince and grabbed her hand.

Beem:	*Lyndal will come for us tonight, but if we're forced to transport we'll meet back in Maidenton . . . in twenty-one-eleven. Got it?*
Trince:	*Beem . . . I want you to know . . .*
Beem:	*We don't have time, Trince – pass on the information*
Trince	*But Beem, I . . .*
Beem:	*Twenty-one-eleven. Got it?*
Trince:	*Yes, Twenty-one-eleven.*
Beem:	*Good*

Beem wondered what Lyndal had given him. While the guards were preoccupied, he carefully opened his hand. He was holding a parcel wrapped in crimson linen embroidered with a pattern of a golden vine. There was something inside. He looked to make sure no one was watching and pulled back the covering revealing seven little sticks. One of them was charred on the end.

These are the sticks that make the smoke. Why would Lyndal give these to me?

He wrapped them up and tucked the bundle underneath his belt.

The rest of the children passed the message along undetected. The last one in the line of communication was Wort. Spinny hesitated, but grabbed his hand.

Spinny:	*How could you have done this to us?*
Wort:	*It wasn't me!*
Spinny:	*You're such a liar.*
Wort:	*I swear it. The guards heard a scream coming from the top of Broadside. When Mr. Scullins took us to investigate, they found a hole. They forced me to come along.*

Spinny was stunned. He realized *he* was the one responsible for the mess they were in. He was overcome with shame and guilt.

"Let's get started," announced Scullins, "I want them marked as soon as possible!"

A horrified silence fell over every person in the room. Never in the history of Keeon rule had such an order been issued.

"But are you sure that . . ." the chief of the guard began.

"Don't you dare question my authority!" Scullins snapped, "They knew exactly what they were doing when they broke the law. They are traitors and instigators of a rebellion, no longer children in the eyes of the system. They will be treated like any other prisoner."

The chief swallowed hard, still in disbelief.

"Even the girls?"

Scullins glanced at Trince and Pria who had turned ashen at the thought of being branded. He paused.

"Make them watch." he sneered, with an evil smirk. "Now get moving! I want them back inside and locked up within the hour."

The guards grabbed the tethers and yanked the children forward. Spinny struggled to hold on to Wort.

Spinny:	*Twenty-one eleven*
Wort:	*What do you mean?*
Spinny:	*We're all going to . . .*

"Stop!" yelled Scullins as he noticed Wort, "I have other plans for this one. Take him and put him . . . I know . . . put him in with his mommy. That's more punishment than anyone should endure."

Wort was plucked from the line and led off in the opposite direction.

"Wait!" yelled Spinny, struggling to free himself, "I need to . . ."

He was immediately seized and gagged. Wort could see the desperation on Spinny's face.

The children were brought outside into the prison's courtyard. Its perimeter was lined with a row of white posts, each with a large metal ring fastened on top. One by one, they were positioned with their backs to a post, while their tethers were fed through the rings. The straps were pulled tight, forcing them to stand on their toes. In the center of the dirt yard, a fire pit was already blazing. One guard fed the fire with wood while another pumped it with a large bellows. It roared and crackled until it became so hot the soldiers were forced to back away.

Trince looked at Beem with tears streaming down her cheeks.

"Please don't do this," she sobbed, "Let's just go now and be done with it."

Beem looked at Trince with compassion. She saw in his face an expression of serious resolve that had never been there before.

"Only if it's too much. Only if it's death," he replied.

"But Meekus is too young," pleaded Pria through her tears, "It's not right to make him endure this kind of pain."

Meekus leaned out from his post.

"I'll be all right," he said with innocence, "I'm not scared at all. The Wisdom told me I would be fine."

"Don't you see? They want to break us," Beem responded, "Scullins is trying to frighten us into telling him everything we know. But we need to stay strong – no matter what happens. We'll know when it's the right time to transport. If we're patient, there might be another way out this mess – so we can all stay together."

"You seem very talkative," interrupted a burly guard.

He grabbed Beem by the neck in a chokehold and lifted him in the air as he untied his tethers. Beem gasped for air. He was led in front of the fire and forced to lie face down in the dirt. The intense heat was almost too much to bear.

"What do you have to say about this, Mr. Talkative?" the guard taunted.

He knelt on Beem's back, pinning him to the ground and ripped his tunic from his left shoulder. A red-hot branding iron marked with an "X" was pulled from the coals. Beem could feel the heat radiating as it was lowered to his shoulder. Horrified, Trince tried to turn away, but a guard forced her to face forward.

"You'd best keep your eyes open, missy, or you'll be getting the mark too."

The guard signaled to his comrade holding the brand. All at once, the burning iron was shoved into Beem's flesh. It sizzled and smoked, emitting the stench of burning skin. Beem moaned as the searing pain shook his body. Waves of nausea washed over him and he fought to remain conscious. The iron was removed. His traumatized body fell limp to the ground. He was dragged away by the arms and dumped in front of the restraining post. The children watched Beem anxiously to see if he had survived the torture. Slowly, he lifted his head off the ground. He looked at his friends and managed a weak smile. Dirt was caked to his lips and face.

"It's not that bad," he whimpered.

His head dropped as he fell into unconsciousness.

The guard laughed.

"That was pitiful," he mocked as he strutted in front the others.

"Anyone feel like talking to Mr. Scullins yet?"

The children remained silent except for an occasional sniffle.

"All right then," he continued, "let's give this little guy his turn."

He clutched Meekus' neck. The girls began to squirm.

"Do you have something to say now?" the guard

queried, but no one said a word.

The same procedure was inflicted on Meekus and finally Spinny.

Scullins was fuming when he entered the courtyard. Somehow, the 'ignorant' Kinsmen prisoners had escaped. Everything was now resting on breaking the children's spirits.

I will make them talk if it's the last thing I do. They will pay for this!

He straightened his coat, wiped the dandruff from his shoulders and sauntered over to where the girls were tethered. Their eyes were swollen from crying and they glared at him with disgust.

"Good," he gloated, full of self-importance.

He inspected the bodies of the three boys. The charred X's marking their backs were blistered and bleeding as they lay exposed in the morning sun.

"Very good!" he reiterated, "Lock them up. And this time, do a better job than you did with their parents. You fools let them escape!"

Without warning, Scullins backhanded the chief across the face. He clenched his fist to strike back but restrained himself. Scullins paid no attention and marched back inside the building.

Lyndal caught Jinx's arm and pulled him behind a food cart.

"What happened?" he whispered, "Why are you here?"

"They found the Stone Room," Jinx explained, "When I got to the clearing I saw torches coming out of the grove. Everyone was captured. I started back to find you, but The Wisdom stopped me and told me to come here."

The place they were standing was too exposed. They moved to a secluded area behind a building where they could talk freely.

"The Wisdom told you to come here . . . and do what?"

"Tell the truth. I'm supposed to tell the people what is really happening here – before the Keeon have a chance to spread their lies."

Lyndal closed his eyes and stood motionless for a few moments.

"Yes – yes!" he agreed, "I sense that too. But, I'm not going to be able to help you with your mission. I must remain hidden until the time is right. I hope what you do will make a way for me."

"What are you going to do?" asked Jinx.

"My first priority is to get everyone out of Punishment House. We still need to proceed with the plan to reunite you with your parents. I trust this is the last time I will have to wear a Keeon uniform, at least for a while."

Lyndal clasped his hand. Jinx felt a surge of courage fill his heart.

"Keep hope alive!" Lyndal whispered.

"Keep hope alive." Jinx replied.

Lyndal checked to make sure they hadn't been seen, and then vanished.

The Kinsmen who had witnessed the commotion in the square were now gathered in groups, whispering amongst themselves. Jinx positioned himself next to a small crowd to discretely listen in on their conversation.

"Why would they imprison children?" asked the bread vendor.

"Didn't you recognize them? Those are the children of the rebel families," answered one of the shoppers, "The ones who had their houses burned yesterday. No doubt they will be banished along with their parents."

"What about Esta Cromwell?" asked a young woman.

Jinx felt a familiar nudge and stepped forward.

"Mrs. Cromwell is the reason our houses were burned."

They all turned to listen to the young man standing before them.

"Aren't you one of the twins?" asked another merchant, "Wasn't your brother taken inside?"

"Yes, he was. As soon as the Keeon realize I'm still out here, they will try to capture me as well."

"But why? What did you do?" asked the woman.

"We did nothing . . . except discover the truth."

They all looked at him with great curiosity. He could feel the opportunity of the moment.

"What truth are you talking about?" asked Mr. Leeds, an elder of the village committee.

"The truth about The Legends, the stories about The Ancients and the Great Departure . . . everything is true. And I have proof! My friends and I found some incredible things the Keeon don't want us to know about. We found them inside a hole."

The crowd gasped.

"But it's not really a hole!" Jinx declared, "It's a group of buildings the Keeon buried to keep us from discovering them. They are filled with all sorts of evidence."

"Evidence of what?" asked another man who had just joined the group.

"Evidence that The Ancients are real!" explained Jinx, "Evidence that proves the Keeon were once Kinsmen like us. Don't you see . . . the Keeon invented the lie about holes being evil to keep us from finding the truth. They're using fear and our own ignorance to control us."

Jinx could see the people were struggling to understand what he was saying. Some shook their heads while others snickered.

"This is too hard to swallow," argued one of the

men, "We've heard these stories before, all about the 'Ancient race.' It's just a bunch of mythology – fantasy stories. I've heard enough."

Some of the people started to walk away.

"Wait!" yelled Jinx, "How do you explain the fact . . . that I can see in the dark?"

Marta Roann laughed aloud.

"Ha! Now you've gone too far. Such nonsense! Let's get back to work."

Jinx watched helplessly as the crowd dispersed.

I told them the truth. Now what?

"Wait," instructed The Wisdom.

"Hold on a minute," announced Rulan Leeds, "I have something to say."

Everyone turned and fixed their attention on the town elder.

"I believe what this young man is saying," he continued, "I think everything he said is true. I know it all sounds like foolishness, but the fact of the matter is . . . the fact is . . . I can see in the dark too. I've just never told anyone."

Immediately the crowd regathered around Jinx and began questioning him. Mr. Leeds approached him and placed his hand on his shoulder.

"Where is this hole, young man? I'd like to see it for myself."

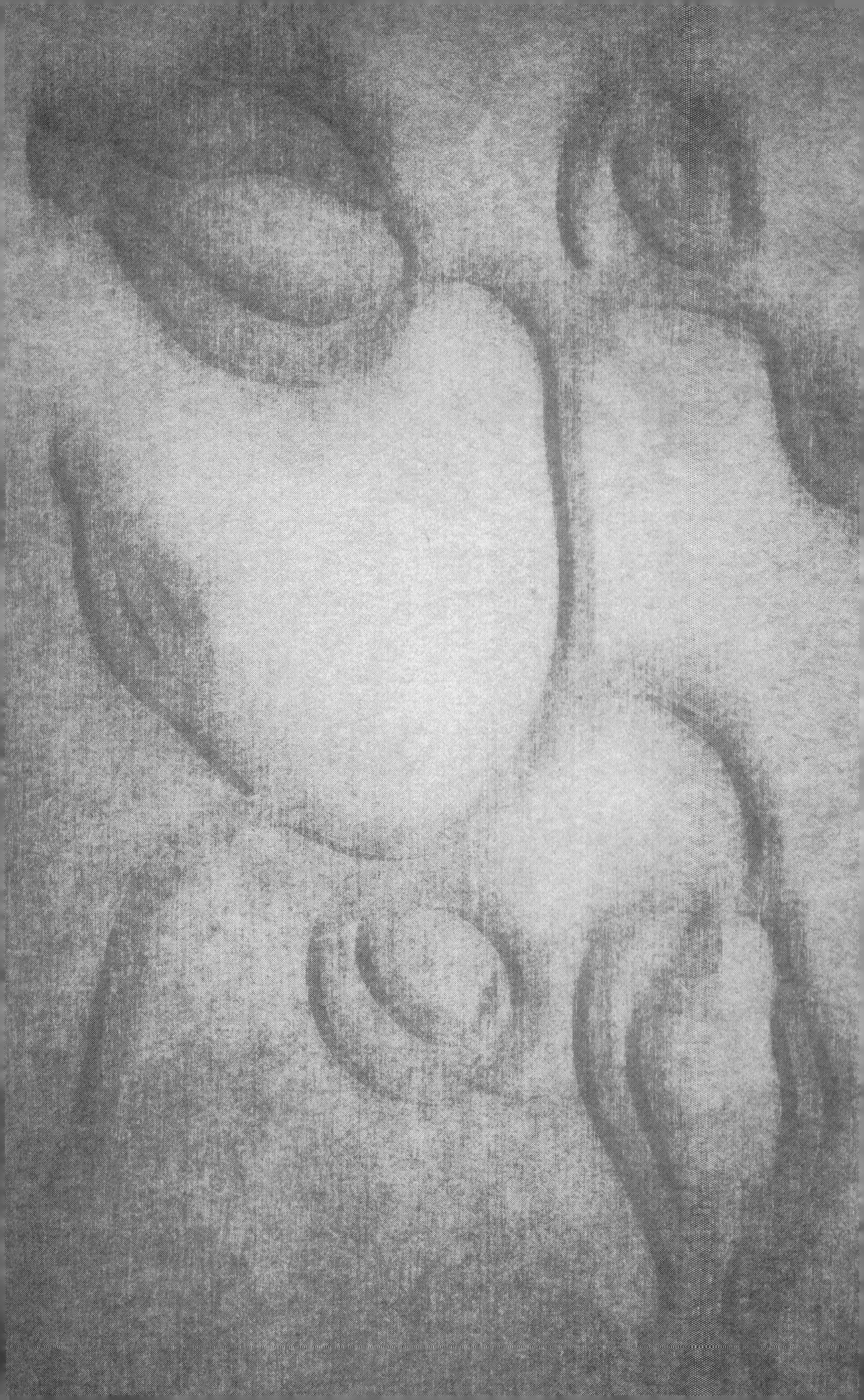

11

Believing My Eyes or Believing Your Lies

"Hey Flyn, what do you think this means?" asked Witzel, who was staring into the hole.

"What are you talking about?" said Flyn.

"This hole," he replied as he kicked a dirt clod into the opening, "You saw all those things down there. What do you think is going on?"

"They don't pay us to think! They pay us to stand here and keep watch . . . and not ask questions."

"Yeah, I know all that," said Witzel, scratching his head, "But don't you think this means something? There were rooms full of furniture and strange objects down there."

Flyn quickly became annoyed with Witzel's stream of questions. He knew deep inside that something important was happening, but his vow to uphold Keeon law took precedence over the truth buried just beneath their feet.

"Those kids must have taken all those things down there," he concluded, "That's why we captured them. Holes are evil and off limits. They broke the law! Now they're going to pay for it."

Flyn thought his explanation was very clever. He proceeded to convince himself it was true.

"You're funny, Flyn," Witzel said with a laugh, "How could those kids have taken all that stuff down there. Besides, didn't you see the walls? They're as smooth as glass."

"Shut up!" Flyn yelled, "You're making my head hurt. Why can't you just leave me alone?"

He snatched up his spear and pushed past Witzel. He made his way through the trees and positioned himself so he could scan the meadow. In the distance, a small group of Kinsmen were approaching.

"Hey!" he yelled to Witzel, "It looks like we're going to have company. Get ready."

Hiking across the field were five villagers led by a young boy. They were headed straight for the two Keeon soldiers guarding the entrance to the Stone Room.

"Look!" cried Jinx, "There they are, just as I told you."

The two armed men stood in front of the clump of trees, looking quite menacing with their spears held in front of them. The group continued forward at a slower pace, uncomfortable with the thought of a confrontation. Jinx urged them on. When they were within a stone's throw of the trees, Flyn stepped forward, pointing his spear at the curious onlookers.

"Stop right there! As of this morning, this entire area is off limits to Kinsmen."

Jinx faced the group.

"It's off limits because there's a hole in the middle of those trees. That's the entrance to the Stone Room and all the other buildings I told you about. In fact, there are structures that go all the way up inside Broadside Hill."

Witzel was astonished by what he overheard.

"Hey Flyn, how did he know that?"

Flyn spun around and pointed his spear at Witzel.

"I thought I told you to shut up!"

"So it's true!" said the elder Kinsman to Witzel, "There are rooms underneath the ground and this is the entrance."

Jinx continued his speech.

"A long time ago this was a great city. Thousands of Ancients used to live here. They worked here and raised their families here. They were incredibly smart and created machines to do all sorts of amazing things."

Witzel inched closer to the group, thoroughly captivated by Jinx's story.

"What sort of things?" he asked, oblivious to his partner's growing disapproval.

"Enough!" ordered Flyn.

He aggressively jabbed his spear at the assembly.

"You are all in violation of Keeon law! You will be punished for even listening to such lies. Go back to your homes NOW before something terrible happens to you!"

Witzel picked up his spear and approached Jinx. The people backed up in fear. He drew back his arm and thrust the weapon into the ground at Jinx's feet.

"What sort of machines?" he asked.

Greatly relieved, Jinx smiled and continued his story.

"Machines that . . . that can make the walls glow."

"It's true!" yelled Witzel, bubbling with excitement, "I saw them with my own eyes – right down there!"

He pointed to the middle of the grove.

"Witzel!" Flyn shouted.

His face was boiling red. He glared at his partner and spewed out a stream of obscenities.

"Would you like to see it?" Witzel continued, completely ignoring the outburst.

Flyn had enough. He took off running toward the village.

"Where do you think he's going?" asked Tessa.

"Don't worry," Witzel said with a smile, "He's just in denial."

Bang, bang, bang! The sound reverberated off the walls of Punishment House. Scullins looked up from his desk and addressed the guard posted by the door.

"Send them away. I'm too busy for Kinsmen issues today," and shooed him out of the room.

A few minutes passed and the guard returned. He cleared his throat to get Scullins' attention.

"Well, what is it?" he said, not even looking up from his paperwork.

"There's a . . . a . . ."

"Scullins!"

He recognized the voice at once and looked up to see his old classmate standing in the doorway.

"Ivan Pincher," Scullins said with a disdainful smile, "At last you've arrived."

Pincher was an imposing man with cruel eyes. Scullins secretly despised him, but loved his methods of dealing with troublemakers.

"I'm glad you came. I can use your help," Scullins continued, "This disturbance is turning out to be worse than I had anticipated. Did you bring anyone with you?

"Of course," Pincher answered with his usual cockiness, "I brought a company of the Black Regiment from the domes."

His voice hushed to a whisper.

". . . along with someone else."

At that moment, a mysterious man cloaked in purple entered the office. The hood of his mantle was pulled forward, obscuring his features. Pincher turned, faced the man and bowed low as he backed away. Scullins couldn't help staring at the visitor, curious as to why Pincher felt the need to bring him along. The stranger faced Scullins and pulled back his hood just enough to reveal his eyes. Scullins dropped to one knee, and bowed his head.

"Sir, it's an honor to have you here," he choked out.

The man looked down at the pitiful creature groveling at his feet.

"Where are the dissidents?" he croaked in a gravelly voice.

"Well sir . . . there have been a few, uh . . . complications."

Trince and Pria sat huddled together in the corner of their cell, sobbing. They held hands, trying their best to comfort each other. Trince wondered if the boys would ever be the same after such brutal torture. The dreadful images were still fresh, refusing to leave their minds. An hour passed and the door to their cell creaked open. Two Keeon guards stepped inside. The girls recognized one of them as the chief, the one Scullins had slapped in the courtyard.

"You're right," he stated to the other Keeon, "This is no place for a girl. I have a daughter back home who is the same age. I don't care what that imbecile has to say, they've suffered enough!"

He walked over to Trince, and looked into her swollen eyes. Her soiled face was streaked with tears.

"You don't know nuthin', do ya?" he asked gently.

Trince stared at him without saying a word. The chief stood up and turned to his comrade.

"Get these two out of here," he ordered, "They've seen enough for a lifetime. If Scullins has a problem with it, he can deal with me."

His partner helped the girls to their feet, led them down the hall and out the back entrance of Punishment House.

"This is your lucky day," he said as he removed the straps from their wrists, "If I were you, I'd keep out of sight until this whole thing blows over."

Pria thanked the guard and ran quickly down the

steps, but Trince wouldn't budge.

"What about the boys?" she demanded, "What will happen to them?"

"It's up to Scullins, missy. It would be best if you forgot you ever knew them. Just be glad the chief took sympathy on *you*."

Pria returned and began pulling frantically on Trince's arm.

"Come on!" she insisted, "We need to get out of here."

Trince was torn. She paused and sensed that Pria was right. They ran with all their might until they were a safe distance from Punishment House.

"I can't believe we're free," said Pria, trying to catch her breath.

Trince nodded as she gasped for air.

"What are we going to do about the boys?"

"I don't know, but right now, we need to find Lyndal. Come on."

"The boy was right!" exclaimed Tessa in amazement.

The villagers moved about the Stone Room in awe, fascinated with their underground surroundings.

"There are pictures of The Ancients down this way," announced Jinx.

The five Kinsmen, along with Witzel, followed him down a corridor and through some connecting rooms. Gasps of wonder echoed through the halls with each new discovery. Some of them ran their fingers along the smooth stone walls as they walked. The warm glow illuminating their way was a marvel they couldn't stop talking about.

Jinx led them inside what appeared to be a child's sleeping chamber. There was a small bed with side rails, a chair, and some playfully decorated furniture – all blanketed in dust.

"Look!" exclaimed Marta, "Here's a doll. Isn't it cute?"

In the process of wiping it clean, she gave it a good squeeze. All at once, the eyes of the doll lit up like little torches.

She screamed and threw the toy to the floor.

"Did you see that?" she exclaimed.

"Don't be afraid," Jinx assured her, "Those are the eyes of an Ancient, just like the people in this picture."

He pointed to an unusual portrait hanging on the wall. It appeared to be lifelike, similar to the image they had of Lyndal.

"See, everyone's eyes are glowing, even the children's."

"All my life I've been told the way we live is true and The Legends are lies," said Mr. Leeds, "Now, in an instant, everything has changed. It's obvious we've been deceived by the Keeon."

The people were stirred by his words. They turned their attention to Witzel who put his hands up in surrender and backed away.

"I . . . I never knew a thing. I'm just as surprised as you are."

"That's true," said Jinx, coming to his defense, "It's been thousands of years since The Ancients lived here. They all transported away when they discovered Beniwan was dying."

"So even that part of The Legends is true," the old man sighed.

"I think it's about time the rest of the village knows the truth," interrupted Gilford Kemp.

He removed the picture from the wall.

"My wife would like to see this . . . and so would the committee."

They all nodded in agreement and began gathering up a few peculiar objects to take with them.

Jinx noticed a change in the atmosphere as the villagers prepared to leave. He had never seen such hope and excitement in his people before. Words like 'freedom' and 'truth' could be heard on their lips. The people who emerged from the hole were not the same as the ones who had climbed in.

Flyn burst into Scullin's office.

"They went inside. I couldn't stop them . . . so I came straight here!"

"What are you babbling about?" shouted Scullins, infuriated by the intrusion. "How dare you interrupt me while I'm in conference?"

The hooded man turned. Flyn caught a glimpse of his eyes and backed away in fear.

"I'm sorry sir. I . . . I didn't realize that . . ."

The stranger touched his finger lightly to Flyn's shoulder, forcing him to one knee.

"Who went inside what?" came the raspy voice inside the purple hood.

Flyn couldn't bear to look into those eyes a second time.

"Kinsmen," he whimpered, fearing for his life, "A group of Kinsmen went in the hole."

The hooded man directed his attention to Pincher.

"Take him!" he ordered. "And bring the rest to me. I want this rebellion crushed – NOW!"

Pincher flew into action, pulling the terrified guard out of the room. The hooded man turned his gaze to Scullins who was nervously fidgeting next to his desk.

"You incompetent fool," he croaked, closing in on his victim.

Scullins, overcome with terror, lost all composure and crumpled to the ground.

"You will tell me everything," the man growled.

Witzel and the Kinsmen gathered as they made their way out of the trees.

"What should we do now?" Marta asked.

"Tell everyone the truth," said Mr. Leeds, "They will have to believe us. Look at these things we have. This is indisputable evidence that The Legends are true."

"The days of Keeon deception are finally coming to an end!" said Mr. Gallow.

"No offense." he said nodding at Witzel.

"None taken," he answered, "This has been quite a day for me as well."

The villagers set out toward Maidenton. It was decided that Rulan Leeds would call a council meeting and present their findings. As they approached the village, however, they could see a company of soldiers on the main path, heading directly toward them. They were not regular Keeon guards. They looked taller and were dressed in sleek, black uniforms. A strange man was in the lead, pulling Flyn, in tethers, behind him. Flyn caught sight of Witzel.

"There they are! They are the ones who broke the law!"

The Kinsmen faltered, not knowing if they should press on or run.

"Don't worry," said Witzel, "I'll take care of this."

"Ho! Flyn!" he yelled, waving his arms, "I have everyone here. I'm bringing them back to the village."

Before Flyn could respond, a soldier grabbed his wrist strap, yanked him around and dragged him back toward the village. The others continued advancing without missing a step. Their approach was ominous. The ground seemed to rumble beneath their feet as they marched in precise rhythm.

"Whatever happens," Jinx urged them, "tell our people what you saw today. Show them the treasures. They have a right to know the truth."

Witzel stood alone, at the head of the group, facing the oncoming threat.

"Don't worry!" he said, "I can handle this."

The soldiers surrounded the group, corralling the terrified Kinsmen together like trapped animals

"Ho there!" Witzel shouted, trying to get Pincher's attention, "We were wondering . . ."

Without a word, two soldiers seized and gagged him, and then tied a sack over his head. They bound his wrists and led him into the woods.

"Where are they taking him?" asked one of the villagers.

"Shhh!" whispered Marta, "Don't say another word!"

They cowered before the intimidating wall of soldiers surrounding them. Pincher stepped into the circle.

"My name is Ivan Pincher. I am the premier Kinsmen representative to the great council that meets in the City of Domes. I am here to act as an intermediary when you are brought before the village committee later today. You are to keep all questions to yourselves as we return to the village. If you feel the need to talk, these soldiers will help you to reconsider. Am I understood?"

The group stood silently, eyes to the ground, all except for Mr. Gallow, who was hard of hearing.

"What if we were to . . ."

Pincher reached over and twisted the man's nose, until he fell to his knees, bleeding and gasping in pain.

He signaled to a guard who gagged and hooded the man as they had done with Witzel.

"Very well," said Pincher, his voice thick with disdain, "Let's try this again. Am – I – under – stood?"

There was no response.

"Good."

He began examining his prisoners, one by one.

"Aren't you a little old to be stirring up trouble?" he asked Leeds.

The village elder was trembling so hard that the picture he had concealed in his tunic slipped out. He tried desperately to conceal it.

"What have we here?" said Pincher, jerking the picture from his hands.

"Oh my!" he said, pretending to be afraid, "I'm sure everyone in the village would like to get a look at this – people with glowing eyes. I'll have to be very careful not to break it."

He dashed the picture to the ground, shattering it into little bits.

"Oops." he mocked, "How clumsy of me."

Pincher turned and addressed the Black Guard

"See if they have anything else of interest."

The soldiers began frisking the Kinsmen. It didn't take them long to collect a small pile of artifacts.

"These are meaningless!" spewed Pincher, "Regardless of what you think you saw down there, this means nothing. The Keeon built those rooms as a trap. The objects were placed there to see if you would obey the law. Your possession of them proves only one thing – you are all lawbreakers!"

Pincher ordered the prisoners to be taken to Punishment House at once. As they approached the village, the two soldiers who had removed Witzel joined them from the woods – but Witzel was nowhere to be seen. They stood at attention before Mr. Pincher.

"Return to the trees and secure the entrance," he ordered, "Once you're finished there, go up the hill and *take care* of the remaining local guards."

The sun was overhead by the time the girls arrived at Lyndal's house. They slipped into the entrance beneath the boulder and activated their night-vision. Pria crouched next to the hole in the stone wall.

"Lyndal! It's us – Pria and Trince."

As they stepped inside the warm cozy room, both girls felt safe for the first time since they had been captured. Lyndal welcomed them with a comforting hug. Their tense bodies finally relaxing in his gentle embrace and they both let out sighs of relief.

"I thought you would come here," he said, holding them close.

"But, how did you know we were released?" asked Trince.

"I'm the 'new guard' who convinced the chief you didn't belong in there. After he saw you in the cell, he must have agreed with me."

All at once, the trauma of the day, mixed with complete exhaustion, overwhelmed Trince. She burst into tears.

"What's going to happen to the boys?"

"It's difficult to say what might happen. The Keeon will always take sympathy on females, but with males

. . . they won't be as easy to get out as you were. But don't worry; they know what to do if it gets too dangerous."

"So what do we need to do to get them out?" asked Pria.

Instead of being crushed by her captors, Pria felt her resolve become stronger and more courageous – ready for a good fight.

"I'll take care of it. We have some advantages that we didn't have when we rescued your parents. I know which cell they're in, and they have the powers."

Lyndal's confidence gave Trince comfort. She wiped her tears and blew her nose.

The three of them sat down on a soft rug by the fire.

"What's our part?" Pria asked, "We want to help."

"Now that you're free, it wouldn't be wise for you go in again – even for a rescue. The smartest thing to do now is join up with your parents and be on your way."

"That's impossible!" exclaimed Trince, jumping to her feet, "Not without knowing what happens to them."

"I have to agree," said Pria, "As long as they remain in Punishment House, we're staying right here." They held tightly to each other's hands and looked intently at Lyndal. He could see he wouldn't get past their stubborn determination or the intense love they had for their friends. He smiled, proud of their decision.

"Very well then, you can stay right here. Besides, I really like Pria's cooking."

Jinx could sense something was wrong. The Wisdom was churning inside him. It felt like something evil was close, but he had never experienced anything like it before. He fought the growing fear but it continued to torment him.

The small group of Kinsmen had been imprisoned together in a damp holding cell. Once inside, several rushed to help their friend, Mr. Gallow. They untied the hood and removed his gag.

Gallow was a tough, old field worker, not one given to self-pity. It took him a few moments to catch his breath.

"I'll be fine," he said with assurance. "But, would somebody please remind me to keep my mouth shut in the future!"

He chuckled and he rubbed his bruised nose.

"This is no time for joking!" snapped Marta, "I'm scared and my husband doesn't know where I am!"

She burst into tears.

"Listen to me," Jinx stressed, "Our greatest hope is to press through this, and hold on to the truth. What you discovered today is the key to setting our people free."

Gilford Kemp slammed his fist against the wall.

"I wish I *didn't* know the truth! I wish I'd never gone down that stupid hole!" he exclaimed, "It was safer to stay ignorant – and go about our business without any trouble."

"That's not true," interrupted Mr. Leeds, "Isn't it better to know the truth and risk dying, or would you rather live the rest of your life as a slave, and die . . . living a lie?"

"Quiet," Jinx whispered, "Someone's coming."

He dropped to the floor and stared blankly at the wall.

Pincher, Scullins and a half dozen soldiers filed in to the cell.

"Take the two women to 'B' Block," ordered Scullins, "and throw the rest of this scum into the pit."

The soldiers ignored him, waiting obediently for Pincher's instructions. Pincher gently nodded at the ranking officer. His men sprang into action, following Scullin's orders to the letter.

As Jinx was lifted to his feet, Scullins recognized him.

"Wait! You're one of those rodent children. How did you get in here?"

Jinx stared at him, not saying a word.

"Throw this boy in with the other brats," he ordered, "I'm getting tired of criminals ending up in the wrong places!"

The guard stood motionless until Pincher signaled his approval.

The prisoners were separated and led to their cells. Pincher turned to Scullins with a malicious grin and stuck out his hand. Scullins, a little confused, took it hesitantly.

"Nice to have seen you again, old friend," said Pincher.

"Are you going somewhere?" Scullins asked.

"No, no. *I'm* not going anywhere," Pincher sneered.

He nodded to the soldiers flanking Scullins. His face turned whiter than normal at the terrible realization of what was transpiring.

"Put him in the pit with the others," Pincher ordered.

"What?" Scullins screamed, "You can't be serious!"

The guards half carried, half-dragged Scullins down the corridor, kicking and shrieking curses. Pincher turned and coolly walked to the front of the building.

The men, including Scullins, were taken to the disgusting cavity below the floor. When the trap door was lifted, it revealed the entire brigade of Keeon guards, chained to the wall.

"There has been a grave misunderstanding," Scullins argued, "Go back at once and report this to Mr. Pincher."

They paid no attention and lowered the men into the pit where they were shackled alongside the others. The soldiers exited without a word. The heavy door slammed across the opening with a thud, entombing the doomed men in the dark. Scullin's muffled cries could be heard as the cell door closed behind them.

At the other end of the complex, Pincher bowed low before the hooded man who was seated at Scullins' old desk.

"They are all in shackles, as you wished." he announced, "And the rebels are contained. The holes are being filled in as we speak, and all evidence has been destroyed. The executioners are simply waiting for my orders."

"Excellent," croaked the stranger, "This must be swift and painful. The Kinsmen of this village need to be taught a lesson."

He paused for a moment growling with amusement.

"Make the executions public," he announced as he stood to his feet, "By the time we finish with them they will understand what it is to live in *real* fear. Make sure everything is cleaned up before the sun goes down."

Pincher remained motionless in his bowed position.

"Yes sir."

The hooded man made his way across the room to the door.

"I'm leaving for the domes. Find me as soon as you return. I want a full report."

Pincher remained bowed until he heard the entrance doors of Punishment House bang shut. He stepped into the hall and signaled to his soldiers.

"You two – go find the village committee members. Have them gather in the town square in four hours. The rest of you, assemble the execution platforms in front, where every eye will see them. We're going to give the village of Maidenton some entertainment they won't soon forget!"

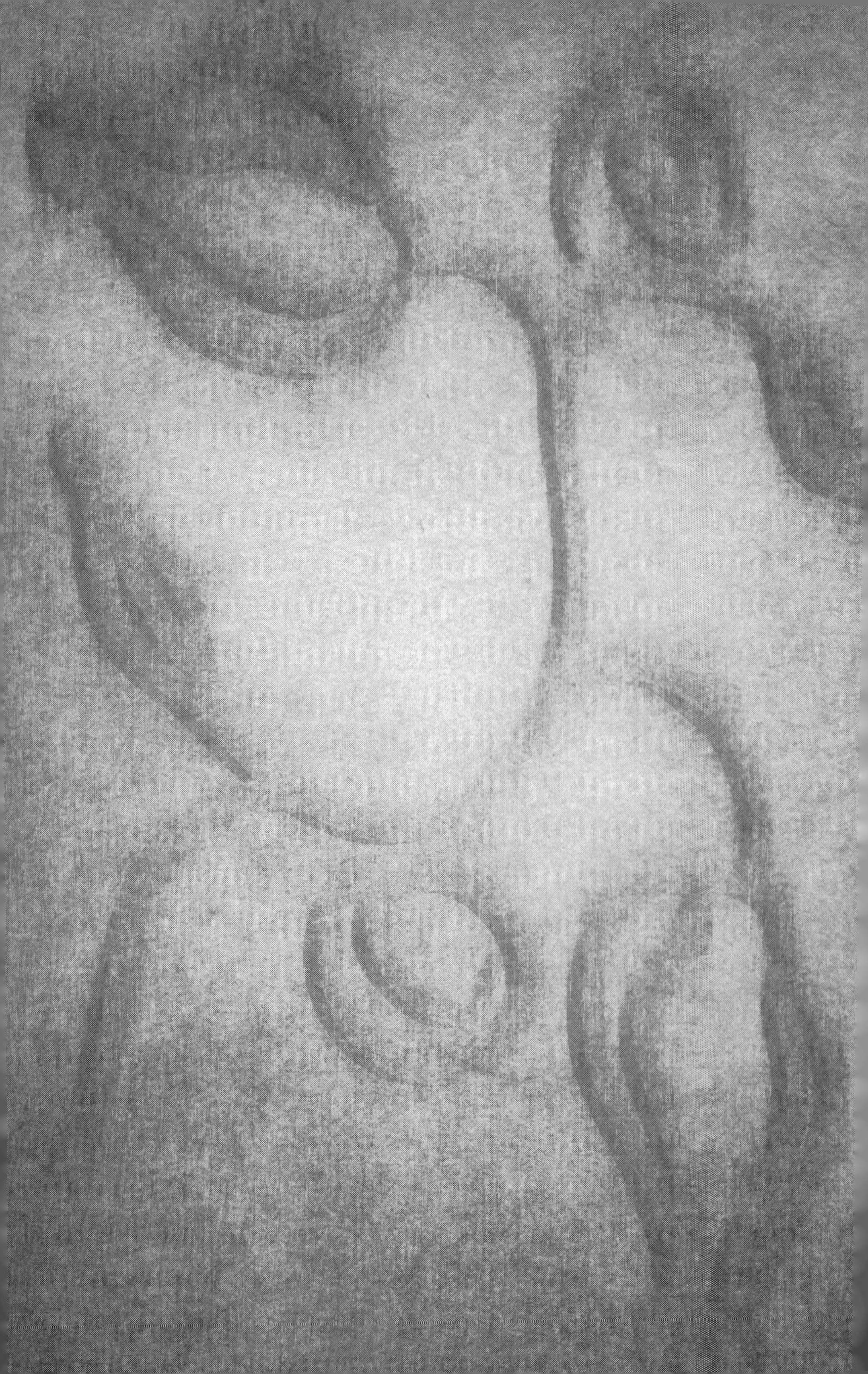

12

NO TIME FOR GOODBYES

"*Something's not right,*" Lyndal murmured.

The girls watched as he busied himself rearranging the books in his library. He was quite agitated and kept muttering things under his breath.

"What is it?" Trince asked.

Her words startled him, snapping him out of his funk. His face softened and he attempted a smile.

"It's The Wisdom," he explained, "It's been stirring inside me for hours. I just felt another wave of something . . . something evil, close by."

Trince's eyes widened.

"I feel it too," she said with a shiver, "I wasn't sure what it was. What do you think is going on?"

"I don't know. I haven't felt anything like this in almost a thousand years."

He sat at the table, pulled on his boots and began lacing them. Then he was lost in thought again. All at once, he turned to the girls.

"I need to get back to the village, right now."

His tone was urgent and they could see the deep concern on his face.

"Don't worry about us," Pria reassured him, "I'll have some of your favorite vegetable pies waiting for you for when you get back."

Pria's attempt at lightening the mood went unnoticed. He hurriedly gathered a few supplies from a nearby shelf.

"I don't know how long I'll be gone," he said, snatching the Keeon uniform from the hook, "Help yourselves to anything you want, but whatever you do, stay out of sight."

He gave them both a quick hug and smiled in earnest.

"Keep hope alive."

Then he vanished.

The three boys sat in separate corners of the large prison cell. Spinny remained bound and gagged. A trio of soldiers stood in the doorway watching their every move.

Jinx was thrown in. He hit the ground hard and slid across the dirt floor. Beem quickly ran to his aid and helped him to his feet.

"Are you all right?" he asked.

Jinx brushed the dirt from his clothing, examined his grazed elbows and smiled at Beem.

"I'll be fine," he said, slapping him on the back.

Beem cried out in pain and crumpled to the floor. The soldiers laughed. Jinx was perplexed.

"What did I do?"

"Look," said Meekus.

He pulled the tunic from his shoulder, revealing the blistered, bloody, X-shaped wound. Jinx stood stunned, realizing the horror his friends had endured.

"I'm so sorry Beem, I didn't know."

"I'll be all right," he replied, wiping the tears from his eyes, "Just warn me next time you want to be so affectionate."

"That's enough," snapped one of the soldiers, "Get back to your corners. You too," he said, motioning to Jinx.

Lyndal materialized in a back alley. The presence of evil was much stronger and much closer.

What is that? Where have I felt this before?

From this vantage point, he had a clear view of the buildings surrounding the square. In the distance, he could see a richly crafted black carriage driving away on the far side of the bridge. He recognized its shape at once and quickly ducked behind a wall.

This is more serious than I thought. What would bring the Shallum to this side of The Sands?

The hooded man was suddenly shaken. Dread and foreboding enveloped him. He spun around, peered through the rear window of the carriage and focused in on a narrow alleyway near the edge of the village. He scanned the area for anything, or anyone unusual, but saw nothing. He snarled and turned, facing forward. The carriage continued on, toward the great sea of sand.

Lyndal was troubled by what he had seen and struggled to collect his thoughts. He walked cautiously into the center square, mixing in with the crowd that was milling about.

Black Regiment soldiers were noisily assembling a large wooden platform in front of Punishment House. All around the town center, shop owners and citizens huddled together in small groups behind their carts. Lyndal moved undetected from group to group, listening in on their frightened conversations.

Something's not right. I need to get inside – now.

Lyndal slipped in to the alley, put on the Keeon uniform and made his way to the entrance of Punishment House.

"Look at this," called one of the soldiers, "We must have missed one."

Two guards flanked him and escorted him to the front door.

"Ho," said Lyndal.

"Ho, yourself," taunted one of them.

They each grabbed an arm as he crossed the threshold and steered him down a corridor.

"Where have you been hiding?"

"I've been . . . on guard duty. Can I ask where you're taking me?"

"We need you to do some more – guarding," the soldier mocked.

They delivered Lyndal to an all too familiar cell.

"Who's in the pit?" he asked as they pried open the door.

"Apparently you are," said the soldier, shoving Lyndal in.

Without another word, the man chained him to the wall.

Lyndal surveyed his filthy surroundings. Shackled alongside him were ten Keeon guards, three Kinsmen and a very upset Scullins. Scullins shrieked and begged for the soldiers to free him but his cries were ignored. The door slammed above them.

"This is a horrible mistake!" Scullins screamed over and over again.

Finally, the Keeon guard sitting to his right jabbed him in the chest, knocking the wind out of him. Scullins sputtered and coughed, completely speechless. For the first time since their imprisonment, the men had some relief from the torture of his constant sniveling.

Lyndal activated his night-vision and transported to the opposite side of the pit. His chains dropped to the ground. He leaned down and whispered into the village elder's ear.

"Don't say a word. I'm going to help you escape."

Rulan Leeds held his tongue and listened carefully to Lyndal's instructions.

Pincher motioned to the captain of the regiment as he entered the office.

"Is the village committee assembled?"

"Yes sir and the platform has been completed."

"Then it's time!" Pincher stated, "Remove the guards from the pit and take them to the inner courtyard. I want them to have time to ponder their future. Make them squirm!" he cackled in twisted delight, "Inform me, once you have them secure. I'll be in front, addressing the rabble."

"As you command," said the captain.

All of Maidenton was gathered in the square. The atmosphere was charged with alarm and confusion. Several large eating benches had been placed in front of the platform, where the committee members were seated, awaiting the public address. As Pincher burst through the doors, the townspeople erupted into a frenzy of shouts, bombarding him with questions.

"What's going on! Where is my husband? Why are there soldiers in our village?" echoed countless angry voices.

Pincher strutted across the stage, relishing the attention and his power to manipulate the situation. He motioned for them to be quiet. The chaos gradually subsided.

"All in good time – all in good time. All of your questions will be answered."

He centered himself on the platform and with great pomp, began his address.

"Today is a day you will never forget, a day that will

become part of your legacy. The story of what is about to transpire will be told to your children's children's children. Now sit back and watch as history is made."

The prisoners were roused from their misery by the sound of footsteps above their heads. Lyndal quickly transported back into his shackles. The trapdoor opened, and two soldiers jumped in. They began releasing the Keeon guards from their chains and one by one, they were pulled out of the pit.

"It looks like you won't be dying – today," said a soldier as he unhooked another Keeon, "Be grateful you're not one of these pathetic villagers."

The guards were overcome with relief.

When they got to Scullins, the Keeon chief intervened.

"No! Not him!" he shouted, "He's not one of us. We want nothing to do with him."

This infuriated Scullins. He began flailing, desperately trying to free himself from his restraints. Without hesitation, the soldier slugged him in the face, knocking him unconscious. A chorus of cheers erupted from the Keeon. Even a few Kinsmen managed weak smiles.

Lyndal was the last in line to be released.

"I would prefer to stay here with the Kinsmen if you don't mind," he said.

"Suit yourself," the soldier snapped, "But you won't get a second chance."

Lyndal nodded and hung his head.

The two soldiers climbed out of the pit and slid the door back in place. The foul stench and oppressive darkness were crushing.

"I'm here to help and I need you to listen carefully," whispered a voice from the darkness, "This is our only chance to escape. We don't have much time."

Gilford Kemp spoke up, "Who are you and what do you think you're . . ."

"Quiet!" demanded Leeds, "This is Lyndal Froam and he is our only hope for survival. Listen closely and do whatever he says."

The boys heard a bustle of activity outside their cell door.

"This is it," whispered Beem, "Stick to the plan."

"What plan?" asked Jinx.

Before Beem could explain, four additional soldiers filed in. Their wrists were bound and they were led to the front of the building, stopping at the large entrance window. Beem quickly grabbed Jinx's hand and transferred the twenty-one eleven plan to him.

Outside, the boys could see a huge crowd had gathered and were being addressed by a man who strutted pompously back and forth on a stage in front of them. Once Pincher gave the signal, the entrance doors swung open and the boys were paraded onto the platform. Shouts of protest broke out. A woman screamed and fainted. The soldiers lined them up against the left side of the newly built wall, tied their feet together and fastened them to the floor. Next, their hands were stretched above their heads and the wrist straps were nailed to the wall.

"Silence!" Pincher bellowed, waving his arms in the air.

The clamor subsided and he continued in a subtler tone.

"We have yet to pass judgment, so settle down and give me your full attention."

He turned to the committee members and began his address.

"According to our report, these young men, along with their families, were part of a secret rebellion that had plans to take over the village."

The crowd erupted again. Pincher motioned to the guards to enforce his command for silence.

"If you are unable to control these outbursts, I will be forced to take these children inside and pass judgment on them myself."

The townspeople quieted.

"That's better," he said with a sneer.

"In addition to the charge of treason, these lads were found early this morning -meeting together – inside a HOLE on the outskirts of this village!"

The people gasped again. Although it seemed improbable the boys could plan an uprising, the thought of being inside a hole was abhorrent to Kinsmen. Pincher watched with twisted delight as doubt began working its way into the minds of his audience.

"But there's more," he announced, "It seems these sweet youngsters have been recruiting others to join in their lawlessness."

Pincher turned to the soldiers.

"Bring the others."

He paused and faced the boys with a cruel smirk, then turned back to the committee, focusing in on them with brutal intensity.

"Consider carefully the decision you make today," he whispered, his voice thick with intimidation, "How you handle these few will determine the well-being and future of your entire community."

He fixed on them with a sinister glare.

The committee members had been set up by Pincher's indisputable argument. They were left with only one choice – and it was unthinkable.

Moments later, the Black Guard returned, escorting Lyndal, the Kinsmen and a delirious, black-eyed Scullins to the platform. The soldiers secured them to the right side of the wall and lined up, at attention, between the prisoners and the stunned crowd.

Pria watched as Trince brushed her hair.

"I wonder what's taking Lyndal so long? He should be back by now – especially since he knew I was preparing his favorite meal."

"He's all right," Trince answered. "He's probably just working out the details of tonight's rescue."

Trince could feel Pria's growing concern. She sat down by her friend, and gave her a hug.

"Isn't it exciting though? We'll be able to see the boys tonight!"

Pria attempted a half-hearted smile.

"I can't wait to see Beem," Trince gushed.

She paused and sighed.

"Because you know . . . I really like being with him."

"I do too," agreed Pria, "It's just not the same without the boys."

"No," said Trince, "I mean . . . I *like* Beem."

"You mean 'like him' like him?"

"Uh-huh."

Pria began to laugh.

"You're just now figuring that out?"

"What do you mean?"

"I could have told you that months ago," teased Pria with a giggle, "It's all over you – the way you look at him, the way you show off when he's around, the things you say about him. It's so obvious."

Trince felt a little embarrassed.

"Do you think he knows?"

Pria took her by the hand and smiled.

"Are you kidding? He's a boy. He won't figure it out for a couple of years."

They both burst into laughter and hugged each other.

"I'm glad I told you," said Trince, "I've been so worried about him. I thought I was going to go crazy."

Pincher paraded in front of the Kinsmen prisoners, scowling and sneering.

"You have all been accused of conspiring with known rebels . . ." he snarled, pointing at the boys,

"And you broke the law by entering a hole. How do you plead?"

Mr. Leeds looked up at him and cleared his throat. Pincher could barely contain himself as he awaited the old man's pitiful plea for his life.

"I'm guilty, I suppose. I don't know anything about any rebels, but I did go inside a hole this morning. It was amazing! The walls were . . ."

"Enough!" Pincher screamed, clamping his hand over his mouth.

The villagers were shocked. It was unthinkable for a Kinsman to ever venture into a hole – especially a respected elder.

Pincher strode across the platform.

"You heard it yourselves! Guilty as charged!" he bellowed, pointing an accusing finger at the captives.

"That's not true!" yelled Jinx, "These people are innocent. I'm the one who took them inside the hole. I'm the one who's guilty. Let them go."

Pincher hurried over to Jinx and yanked his head around to face the crowd.

"Again!" Pincher announced, "Guilty as charged . . . and from his own lips!"

He faced the committee.

"There is no need for further discussion. By their own admission, the people standing before you are guilty of every charge levied against them!"

Pincher motioned to the soldiers. Each of them

positioned themselves directly in front of a prisoner – one on one – and lifted their spears awaiting Pincher's command. A hush fell over the crowd, as they stood overwhelmed by what they were witnessing. Scullins, who had just come to his senses, mustered all his strength and cried out.

"Wait! What about me and this Keeon guard next to me? We're not guilty of anything. Why are innocent men standing among these criminals?"

"You, Mr. Scullins, are not the concern of these people," announced Pincher, "You interfered with justice. Your sentence came this morning when I found you shirking your responsibilities. But who are you?" he said as he approached Lyndal, "I thought I had my men release all the Keeon guards this afternoon. So why are you standing here?"

Lyndal kept his head down and began to speak.

"*I* am the one you're really looking for."

Pincher looked surprised and turned to the captain for an explanation. He had no response. Pincher scowled and motioned for Lyndal to continue.

"Go on . . ." he said impatiently.

"*I* am the reason everyone is standing on this platform today," said Lyndal.

His voice grew louder with every word.

"*I* am the reason families were arrested and their houses burned. *I* am the reason these children risked their lives to search out the truth. *I* am the reason that you, sir, have spent your whole life trying to cover it up."

Lyndal transported a few inches in front of him causing his restraints to fall to the floor. He lifted his head and faced the crowd. His eyes glowed and sparkled as if they were on fire.

"You see – *I* am an Ancient!"

Pincher staggered and fell backward, gripped with terror. He reached out in desperation and clutched the leg of the soldier in front of him.

"Kill him! Kill him!" he croaked.

The soldier was momentarily shaken by Lyndal's appearance, but quickly regained his composure. He pulled back and hurled his spear at the man with the fiery eyes. Lyndal vanished. The people watched amazed as the spear flew past its mark and clattered onto the entryway of Punishment House.

"He's an Ancient!" yelled Meekus, "The Legends are true!"

The rest of the prisoners began shouting in agreement.

"The Legends are true! The Legends are true!"

Pincher pulled himself up to one knee, his face dripping with sweat.

He screamed hysterically at the soldiers, "Kill them all! Now! Now!"

The soldiers let loose, hurling their spears as the crowd cried out in horror. The dull thud of spear against wood echoed through the square. Their shafts were still vibrating, embedded in the wall where the Kinsmen had been just moments before. But every prisoner had vanished – all except for Mr. Scullins.

He moaned and writhed in pain, struggling to choke out his final words, "The Legends are tr . . ."

He flopped forward, his lifeless body hanging from the spear that pinned him to the wall.

"The Legends *are* true," stated one of the astonished villagers.

"The Legends are true!" he reiterated with increasing passion.

Others began to echo his chant until all the Kinsmen were crying out in unison –"The Legends are true, The Legends are true!"

Lyndal looked down on the scene from the balcony he had transported to. Satisfied that all the prisoners had made it safely away, he removed his Keeon uniform and transported home.

Pincher and his troops fled inside Punishment House before the angry mob could get to them. The heavy door was barred while he shouted orders.

"You are not to let anyone in. I am leaving and won't be back for a few hours. Secure the village while I'm gone. Don't let any of these ignorant peasants leave. If the situation becomes violent, use force. The sight of a few dead Kinsmen should bring them to their senses."

The small entourage slipped out the back door of the complex and hastily stole away from Maidenton.

"I'm back!" Lyndal announced from his sleeping chamber.

The girls felt a flood of relief at the sound of his voice.

"We saved you some food!" Pria replied.

"It smells wonderful. I'll be right in."

Lyndal hesitated. There was no easy way to explain to the girls what had just happened. He walked into the kitchen and was nearly knocked over as they smothered him with hugs.

"You were gone so long, we were beginning to worry. But now that you're back, we want to know everything. What's the plan? Do we get to help with the rescue?" asked Trince excitedly.

She was barely able to contain her excitement at the thought of seeing Beem again. Lyndal looked into their happy faces. He was overwhelmed with compassion and regret.

"I'm afraid there is not going to be any rescue," he said, "Everything has changed."

"What do you mean?" demanded Trince as she clutched at his sleeve. The joy of the previous moment evaporated and the girl's faces drained of all color.

"Calm down!" he reassured them, "Everyone is safe."

"You had me worried," exclaimed Trince, letting out a sigh of relief. Pria giggled nervously and sat down next to her friend.

Lyndal leaned forward, took the girls hands in his and began to explain. "I don't know how to tell you this . . . so I'm just going to say it. The boys had to transport."

They stared blankly at him as the implications of his words sank in.

"I'm so sorry," he continued, "It was life or death. They had no other choice."

"But that means . . ." Trince said, her eyes welling up with tears.

"I'm afraid so," said Lyndal, handing her his handkerchief, "But take joy in the fact they're safe. They all made it out alive – even the Kinsmen."

"What Kinsmen?" asked Pria as she wiped the tears from her cheeks.

Lyndal proceeded to tell them everything. His description of the situation was so gripping, it provided a temporary distraction. But when he got to the part where everyone transported, Trince burst into tears again.

"I already miss them," she sobbed, "And I never got a chance to say goodbye. He'll forget I ever existed."

"Listen to me," urged Lyndal, "Your bond of friendship is held together by something distance and time can never destroy – love, real love. You have a love that has been tested and proven through your struggles and sufferings. This kind of love is an amazing force. It's more powerful than anything in the universe. It can overthrow kingdoms, save worlds, free captives, and defeat evil. Don't you see? This love will keep your hearts knitted together no matter how long you may wait to be reunited. I understand very well what you're feeling right now – so believe me when I tell you – everything *will* turn out all right in the end."

The sun had set and the night mist spread a thick blanket over the countryside. A sleek ebony carriage, forty Keeon soldiers, and a small contingent of the Black Regiment crossed the bridge into Maidenton. The Keeon moved in, silently dispersing throughout the village. The rest of the entourage made their way to the entrance of Punishment House.

The scene looked very different from the chaotic confusion of the preceding day. The square seemed peaceful with one exception. The gruesome specter of Scullins shriveled body, pinned to the wall. It served as a reminder of the remarkable events that had recently taken place.

Torches blazed around the perimeter of Punishment House. A wall of guards surrounded the prison. As he neared the entry, Pincher seized a soldier posted by the door and shoved him against the wall.

"Where's the boy?" he demanded.

"Right where you left him sir," answered the soldier.

"Does he know anything?"

"No one has entered or left the cell," the soldier responded, "He knows nothing."

Pincher seemed satisfied with his report and loosed his grip from the man's uniform.

He escorted the hooded man down the main corridor. Two soldiers followed close behind carrying the heavy, elaborately crafted boxes they had just pulled from the carriage. Each wooden box was stained the color of crimson, with a hinged lid on top and a small circular door on one end.

"Set the boxes down and be careful with them," Pincher ordered as they crossed the threshold into the cell.

The men gently lowered their cargo to the floor.

"Lock the door behind you and remain at your post until we tell you otherwise."

The door slammed shut.

Mrs. Cromwell jumped to her feet, brushed off her dress and bowed low before the men. Wort came alongside her and held tightly to her hand. Pincher was fuming. His expression became distorted as he jabbed his finger in Wort's face.

"Listen carefully to me you little rodent," he spewed, "You have only one chance for survival."

Without warning, Pincher lunged at Mrs. Cromwell. He grabbed her by the throat and slammed her against the wall. With his free hand, he unsheathed his dagger and pressed the point into her neck just deep enough to draw blood.

"I . . . I . . . I don't understand," she gasped.

"Shut up, you stupid, ridiculous woman," he snarled, "Do you think we care the least bit about you? You are nothing but a coward and a traitor and all your friends despise you!"

His words ripped her to the core. She began to whimper and tremble uncontrollably. She looked at her son in utter desperation.

"Do whatever this man tells you to," Pincher demanded, turning to Wort, "If you hesitate, complain or even so much as flinch, I will kill your mother right here – right now. Am I making myself clear?"

Wort was traumatized by the man's cruelty. Who was he and why was he there? He wondered what had become of Mr. Scullins. He was confused. He knew he had broken the law and would be punished, but this strange man seemed to be searching for something else. Wort was out of options.

"Y . . . yes sir," he answered.

He felt The Wisdom rise up inside him.

"Transport – transport away, NOW."

Wort was paralyzed, terrified for his mother.

The hooded man approached him. Wort could sense something terrible and backed away in fear. The man pulled the covering from his face. Wort gasped in horror. His eyes were bottomless pools of murky darkness. Despair and death lived inside their depths. Wort tried to cry out but the man grabbed his face and forced his mouth open with a claw-like hand. With the other hand, he pulled something from his cloak.

"Swallow," growled the man as he shoved the smooth round object into Wort's mouth.

He covered his face until Wort began to suffocate. He writhed in torment. Tears rolled down his cheeks and he began to gag. It was too big to swallow. Should he transport, or should he obey the man? Pincher's knife pressed harder against his mother's throat. She moaned in pain. Wort couldn't take any more. With all of his might, he swallowed.

Suddenly the man released him and walked away. Wort stumbled forward, struggling to catch his breath. His mind became muddled with a million disconnected thoughts and images. He felt dizzy. The people in the room became distorted. The face of his mother faded into a blur as he slid down the wall. Then everything went black.

Pincher called to the sentries to remove Mrs.

Cromwell. As soon as she entered the hallway, she collapsed and became violently ill. Wort remained unconscious on the cell floor. His body began to twitch and jerk. The soldiers gagged him, tied a sack over his head and inserted his hands into the circular openings in the two red boxes. Pincher hovered over him like a bird of prey and prodded him with his boot.

"At last we have a link to The Ancients," he gloated, "I've been waiting for an opportunity like this my whole life."

Pincher cackled with glee as he rubbed his hands together in satisfaction.

"Be sure to keep him alive," warned the hooded man, "If he dies, he will be of no use to any of us."

Pincher nodded in agreement.

"I must return to the domes," stated the Shallum Lord, "The Grand Council convenes in two days. Report whatever you discover to me as soon as you can."

"Now that I have my experiment under way, I might be a little preoccupied," said Pincher with a smug look.

The hooded man turned to leave.

"Before you go, what shall I tell the villagers now that they believe The Legends are true? They have seen the eyes of an Ancient, and witnessed transporting . . ."

Without hesitation, the hooded man answered.

"Tell them what they *want* to hear. Use the facts to conceal the truth. Create the perfect counterfeit. It's what you do best. They haven't had enough exposure to the truth yet to distinguish the difference."

Pincher bowed low as the hooded man exited the building. He watched the Shallum carriage pull away and disappear into the black. He stood pondering the words of his dark mentor.

"This is going to be more enjoyable than I thought," he said to himself, "I can't wait to teach these fools about the truth they *think* they discovered."

He motioned to the captain of the Black Guard.

"Prepare to convene the village council, first thing in the morning. Tell them of our plans to draw up a peace treaty. The first thing we must do is win their trust."

"As you wish," replied the captain.

He turned and headed toward the barracks to brief his men.

Confident the rebels would never return to Maidenton, Ivan Pincher set about rewriting The Legends of The Ancients.

The End

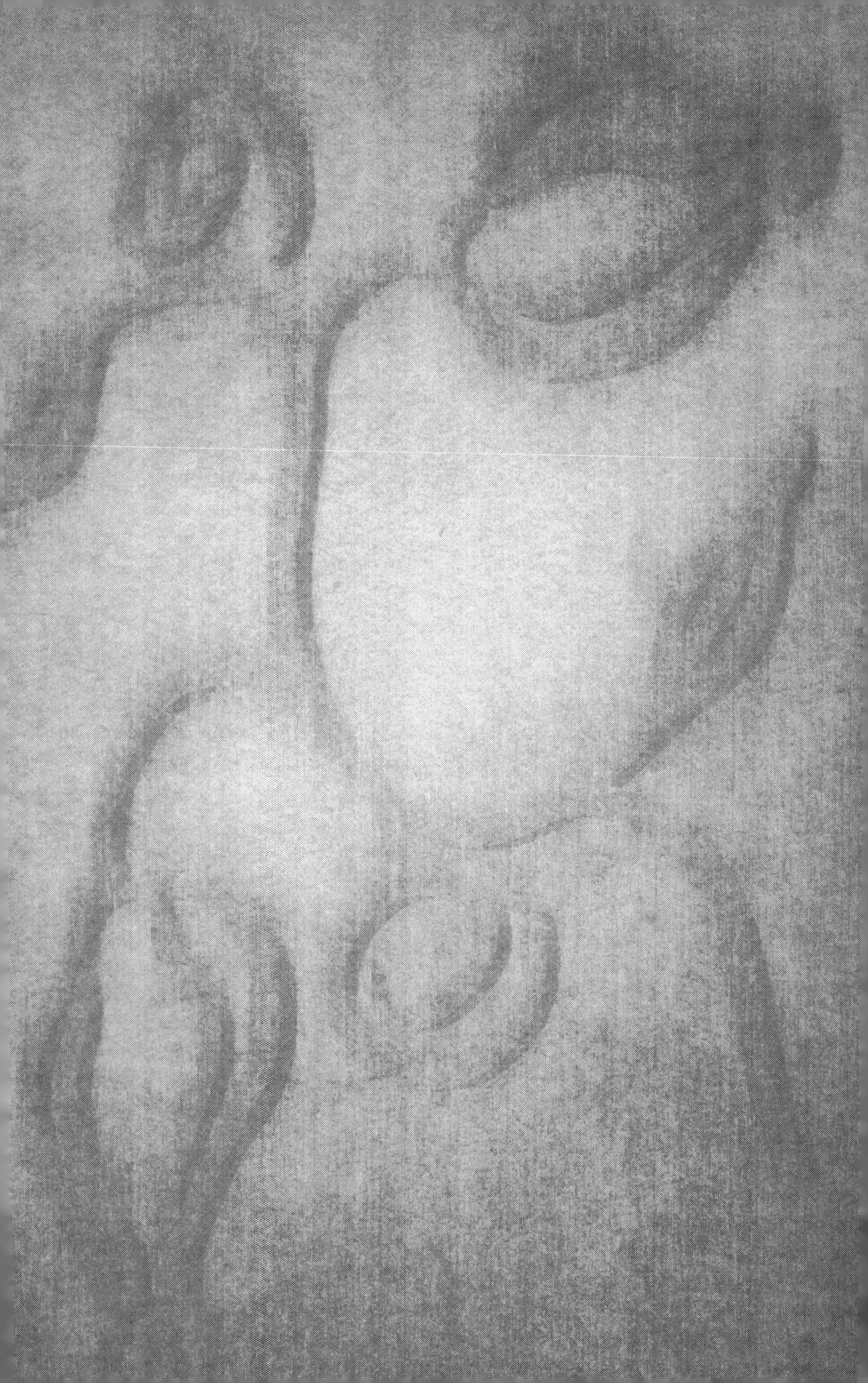

Thank You

My deepest thanks goes to the following people: Jeremy, Diana Moore, Diane C, Wes, Tinker, Lisa, Drew, Tina, JC, Marilyn, Michelle Lee, Nora, Jeff, Doug, Nathan, Nerf, Wynd, Nikki, WordSharp, Sarah, Smoo, Karen, the IW group, the TTerbush Clan, and the love of my life; Jennifer. You guys ROCK! Thanks also to the numerous friends and family who continue to encourage me in putting these stories on paper – you know who you are and I love you.

ABOUT THE ILLUSTRATOR

Sci-Fi Book Cover Designer was founded by illustrator and "Sci-Fi Book Design Specialist", Nathan D. Fisher. Since 1995, Nathan has brought a deeply personal sense of caring and dedication to every project he has taken on. He has combined his years of experience and expert skill with his boundless passion for the science fiction genre, to bring his clients unique artwork they can proudly use to adorn their novels.

Be sure to visit the following web sites:

TomTerbush.com

Beniwan.com

Missinglid.com

ScifiBookCoverDesigner.com

19107183R00195

Made in the USA
Lexington, KY
06 December 2012